# VENETIAN TRADE

The two young men stood facing one another, one in a robe of finest silk patterned in rich colours, the other wrapped in a cloak of coarse threadbare fabric saturated with brine, dirt and urine, yet neither felt the need to cover himself, or to avoid the other's eye. They met as countrymen far from home, and they met as equals. Despite the hubbub on the canal below, there was a stillness in the room. Rob tried to think of something to say, but no words came, and he gave up. If his lordship was content with silence, why should he not be?

After a moment Rob felt a sharp quickening, and looking down he saw that his cock was sticking up, as was another half-hidden among folds of rich silk.

First published in Great Britain in 1999 by
Idol
an imprint of Virgin Publishing Ltd
Thames Wharf Studios,
Rainville Road, London W6 9HT

ISBN 0 352 33300 6

Cover photograph by Colin Clarke Photography

Typeset by SetSystems Ltd, Saffron Walden, Essex
Printed and bound in Great Britain by
Mackays of Chatham PLC

# VENETIAN TRADE

Tom Granville

To Stephen

# SAFER SEX GUIDELINES

These books are sexual fantasies – in real life, everyone needs to think about safe sex.

While there have been major advances in the drug treatments for people with HIV and AIDS, there is still no cure for AIDS or a vaccine against HIV. Safe sex is still the only way of being sure of avoiding HIV sexually.

HIV can only be transmitted through blood, come and vaginal fluids (but no other body fluids) passing from one person (with HIV) into another person's bloodstream. It cannot get through healthy, undamaged skin. The only real risk of HIV is through anal sex without a condom – this accounts for almost all HIV transmissions between men.

### Being safe

Even if you don't come inside someone, there is still a risk to both partners from blood (tiny cuts in the arse) and pre-come. Using strong condoms and water-based lubricant greatly reduces the risk of HIV. However, condoms can break or slip off, so:

* Make sure that condoms are stored away from hot or damp places.
* Check the expiry date – condoms have a limited life.
* Gently squeeze the air out of the tip.
* Check the condom is put on the right way up and unroll it down the erect cock.
* Use plenty of water-based lubricant (lube), up the arse and on the condom.
* While fucking, check occasionally to see the condom is still in one piece (you could also add more lube).
* When you withdraw, hold the condom tight to your cock as you pull out.

* Never re-use a condom or use the same condom with more than one person.
* If you're not used to condoms you might practise putting them on.
* Sex toys like dildos and plugs are safe. But if you're sharing them use a new condom each time or wash the toys well.

For the safest sex, make sure you use the strongest condoms, such as Durex Ultra Strong, Mates Super Strong, HT Specials and Rubberstuffers packs. Condoms are free in many STD (Sexually Transmitted Disease) clinics (sometimes called GUM clinics) and from many gay bars. It's also essential to use lots of water-based lube such as KY, Wet Stuff, Slik or Liquid Silk. Never use come as a lubricant.

**Oral sex**
Compared with fucking, sucking someone's cock is far safer. Swallowing come does not necessarily mean that HIV gets absorbed into the bloodstream. While a tiny fraction of cases of HIV infection have been linked to sucking, we know the risk is minimal. But certain factors increase the risk:
* Letting someone come in your mouth
* Throat infections such as gonorrhoea
* If you have cuts, sores or infections in your mouth and throat

**So what is safe?**
There are so many things you can do which are absolutely safe: wanking each other; rubbing your cocks against one another; kissing, sucking and licking all over the body; rimming – to name but a few.

If you're finding safe sex difficult, call a helpline or speak to someone you feel you can trust for support. The Terrence Higgins Trust Helpline, which is open from noon to 10pm every day, can be reached on 0171 242 1010.

Or, if you're in the United States, you can ring the Center for Disease Control toll free on 1 800 458 5231.

# One

---

Rob's nostrils itched as he came up on deck, and paused to button his trouser-flap. The air had soured since they had entered the lagoon, but before him lay all the spectacle of Venice. After weeks at sea, a scene of such magnificence and confusion, of variety on land and water, of movement and colour, numbed his senses. But soon a more urgent sensation demanded his attention. He ran a hand across his arse, and swore under his breath. The fresh stripes were as hot as mustard, but he knew better than to show his pain. Nor was he yet out of danger. Below him, at the foot of the stairs, the quartermaster was still lurking, and snapping his rope's end against his thigh as if unsure that its work was done.

In his time he had taken his fair share – and more – of hidings, and had never thought to complain. After all, he was still a young man and headstrong. But that was before he had signed on the *Dawn Treader*, bound for Patras out of Greenhithe docks with Venice as first port of call. He had been looking for adventure and good company, and was prepared to take in his stride the rough and tumble of life below deck. He had proved his courage by climbing the rigging in rough seas off Finistere, and had held no grudges when two sea-dogs had laid siege to his hammock while he slept. One jolly old fellow had slid in beside him, while the other held him still and whispered promises of pleasure and

1

protection. One showed off a stiff cock, and before Rob could protest, he found himself rolled over and his arse probed. There was a struggle, and some laughter, but in the end Rob's firmly clenched buttocks guarded his entrance. When the other dog had no better luck with Rob's mouth, whose strong white teeth proved an effective portcullis, both the old devils gave up the hunt.

On other occasions Rob had defended himself with his fists, and had borne his bruises with pride. Even so, as his manhood blossomed in the bracing sea air, he had begun to learn that it is not always sufficient only to defend oneself, and let all others go hang.

A stowaway had been discovered. He had been hiding for three days in the rope room. Paraded below decks by bullies, who hoped to make him their plaything, the miserable young man had stared straight ahead as if the very essence of him had frozen. As Rob watched the cruel sport he felt a prick of conscience, and intervened to shame the taunting mob. As he spoke the lad had turned towards him with trembling lips, and a look of haunting gratitude in his pale beseeching eyes.

The men, knowing their quarry had found his champion, had moved on and left the two young men alone. That night, as Rob lay in his hammock reading his treasured collection of ballads and songs, he had felt a hand on his shoulder. This tentative touch, and its gentleness, told him that this was no nocturnal opportunist come to try his luck. Accordingly he made no sound, or objection, as a slender figure hoisted itself into his hammock. Rather, Rob blew out his candle, and was greeted by a warm salty kiss.

Had they not made such a handsome pair, among so many gnarled and grizzled faces, the officers and more hard-hearted of the crew might have objected to the way the young lovers made no secret of their affection. Rob was a fine-looking young man, with hair the colour of ripe wheat, and eyes as bright and blue as any tropical ocean. His body was limber, and well proportioned, being wide at the shoulders and a little less so at the hips, and once he got his sea-legs, he strode the decks with all the confidence of an English seaman. The stowaway, on the other hand, had to make up in character and sweet good looks for what he lacked in strength and confidence. But with food and rum in his belly, and under Rob's ever-watchful eye, he soon learned the ropes as his chest deepened and his arms and neck thickened. By the time the *Dawn Treader* had passed Gibraltar, he had discovered how to outpace trouble by racing up the rigging faster than any pursuer. Moreover, he showed rare skill with the penny whistle. The spring nights began early in the Mediterranean, and the sailors would dance on deck under swaying lanterns that cast deep, ever-moving shadows. Tots of rum would be passed round while the ship bucked and creaked as she headed into the warm night wind. And when the crew stumbled below to fall into their hammocks, the hardy old salts would call out thanks to the stowaway and recall other voyages blessed by young sailors with a talent for music.

While others slept Rob took his pleasure with the stowaway, who was as well hung as his lips were full. At first they had merely shared kisses, and used their hands to explore and excite one another. If one achieved relief, the other would wait until the spasm had subsided, and then reach for the other's hand, and make a circle of the thumb and forefinger, and use it to rub his own sore overused cock until the foaming liquid burst forth. It was innocent compared to the rougher exertions under way in the hammocks rocking on every side, but young men learn fast. After a few nights together, Rob discovered there were better uses for his cock than rubbing it against a friend's thigh, or having him yank it until the come shot up into the darkness. He learned that a cock will slip easily up a grateful friend's arse, and feel at home there, and that a nipple sucked and chewed will stand erect and flood the chest with sensations quite as intoxicating as rum. And so they passed the long nights in discovery of themselves and each other, expending their lust upon each other, and sealing their affection with kisses. The dreamy easy hours passed, and in the morning they would yawn and shake themselves awake like young animals. As they stood naked in line for the morning wash – a bucket of seawater tossed over each man – they would stare deep into each other's eyes, scarcely blinking as the cold water drenched them. Few among the crew were inclined to deny them their simple pleasures, or give in to the temptation to join their sweet union.

And then, one brilliant morning as the *Dawn Treader* sailed through choppy waters off Sicily, there was a terrible cry from the rigging, and a shadow, as fleeting as any seabird's, passed over the middle deck. There was no sound of a splash, and no cry for help. Nothing was to be seen on the water's surface. The stowaway had been swallowed amid the sea's empty turbulence.

After that Rob seldom spoke, but he knew he was not meant to be a sailor. And the old salts knew it too, and kept their distance as if he were as cursed as the albatross.

All except the quartermaster, who felt no superstition, and saw only opportunity.

From then on, day in and day out, this burly fellow, with his bulging stomach, and long black beard, would call Rob from his duties to feel the sting of the rope's end that always dangled from his belt. He seldom offered a reason, and in truth none was necessary. Rob had only to look into his tormentor's black eyes to see the lust bubbling there. Some of those watching were inclined to think Rob was receiving no more than his deserts, and would nudge one another, amused by the way the quarter-master licked his lips as he ordered the young seaman to strip to the waist, or drop his bell-bottoms, and receive the lash. And these whippings were only the public part of the quartermaster's discipline. For private use he had inside his trousers a length of more fleshy rope. Whenever he caught Rob off-guard he would drag him below deck into a quiet corner and order the young seaman to his knees. As Rob sucked and gagged on the soft dripping cock, he would swear vengeance, as had many helpless souls before him.

But now escape was possible. Surely in Venice it would be easy to disappear. Was it not the city of disguise, where masks and cloaks were the common garb? If he could not find refuge along unlit canals, or through low doorways leading into secret gardens, he would deserve to suffer the rope's end.

There had been talk below deck of the dangers of Venice. Old salts warned of women who were not really women, of thieves and cut-throats lurking in the shadows, and of justice by summary

4

execution and unspeakable torture. It was said that a plague raged, which in its most infectious phase restored to the raddled and old the lost beauty of youth, until as death drew near the skin cracked and the putrid reality was laid bare. But Rob was not in a mood to heed warnings. All he wanted was to set foot on firm ground, and be rid of the *Dawn Treader*, whose foppish officers strutted the decks with nosegays pressed to their nostrils, while the common sailors knelt at their feet to scrub and sluice. Never again would he lie below deck, in fear for his honour, amid the stench of shit and rotten food. Never again would he sleep on his stomach to heal the stripes across his back or arse. From now on he would live by his wits on dry land.

He turned to look back towards the open sea, and bid it farewell, but his eye fell instead upon the galley ships moored nearby. Under the blue sky, they made a fine sight, with gleaming cannons lining their decks, their prows and tiered bows decked with flags of gold and purple. Small craft huddled round them, and crowds had gathered on the quayside. Rob had heard tales about these mighty vessels, and the suffering of those forced to spend their lives under the lash as they strained at the oars. Once he would have stared at the scene, awed by its beauty and cruel reputation, but he had suffered himself in the cause of nautical splendour, and he turned away with a shudder of disgust.

The great bell on the Campanile tolled midday as Rob crossed the grand piazza. He had bade his shipmates a cheerful farewell, and promised to meet them on the Rialto at dusk. But he hoped never to see any of them again. He would start life again, here in Venice, where all the world's riches were displayed, and all its vices too. With luck and cunning he would find his fortune soon enough, and afterwards return home to England a rich man.

Everywhere he looked there was something to astonish his young eyes. Outside St Mark's a man was letting off fireworks in broad daylight, and a band was playing a fanfare, not with any hope of silencing the crowds but perhaps to encourage the hubbub. Here, whores were selling themselves from the back of an elephant led on a chain, there two young dandies walked arm in arm, their bulging groins attracting admiring glances from a procession of priests leading a scarlet-robed cardinal to prayer. Nearby a bear danced with a man wearing a gypsy's skirt and a pair of Siamese twins crouched in a cage, one weeping, the other laughing. Tourists in their national costumes were pestered by hawkers, as eager to show off fine legs and behinds as their tawdry goods, while groups of thieving children went skipping by, jabbering in foreign tongues. Never in his life had he seen such busyness, or so many people of so many kinds.

Everyone seemed friendly, nevertheless, and he had to admit that the young men were well dressed and handsome, but none spoke English, which was a pity. He felt lonely amid so much novelty and longed for someone to talk to.

Passing under the colonnade at the far end of the piazza, he found himself in a narrow, but still crowded street. In every corner some trader had set out his wares, and everyone seemed to be arguing or laughing, carrying great bundles on their backs, or ambling along like lazy peacocks showing off their finery. He had been expecting the Venetians to be like the Italians he had come across in London, fellows with well-knit bodies, bulging loins, dark oily hair and gleaming eyes and teeth. However, here there were as many with fair or red hair as were to be found among the lads in the villages and orchards of his native Kent. If he could only make himself understood, he was sure he would soon make friends.

The narrow pathway opened into a wide walkway alongside a canal. Ladies and gentlemen were being helped from gondolas and making their way into a restaurant. The smell of cooking was in the air, mixed with ladies' perfume. Rob paused to watch the scene, impressed by the unhurried dignity of the rich. One of the party was a fine figure of a man, tall, slender and dark, with a trim beard and hair that fell to his shoulders like a sheet of black liquorice. This fellow paused when he saw Rob staring, and looked him up and down, as if he had been offered some trifle for sale, and then smiled and used the palm of his gloved hand to blow him a kiss. Everyone was laughing. Rob felt his cheeks redden, and would have said something, but the man was already entering the restaurant.

Life below deck had been nothing like this. Here was a world full of possibilities, of the unexpected, and the novel. He walked on with a spring in his step. Nevertheless he soon felt a pang of hunger, and clutched at the few coins in his pocket. Would they be worth anything in Venice?

The streets and passages were confusing: Rob had been expecting wide canals filled with magnificent craft and bobbing gondolas, but in this quarter of the city the alleys and canals were narrow and crooked. His high spirits faded, and all at once he felt chilled, lonely and lost. As he wandered on the crowds began to thin, and soon the city around him was still, except where the water lapped at the edge of the canal.

'*Inglese*? English?'

Rob looked round but saw no one.

'Sailor boy. Over here.'

Despite his alarm at not knowing where the voice came from, Rob was delighted to hear his own language. In a shady corner he saw an old trader. He had not noticed him before, which was not surprising because the man had little to sell.

'Sailor buy nice shirt. Sailor boy look good in nice shirt.'

Rob drew close. The man seemed like any other trader – rather short, with a swarthy complexion, blackened teeth, and oily hair scraped back in a pigtail. Laid out on the ground before him were a few brightly coloured kerchiefs, fancy embroidered carnival hats, a couple of grotesque masks, and a conjuring stick decorated with bells.

'A shirt?' Rob almost jumped at the sound of his own voice.

The man smiled and stepped to one side. Behind him, hung against the wall, were half a dozen shirts. He beckoned Rob closer. 'Nice shirts for sailor boy.'

'You speak English?' Rob would have looked at the man, but his eye was on the shirts. After weeks in white uniform, it would feel good to wear bright colours.

'Limehouse, Shadwell, the great Tower of London.'

Rob wanted to laugh at such familiar names spoken in so strange an accent, but a chill of doubt stopped him. Why was the man selling his goods here, so far from the crowds, and why had he so few to sell?

'Nice shirt, sailor. Try.'

7

Rob felt in his pocket for his coins, and showed them to the man. 'That's all I have.'

The man found this very amusing. He shook with laughter as he unhooked one of the shirts and handed it to Rob. 'Money good. Very good.'

The material was rich to the touch. How soft it would feel on his back after coarse linen. He handed it back to the man so that he might pull off his white sailor's shirt. A sound, rather like a sigh of satisfaction, made Rob look round. He still had his hands over his head, and was struggling with the sleeves.

A gondola had appeared, no more than a few feet away. The gondolier, oar at the ready, was staring at Rob. So, too, was his passenger, a tall young man in a leather jerkin, who was lounging in his chair smoking a clay pipe.

The breeze was cold and Rob shivered. Although life at sea had cured him of any modesty in the company of men, he felt uneasy at being half naked. And watched by three strangers.

# Two

The English sailor made a fine sight as he pulled his white shirt over his head. The man lying on a bed of cushions in the gondola knew that he had found what he wanted. His loins stirred as he drew on his pipe. Reaching inside his jerkin he produced a black purse, which he tossed to the gondolier, whose tobacco-encrusted lips parted in a lecherous sneer. No words were needed; such was the understanding between them. The gondolier shipped his oar, and pulled the boater down over his eyes, before jumping on to firm ground.

The man left in the gondola was well pleased. His name was Gaetano, and he was from Naples where he had recently cut a man's throat. It had been his experience that the Venetians seldom asked questions, and never if paid well. Such discretion made their city an excellent place to lie low, and enjoy the fruits of crime, whereas Naples was full of spies, gossiping priests and informers. In Venice all a man needed, if he had gold, was the service of an understanding gondolier. It had not taken Gaetano long to find one.

This black-hearted fellow knew all the secrets of the city, including those addresses where pleasures were to be found that would have caused scandal in Naples but in Venice raised not so much as an eyebrow. But such delights did not come cheap, and before long Gaetano had wearied of the cost. It cut against the grain to pay for things he had so often won for free by stealth and trickery. He ordered his gondolier, henceforth, to steer clear of all houses of pleasure, and instead to cruise the canals in search of wild things, untarnished by use or sale.

And so, that chilly afternoon, as the gondolier went to do his master's bidding, Gaetano lay back and watched the young Englishman struggle with his shirt. Both arms were raised above his head, which allowed an unimpeded view of his broad shoulders, fine white chest, button red nipples, and flat belly.

Gaetano had to shift his backside to ease the pressure in his underclothes caused by his stiffening cock. Right beside it, and as hidden from view, his trusty knife was lodged in its leather pouch. He sighed, half in anticipation and half from the pure pleasure of seeing such a perfect form displayed. He was an evil man, but his dark purposes had sharpened, not blunted, his appreciation of those things that aroused his lust.

It was becoming clear, meanwhile, that the Englishman was beginning to regret his deal with the trader. No sooner had he got the new shirt on his back than the trader's manner had changed. No more encouraging smiles and broken English; instead a flood of Italian, a raised voice, a finger poked in the chest, and demands for money – Italian money, not the coins the Englishman offered. These were tossed on the ground to be spat on.

From the way the young man was staring round Gaetano guessed he was thinking of making a run for it. That would have been a pity, and he was pleased when his gondolier reached the scene of the dispute and put an arm round the Englishman's shoulders. He smiled and patted the fellow reassuringly.

In a moment of crisis, help is always welcome, but it was obvious that the English sailor was not convinced that the gondolier was trustworthy. This amused, but did not surprise Gaetano. Despite his hat decked with ribbons and the richly embroidered gondolier's jacket, there was no denying that his boatman had a most sinister air. Was it the fleshy face that disturbed the Englishman? Or could it be his thick reddened neck? Or breath that smelt of chewed tobacco?

But the trader willingly accepted a silver coin from the rascal, and the Englishman did not protest when led firmly towards the gondola.

'Nice shirt for nice boy,' the trader called after them, and laughed. A moment later there was another shout, 'English boy, nice shirt.' Another laugh, then silence.

Gaetano watched with satisfaction as the small comedy came to its conclusion. When things went smoothly from the start, more often than not they went smoothly all the way through to the end. He propped himself up on an elbow, and took his pipe from his mouth. He gestured to the English sailor to step on board. 'Rialto. Yes?'

The young man nodded, but when the gondolier jumped on the prow and held out a hand, the Englishman refused it, and stepped on board with a seaman's lithe grace.

'Me Gaetano. What your name?'

'Rob, sir.' Although he struck a manly pose, hands on hips, and rolled easily with the swaying craft, his fair cheeks had turned scarlet. 'I'm meeting my friends at the Rialto . . . They have money . . . to repay you, Sir.'

Gaetano did not understand, but smiled and invited the sailor to sit. He put his pipe back in his mouth and snapped his fingers at the gondolier. Despite his eagerness he told himself there was time for everything he had in mind. There was no need to worry. No need to hurry.

The gondola moved as silently as a sledge through fresh fallen snow, and caused barely a ripple on the canal's dark glassy surface. Rob, who had become used to life on the *Dawn Treader*'s pitching decks, felt as if he were floating on a magic carpet. With his head resting on silk cushions, and his recently whipped arse soothed by a chair strewn with Turkish rugs, he closed his eyes and surrendered to the pleasure of so much softness after weeks of discomfort. Beside him the Neapolitan's pipe sent up clouds of perfumed smoke, which tickled his throat and further teased his senses. The gondolier began a slow melancholy song. His deep voice echoed softly off the mouldering walls. Looking up he saw patches of blue sky, and the evening sun shedding a gold brilliance across the tops of the buildings.

They floated on.

By nature Gaetano was an impatient man, and always eager to get down to the business of the moment. But he could not call out to the gondolier to go faster, and he could not risk passers-by seeing him lay his hands on his sleepy young companion. Even in Venice a man needed a cover of darkness for what Gaetano had in mind.

Before long the gondolier turned his black craft into a narrow waterway. It ran a short distance between high walls, then turned again. On one side there was still a high blank wall, but on the other a small yard filled with half-carved statues, garden pots, and all the bric-à-brac of the stonemason's trade. The surrounding buildings were too high to allow the sun to enter the dark well, and the air was chill and damp.

Rob, who had drifted into sleep, woke with a start as the gondolier jumped ashore. 'Rialto?' He looked around in alarm. 'Where are . . .' As he spoke he turned and caught the look in his host's eye.

Gaetano was putting out his pipe. He tapped it against the side of the gondola and carefully placed it in a silken pouch attached to his belt. This done, he leaned forward until his face was close to Rob's. He was ready to make his move.

He ran a finger down Rob's nose and toyed with his upper lip. He prayed there would not be too much of a struggle. After all, he wanted only to possess the young sailor – there was nothing to steal, no ransom to collect, nothing to be gained by taking his life. If the sailor were wise, and saw the message in his eyes, he would realise he was no match for a Neapolitan, and might still escape with his life, if not his honour. And what price did honour carry in the back alleys of Venice?

Although Gaetano knew nothing of mercy, having never been shown any by the demons that drove him, it was with something akin to melancholy that he embarked upon his seduction. There was little cause to rejoice, but he knew he must go on. Only through the satisfaction of his desires, unfettered by conscience or restraint, could he find brief release from terrors whose lash cut deeper than any rope's end.

Nevertheless, he used gentleness at the start. He was curious to kiss the sailor's lips, as he fancied there might still be traces of brine on them. There had been, he remembered, on the face of a Pole he had kissed one rainy night in Livorno after slitting his throat. So he used his lips to disarm and quieten the Englishman, who was already starting to struggle. The well-toned muscles displayed earlier were as strong as they looked. Gaetano whispered nothings in his ear, and pressed his mouth against the red lips and smooth rosy cheeks. Why did fair men never grow beards? Were they some species of woman? Was it not natural for those with bristles on their faces, and hair on their chests, to fuck them? He placed a hand lightly where the cock lurked inside the bell-bottoms, and was glad to feel movement and hear a tremulous sigh of pleasure. With his free hand he plunged inside his own breeches to grasp the fleshier of the two hard weapons snuggling there. He was a master of the arts of using them both, separately or together, but for now was content to confine himself to the one made of gristle stiffened by blood.

He knew he would have no trouble from the gondolier, whose only concern was to ensure that neither blood nor any other spillage stained his cushions and rugs. Indeed, the surly fellow was more concerned to suck on his tobacco and savour its flavour than to interfere in what might happen under his nose. So long as he gave the fellow silver and gold he would keep his mouth shut. Gaetano knew the man had served as a jailer in the Doge's dungeon, and must have been witness there to many raw exits from this world. If things got out of hand, he would deliver a *coup de grâce* without hesitation or qualm. What he had done before, he could be relied upon to do again. In the morning he would send him to pray for their souls in San Marco. The Lord smiled on confession, as he smiled on all Venetians.

# Three

---

Rob told himself to relax. There was, he had to admit, something intriguing about the man. Perhaps it was because he was a foreigner. Although he was as tall and slender as himself, he was swarthy, with skin the colour of burnt custard. His hair was black and curly, and he had fashioned his beard along his jutting chin to meet in a thick tuft that gave him the look of a cunning goat. Close to, he smelt of tobacco and garlic, and dense hair protruded from his sleeves and spilled from his collar. There was about him a sense of energy and strength quite unlike that of any Englishman.

Besides which, Rob told himself, the man might want merely to fondle him. When others had done the same, he had not always objected. And with the young stowaway in his arms he had come close to happiness.

The man's hand was stroking where his cock lay. It stiffened as suddenly as lit tinder. The man's breath was warm on his cheek, and his dry lips almost cool on Rob's. The sharp tang of pipe tobacco was pleasing. It reminded him of the men who used to come hop-picking back home. Perhaps it would not be so bad to let the man have his way. It had been a while since he had used his hand to jerk gluey liquid from himself; and it felt so good to be kissed and stroked.

He felt his trouser flap being unbuttoned, and his hard cock sprang free. The Italian gasped. It was a fine yeoman's piece, thick and of generous length – Rob had been told often enough that few men were as well made. A spasm of fierce pleasure ran through him as the man gripped this imposing organ, and kneaded it like bread-dough.

Rob was aware that Gaetano was warming to his task. The Italian held the mighty cock in his hand and bent forward to kiss it. As he did so he let out a small cry of triumph and, as if intoxicated, pushed back the foreskin to reveal the shining head. He used his tongue to tickle it until Rob cried out with pleasure.

The Italian let go of the cock, and looked up at Rob as he put the fingers of both hands to his lips. He grinned as he used his tongue to smear them with his saliva. Rob felt a tremor of fear run through him, which immediately became mixed with a rootless, overwhelming sense of anticipation. It was as if something were coming towards him which he had been waiting for all his grown life without ever knowing what it might be. A knot seemed to loosen at the very core of his being, and he let out a deep groan as Gaetano shifted him gently on to his side, and then, more robustly, laid him flat, face down, on his chest and stomach.

If Rob had not known before, he understood then that he was to be fucked, and well, and without delay.

But first there were preliminaries. Rob heard Gaetano call out to the gondolier, and a pair of rough hands began to strip away his bell-bottoms. His new shirt was torn off his back. The chilly breeze lapped against his bare arse until, to an accompaniment of coarse laughter, he felt his arse-cheeks pulled apart so as to let the cold air into the damp narrow valley. A cushion was shoved under his belly, and his legs were forced apart. Warm spittle was spread across his hole. Often in boyhood he had wondered how farm animals in the marketplace must feel as they were tied and trussed. Now he knew. While he found nothing resembling pleasure in the powerful sensations flooding his system, they nevertheless expunged all fear. There was a confidence in the way he was being used that left him scorched with excitement. Every sinew in his treacherous body was ready to experience violation. Never in his life had he been so alive.

Out of the corner of his eye Rob saw Gaetano loosen the knot in his braided belt, and with sure fingers unbutton his breeches. Rob told himself he should look away, or close his eyes, so as to fill his mind with images that might protect him during his ordeal. But he could not take his eyes from Gaetano's groin, where a fine cock was rising from a mass of linen and dense black pubic hair. As it grew it swung from side to side as if searching for something. For a moment Rob experienced a sense of guilty pleasure. It seemed right that if he were to be taken, he should be taken by a proper length of manhood. But when Gaetano mounted him, put a hand over his mouth and used the other to guide the hard gristle deep into his crack, Rob's connoisseurship turned to panic. He wriggled like a ferret. But it was no use. The stiff cock had found its target, and a piercing pain announced the invader's arrival at the gateway that led to the treasured void beyond.

For a moment Rob resisted as he had his first night out on the *Dawn Treader*, but there he had had the protection of the hammock. This time he had been easily overpowered, made ready to be prised open and entered.

It was as if a battle were being fought in his mind: on the one hand the warrior within ordered his defences to be closed, and he clenched himself so tightly he managed to repulse Gaetano's first breach, but then the party of surrender spoke, soft with reason, of the wisdom to be gained from experience and acceptance. As Rob listened to this siren voice he permitted a slight loosening in his backside, which Gaetano sensed like a thieving fox. With a hoarse curse whispered in his ear, Rob found his face crushed into the coarse fabric of the Turkish rugs as Gaetano shoved and pummelled and thrust with all his might. He broke through, and drove deep into the cavern beyond. Although Rob felt the invasion only at the entrance, the very numbness inside him was evidence of the spaces within that were being lost to violation.

The searing pain did not last. Pure sensation returned to ripple through his body. Rob prayed that the worst would be soon over. On his father's farm he had once seen two fellows in a barn coupling like dogs, and they had not stayed together long. He told himself to be prudent, and lie still until the humping demon was spent.

But that would take a while, and in the meantime a still more unsettling storm was gathering strength inside him. It could not be long before it broke. It was as if a slithering snake had been let loose to roam deep inside him, and was coiling and uncoiling in fury, stirring up a devilish infestation of teasing itches, pleasurable wriggles and hot pinpricks.

His captor whispered in his ear, and bit into the back of his neck. He was warm and heavy and wet with sweat.

Rob's heart was hammering. He was sweating and his teeth chattered. He felt occupied, and possessed by an evil energy writhing in his guts. Would it not be better to die than suffer more humiliation?

And yet, once again, as the Italian's cock slid in and out, voices inside him whispered of siding with the invader. And his body's treacherous senses delivered slithers of pleasure among the pain, like traces of gold in mud. These swelled as his body, always eager to welcome fresh sensations, and indifferent to their cause, celebrated this latest novelty by releasing a flow of sensation, which spread out to find its level in every limb, joint and sinew. Its backwash met fresh waves of pleasure until Rob felt himself in a paroxysm of raw feeling. He panted, emitted ecstatic snarls, and gasped for breath. His cock twisted sideways as it expanded to breaking point. Every muscle was striving for relief.

The moment was approaching. The long ascent was almost over. He was at the summit.

Time, and the world itself, stood still.

The climax erupted deep in his invaded guts, and from there began the sublime descent through hitherto undreamt-of pastures of the purest delight. Every sated nerve ending seemed transformed into sharp crystals shining with light. Every cramped muscle purred as it gave up the struggle. Rob heard a rushing sound in his ears, and opened his eyes to see his thick come spurting sideways from his twisted cock.

The ecstasy soon subsided. Long as the climb had been, the journey back was steep and short. With a last groan he shuddered and sank into spent nothingness. The Italian was still pumping at his backside. Nothing had changed. There was no end in sight. His climax had merely been the dazzling mask of a defeat so absolute his mind still could not fathom its scale.

A final spasm ran through his groin. The rugs under him were wet and imbued with come. He tried to shift himself and settle his cock back under him. Some more juice bubbled from his aching cock.

Rob could hear his conqueror on top of him, riding him in triumph, cursing him, straining for breath. As the tides ebbed inside him, Rob felt another climax coming, this one the Italian's, as his snake danced in a frenzy. There was nothing Rob could do. His body was exhausted. He could only wait and submit.

And pray it would soon be over.

# Four

The Italian's climax was quick to arrive, and quickly spent. Afterwards he did not linger, but withdrew with a single movement. He rolled off Rob and lay on his back.

Sensing the Italian had no further business with him, Rob roused himself from gloomy thoughts. The important thing was to get away.

The air was chill and shivers ran up and down his back. His teeth were chattering. As he stretched his legs to pull on his trousers, he noticed the Italian open his silk purse. His dripping cock dangled from his fly. Rob wondered whether the man was going to toss him some silver or gold. However, the Italian preferred to reward the gondolier. The two men stood on the prow and whispered as the coins changed hands.

Then, after the briefest glance back at Rob, the Italian jumped ashore. He paused to tie the knot in his belt, stuff away his cock and button his fly, before picking his way through the stone-mason's yard and disappearing into a narrow alleyway.

His departure was so sudden that Rob simply watched him go – not that he had had in mind anything to say: he was too confused. The Italian had forced himself on him, it was true, but Rob was too honest a man not to admit that the experience had been as pleasurable as it had been unexpected. It was true that he had surrendered, but he was alive, unlike the young stowaway on the *Dawn Treader*. Compared to death, always lurking, nothing else mattered much.

Rob retrieved his shirt. It was grubby, but once on dry land he would brush himself down. It was still early evening, and the night might bring fresh adventures.

Of one thing he was sure: it would take more than an encounter with a lustful Italian to persuade him to return to the ship. Life would be hard, no doubt, but he was young and resilient. One way or another he would look after himself.

Rob got to his feet, and glanced down to make sure he was properly dressed. Only then did he look up at the gondolier, who was still standing on the prow. Rob was about to salute him, to show that he was himself again, and that there would be no hard feelings, when he saw that something was amiss. As Rob had been buttoning his trouser flap, the gondolier had been unbuttoning his. He now stood, oar in hand, legs apart, grinning while he pulled on a long limp cock.

This was too much for Rob. With an impatient grunt he jumped up on to the walkway. He meant to get away – the gondolier was unlikely to pursue him while his cock was hanging out. But he moved a little too slowly. With surprising grace the gondolier leapt off the prow and blocked Rob's way. He raised his oar. There was no way to avoid a confrontation so Rob pointed down at the suddenly erect cock and shook his head. He spoke in English, and tried to smile. There was no point in upsetting the man. But instead of putting away his cock and standing aside, the gondolier began to pull on it more vigorously while making strange hissing sounds. He still held the oar as if he might use it to clobber Rob.

Unsure what to do, Rob glanced round to see whether there was any way out of the yard other than the alleyway. For a moment he toyed with the idea of jumping into the canal and swimming for it, but he remembered what the old salts on the *Dawn Treader* had said: every mouthful of canal water was contaminated by the plague.

As Rob wavered the gondolier pounced. He used his oar to whack Rob on the shoulder so that he fell back sideways into the gondola. In an instant he was on top of Rob, who once again felt his new shirt being ripped from his back. This time it was put to use in tying his hands behind his back. Then his bell-bottoms were tugged down, and a rough hand ploughed under his arse to probe the cleavage between his buttocks. A thumb was pressed against the hole, and would have passed through had not Rob let out a loud protest. The gondolier took a scarlet silk sash from around his waist, and forced it into Rob's mouth. He turned Rob over so that he lay, as he had only minutes before, on his stomach, his face once more rubbing against the rugs.

Rob was full of rebellion. This time no voices suggested surrender for the sake of experience. He knew he must resist, but the gondolier was strong and clearly determined to enjoy what his master had enjoyed, as a servant might chew on a piece of meat left over from a feast. Rob felt the full force of the pounding cock drilling his insides, but his body did not respond and his mind remained clear and calm.

He saw the danger he was in. No pirate, once he has found treasure, will hesitate to scuttle the vessel he has boarded. One way or another Rob had to get the better of his tormentor.

The gondolier was offering no chances. He was as skilful at manoeuvring his cock as he was with his oar. Every now and then he would withdraw, use a thumb to keep the opening loose while his fingers scratched the back of the scrotum. Then he would ease his thicker stump back in. His thrusts were energetic and went deep, but as the pace quickened they grew crude and hurried. His skills seemed to desert him as his climax approached. Rob sensed the man was ignorant of the arts of control and delay, and would not, therefore, be long about his task. He decided to bide his time, and managed to spit out part of the silk suffocating him while lying under the weight of the wretched man.

He did not have to wait long. The cock pumped away like a piston out of control. As the stabs became frantic, and the gondolier panted and writhed, cursing God and the saints, Rob knew the time to act had arrived. Before long the gondolier would be lost to the world as he was consumed by spasms of delight.

Rob waited until the gondolier cried out, like a man both in ecstasy and in fear for his soul, and then, as the frenzied jerking continued, he seized all his strength, his will to survive, and thrust his backside into the air. For a moment nothing happened, and Rob feared the gondolier had somehow become attached to him, but then the dazed villain seemed suddenly to give up the struggle, and slumped backwards off Rob. He lay groaning as his teeming cock flooded the rugs covering the seats.

There was no time to lose. Rob tore at the shirt binding his hands, and freed himself. He spat out the silk gag. Without bothering to pull up his trousers he made for safety.

Putting thoughts of revenge from his mind, he scrambled down the gondola, hoisting his bell-bottoms so that he could leap for firm ground. Looking back he saw the gondolier reach for his oar. His eyes were wide with surprise, and his cock still hung free as it frothed and pulsated.

Rob ran towards the alley, then tripped and fell headlong into the debris and mud. As he lay he mustered a few words of prayer. Then there was a whooshing sound, and a terrible light erupted in his head.

An hour later, under a cloudy evening sky, the gondola reappeared from its cul-de-sac. Inside Rob lay unconscious, wrapped head to foot in a Turkish rug, oblivious to the hostile world around him. The gondolier guided the craft slowly through the traffic until it reached the Grand Canal. Once across the busy thoroughfare he would feel safer. His master had been well pleased with his English conquest, had given him three pieces of gold and promised five more the next time he provided such excellent sport. The gondolier did not mean to forfeit them because the body of an English seaman might wash up on some grandee's doorstep. Venice held her secrets to herself, and her subtle tides allowed no bodies to escape to the lagoon, just as her canals were too shallow to drown anything for long. He knew a place, however, that was dark and forlorn, and not too far away. If he dumped the body there, it would be one among many. He would be safe from discovery.

# Five

——

At first light a dozen gondolas rounded the corner on the Grand Canal below San Toma. There was little traffic at that hour, and in each craft curtains were tightly drawn across the wooden shelter to exclude prying eyes from the debaucheries within. Hired musicians sat in each bow, and the gondoliers' splendid livery gleamed even in the misty morning light.

None of this was appreciated by the honest Venetians waiting to cross the canal on their way to work. They had heard rumours about the Palazzo Ferri, and the evil appetites of the English nobleman who lived there. Most simply looked away, although a few women took the precaution of crossing themselves and muttering prayers for protection. One man, however, stared unblinking at the approaching convoy and, as it passed, shouted a curse and spat. But his glob fell unnoticed by those returning from their pleasures.

One gondola led the way by a length. Its oarsman was a fresh-faced muscular young man, who wore a sash of gold and purple across his jerkin, while the ribbon-ends decorating his hat fluttered girlishly about his handsome features. An ancient castrato, bedecked in fake jewels, stood uncertainly in the bow, and poured forth a fashionable aria, while behind the curtains Lord Damiens lay with two young noblemen of dissolute appearance.

They snuggled close together between him and a couple of bare-bosomed whores. It was a scene to provoke scandal, but the milord's companions were merely stooges and scarecrows, there to frighten away those likely to disapprove or gossip. Indeed, Lord Damiens' sense of good taste prevented him from touching the women – except to brush away a mosquito troubling a powdered nipple – for his proclivities lay in directions that ensured the young noblemen's virginity would remain secure should such a thing still be burdening them.

However, the objects of his lordship's desires were not far away. As the convoy reached the landing at the Palazzo Ferri, the great gates opened and footmen appeared carrying lights. It was these fellows who quickened Lord Damiens' pulse. Some had coarse, brutish faces, which contrasted oddly with their powdered wigs and lacy cuffs, while others were undeniably pretty in their young manhood.

Damiens pulled back the curtain and let in the fresh morning air. He breathed in deep relief, and suddenly felt nostalgic for England. He wanted no more illusion, no more rooms sparkling with candles and looking glasses. He had had his fill of music and dancing, gaming and flirting, of painted faces, perfumes, flowers and frills. His senses had been toyed with for too long. It was time for action. He wanted what he always enjoyed best after a night of amusement: an honest fuck.

As he stepped on to the landing stage he waved impatiently to the footmen to follow him. He would parade his servants and choose one to fuck. If the sundry whores of both sexes, impoverished noblemen and -women, Englishmen on the grand tour and others eager to be debauched found themselves deprived of light as they stumbled from their gondolas, so be it. He was in a hurry for a fuck.

The footmen knew what to expect. The gambling men among them had placed bets on who might be chosen, and a few optimists had already greased their arseholes. Most nights the milord took two men to bed, which in a household of nearly fifty – and given that he had no favourites – meant each one could expect a lordly rogering a couple of times a month. Most went gladly, not least because the tip and breakfast were generous enough to console those who felt their manhood abused. On the other hand, when the milord's appetite was at high tide, he would focus on one at a time. The poor fellow chosen seldom smiled as he followed his master to the great bedroom. The milord's cock was thick and long, and was used with energy and expertise, and without much regard for its recipient's comfort.

The footmen were assembled in the ballroom, where they stood chattering among themselves as they straightened each other's wigs and cuffs and buffed their slippers on the back of their stockings. When the English valet cracked his riding-whip against his thigh as a sign of their master's approach, they all stood to attention, like soldiers in civic camouflage.

Some days Damiens would choose with care, and would have his servants loosen their shirts and lower their breeches, to remind himself of each man's charms or shortcomings. That morning, however, he swaggered down the line with his eyes straight ahead and merely whispered a name to his valet.

'Renzo to his lordship's chamber.'

The parade broke up. Sympathetic hands slapped Renzo's broad shoulders, and patted his neatly formed backside. There would be no sleep for him.

At the palazzo's rear entrance, meanwhile, where the rats swarmed at the canal's edge to seize the morning slops, a kitchen drab stood on the steps staring down at the water. After a few seconds she dropped both the buckets she was holding, and put her hands to her face. She screamed. When nothing happened, she screamed again. Before long a man appeared. They stood side by side, both pointing down into the murk as if unable to believe the evidence of their eyes.

A rolled-up carpet was floating in the water. There was nothing unusual in that. Nor was it rare for dead bodies to turn up in the canals. What upset the servants was the sight of such a young, handsome face, with rats tangling in the golden hair.

Odder still, the young man blinked. He was alive.

★

The master's bedchamber was on the floor above the *piano nobile*, and shared with it one of the finest views in Venice. In one direction lay the crowded Rialto Bridge, while in the other the Grand Canal stretched down towards San Toma, lined on either side with the finest palaces in Europe. The room was bare except for a massive bed, a few oak chests, a writing desk, and some standing mirrors. The walls were draped with fine Flemish tapestries, and dappled morning sunlight reflected off the water below played across the ceiling.

As Damiens entered he paused to examine himself in a mirror set in the centre of the room. He was not pleased by what he saw. Although he was still in his early twenties the bloom had gone from his face: too many nights spent at the gaming tables, too much wine, too many of the extravagances taken for granted in Venice but unknown elsewhere had left their mark. Despite his valet's best and often frantic efforts with powder and rouge, something had been lost since he had left England. He had arrived in poverty, with nothing but his title and lordly ways, and had made himself rich again, but at a cost. He was not a sentimental man, and he saw clearly that beneath the pose, the clothes, the jewels, and all the effects of money obviously spent, there lay an exhaustion, which filled the void left where innocence, hope and love have departed.

Even so, Damiens was not entirely in despair. Tall and thin, with pale skin, and eyes a shade darker than his hair, which had the colour and sheen of polished horse-chestnuts, he was still a fine figure of a man. And he prided himself that new riches and his manner – so haughty and yet so languorous, so brutal but with such an eye for grace and beauty, and a temperament so affable one moment, so cold and demanding the next – had won the respect of all Venetian society.

And his servants feared him, as was right and proper.

A movement behind made him start. He turned and saw young Renzo waiting. Damiens had chosen him because he was tired and knew Renzo to be a willing fellow, always eager to please his master. Of course, he feigned distaste for the sexual duties required of him, but Damiens did not mind that. Enthusiasm would have been unbecoming. And the young servant had a well-knit body, healthy flat stomach, a chest free of hair, and an enticingly rounded backside, which promised rare pleasure to all who might take possession of it. Damiens had only to look at the cheery red lips and thick floppy hair, the ripe erect nipples, and take note of the alert but half-fearful look in the dark eyes to know that he had made the right choice.

Not that he had expended much thought on the matter. Renzo, after all, was merely a footman, the simple son of simple peasants. Despite all his training, he could know little of fancy ways and manners. He was a good servant, and good for fucking, but that was all. When his nose ran he wiped it on his lace cuffs, or used the edge of fine linen sheets, and there were other habits just as disgusting when practised in a gentleman's household. Stripped of his livery he looked a dolt. He was, Damiens knew, a bumpkin, and deserved to be whipped. He nodded to his valet, who was standing by ready to perform just such a task.

That was the trouble with servants. They were all so alike. It was not just the wigs and livery. They were humble and eager in the same way, and had the same vulgar habits and manners. Damiens had learned in the British army that no man chosen from the ranks should be permitted to enter a gentleman's bed unless he had first been stripped, hosed down, deloused, flogged, powdered and perfumed. And so he watched with jaded eyes as his valet took his riding-whip to Renzo's backside.

The valet, a most reliable fellow by the name of Titus, was an expert arse-tamer. He had Renzo bend over the side of a low chest, so that his tight buttocks were nicely exposed. Titus had an Englishman's delight in punishment, and in his hands a riding-whip was a fearsome thing. He took as much care to aim a stroke across the bare arse as he did when tying the knot in his master's cravat. He landed the first few cuts low, at that sweet place where the curving buttocks give way to the firmer flesh at the top of the leg. He followed those with two hard strokes, which he laid one on top of the other in the centre of the arse and then, using a flick of the wrist to excellent effect, he put on several seemingly light blows that criss-crossed the area to artful effect.

Damiens felt himself a little aroused. The servant was a sturdy chap, well able to withstand the blows, and there was no denying

27

the wicked charm of seeing an attractive lad well thrashed. Without doubt Renzo would soon revert to spitting on the floor, belching, farting and scratching his arse, but for the time being the chastisement was doing its work well. The firm arse was wriggling and its owner begged for mercy.

When Titus finally lowered the whip, and took out a handkerchief to mop his brow, he ordered Renzo to make no more fuss and get his well-striped backside on to his lordship's bed. Shorn of wig and clothes, the tearful footman looked younger and more charming as he lay among the sheets, wiping his eyes with his fingers. And there was something about the way his head fell back into the pillows that appealed to Damiens. Hitherto, he had no more in mind than a good fuck. But as Titus turned his attention once more to Renzo, placed the weeping servant on his side, and rubbed olive oil between the buttocks to loosen the hole, Damiens' bored expression turned to one of intrigued delight. For dangling from Renzo's groin was a truly exceptional cock.

Of course, such a thing was not meant to interest Damiens, cocks being neither here nor there in the catalogue of a gentleman's pleasure. A decent bum-hole was what mattered, not the bummer's cock. And yet . . . what splendour there was in the wilful coil stirring among the bedlinen. Did it not part the pubic hair most charmingly? And demand to be worshipped? Should not even a lord bend to venerate such an idol, no matter who owned it? And would it not be good to feel such a length of warmth and strength against the back of the mouth?

Ignoring his valet's gasp, Damiens knelt beside the bed and took hold of the cock. Slowly he ran his hand down to its base and squeezed. The head sprang from its covering, and a dribble of moisture oozed from the slit. Damiens reached underneath for the balls and grabbed them. He might be on his knees before his servant, but he would not allow the fellow to imagine he would be getting off lightly. He tightened his grip until Renzo buried his head in the pillow. Damiens smiled. Things were as they should be. He was in command, and there was no reason why he should not take the cock and balls in his mouth to enjoy as he might some particularly delicious cakes. Wasn't a gentleman always under an obligation to investigate unusual phenomena?

It had been a long time since he had sucked a man off. The last time had been in the army with a brother officer who had wrestled him to the ground in the riding school. That incident had taught him that it was best to suck hard and deep, and to breathe through the nose, for as long as it took for the flood to arrive. Even afterwards it was wise to stick with the task until the last dregs were out.

Damiens was enjoying himself. Having been raised with all the privileges of his class, it amused him when things went topsy-turvy. Renzo would have been expecting to be whipped . . . and he had been. He would have expected to be laid on his stomach and fucked . . . and might still be, but what he had not been expecting was to be sucked as dry as the desert by an English milord known to hunger for arseholes rather than cocks.

When Renzo reached his climax, he did not warn his master of the impending flood. There was no time. With an agonised gasp, he reared up and, taking his master's head in his hands, pressed it down on to his spouting cock. For a moment Damiens choked and fought to be free, but Renzo used his peasant's strength and instinct to keep the aristocrat's head in place until he had emptied the whole of his load.

The valet provided a bucket for his master to spit into, and used towels to wipe him clean. He was shocked. He had believed himself in service to an English milord, and it was not proper for such gentlemen to suck the cocks of Italian domestics. He did not like to see his master with white glue dribbling from his mouth, while his footman lay on the bed groaning with pleasure. It was the world turned upside down. No good would come of it.

# Six

───────

Rob was not sure whether he was among the living or the dead. It was difficult to tell when his body was numb, his head ached, and all the eye could see was wizened old faces, with gaping mouths chattering in a tongue he could not understand. But whether dead or alive, he knew he had been on a strange journey.

His survival had not been entirely a miracle. At the last moment the gondolier had sliced through the rope tying one end of the carpet in which Rob lay unconscious before tipping it into the canal. The rascal was not often moved to mercy, but had once guarded an English sailor in the Doge's prison – and he had never forgotten the way the lad had bent to receive his cock up his arse. And there had been something sweet in his surrender to torture that had melted the frozen core that passed for the gondolier's heart. So it had seemed no more than the devil's justice that he should give a chance to another English sailor, one whose buttocks were as full and as firm, and whose eyes were as willing as those that had stared up at him in the dungeon's gloom.

Rob had drifted unconscious. At some point a scavenger had hauled the carpet from the water, but on seeing what it contained had thrown it back. All night, as he drifted, he dreamed of England. Life there had not been without pain and sadness, and he had signed on with the *Dawn Treader* without regret. But his heart had been full of hope back then; and as he lay close to death in liquid filth, his mind returned to his England.

Images strange and familiar, like someone else's memories, flooded his mind's eye. He was back home in Kent, on the day of the Ashford Fayre.

He had sweated long hours in his father's orchards, and was ready for amusement. With his friend Angus, a Scottish lad recently arrived from the north, he had strolled through the town. They tested their skills and strength in the side-shows, drank cider and chased some girls. Later they boxed each other for the few pennies tossed in the ring, and afterwards allowed a jovial chap to buy them ale in an inn where there was music and dancing.

Rob and Angus were as unlike one another as true friends should be. The Scottish lad was dark with powerful shoulders and arms, a deep hairy chest and a wide hairy arse, whereas Rob had fair skin and a slim figure full of grace. But Angus never took advantage of Rob, and if they fought, their bouts were always good-natured and quickly subsided into wrestling and laughter. For Rob, even Angus's Scottish accent, so laughable to Kentish ears, had come to sound like gay music.

That evening, at nightfall, the Fayre continued merrily. Neither boy wanted to go home while the girls were still dancing, the inns were open and flares lit up the town square − not while there were jokes to be shared and the night air was warm and still. There was work to be done in the morning, but even so they did not hurry, preferring to forget their fathers waiting at home. And when they did finally leave, after a last drink and a song, it seemed natural that they should stop and carve their names on a tree, then climb it and fall out of it. And afterwards get lost, although Rob knew the road as well as any.

So perhaps it was not so surprising that when they reached the cottage where Angus lived the night was fading fast. Birds were singing. Rob was ready to say goodnight and hurry home to climb in at the window and catch an hour's sleep. But Angus saw that the lights were on in his house: to go in would be to walk straight into a hiding, and his arse was still warm from the last one.

Rob did not need much persuading to stay out so they wandered down past the orchards towards the fields by the river. There they lay under an oak. It was going to be another warm day and all chance of sleep was gone. Only the effects of the cider lingered.

Or was it something stronger than cider that made Rob feel so light-headed and happy? The two boys lay side by side, and tried to make music from pressing blades of grass to their lips. Rob wondered why everything Angus said seemed so wise and proper. And why . . . why did he feel so strange every time he looked at Angus? What was that quickening, that flush, stirring and tightening in his chest and groin? What did it mean? And did Angus feel the same?

Neither went to work that day, and neither escaped a thrashing that evening. But it had been worth it, a thousand times over. In friendship their lives had changed. Both boys had been lonely, without knowing they were. Both had much to say for themselves, but had never been heard. For the first time they had spoken from the heart, and opened their hearts to listen. And they had shared their dreams, and hopes, had seen a future for themselves as bright as the sun shining that morning over the orchards of Kent.

That was their only day together. Their fathers, concerned that their sons should not fall into idle and drunken ways, forbade them to meet again, and used their belts to make sure the point was taken. Angus, being a little older and with a resolute character already formed, left home in fury. When Rob heard what had happened, he was inconsolable. Too young to fathom his loss and its meaning, he drifted about the farm, seldom speaking, and never smiling. His father, no less at a loss to know what to do, told the boy that if he worked hard for the rest of the summer he would let him go with his blessing and a few shillings in his pocket.

At harvest time Rob heard that Angus had signed on as an able seaman at Chatham docks, and was most likely already fighting the French. He went and sat under the oak tree by the river. Later that evening, with his father's handshake still warm on his palm, he had set off on his own journey.

32

These memories drifted through his mind until, in pain and dizziness, his consciousness returned. He found himself dragged from the water, and laid out to dry on a marble slab in the cold dungeon of the Palazzo Ferri.

# Seven

In the great bedchamber of the Palazzo Ferri, where Renzo lay sprawled among the tousled sheets, Lord Damiens had regained his composure. He had his valet rub him down with towels and scrub out his mouth with salted water – an unpleasant process, but Damiens wanted rid of the fruity flavour of Renzo's come. Besides which, there was business to attend to, and he still had not had his fuck.

While he dressed, Damiens sent for his senior servants so that they might receive their instructions. They entered like a troop of ancient soldiers begging for charity, four portly figures marching one behind the other, each clutching to his chest a notepad, or files containing bills and correspondence.

Damiens enjoyed shocking these old gentlemen, who had between them served so many masters in so many great houses that they seemed scarcely aware of where they were or who they were serving. There was not much sport to be had in Venice, so Damiens would often make them his prey. Accordingly, he had Titus dress him in a richly brocaded silk dressing-gown, which was left open at the front.

The servants watched in silence as Lord Damiens lit a cigar, and asked for a glass of champagne. He ordered young Renzo from the bed, and had him stand, still naked, behind the large desk over which a mass of papers was spread. Titus, knowing what his master was intending, stood by with the olive oil, once more ready to rub the soft thick liquid between the cheeks of the servant's backside.

Lord Damiens hated fucking a raw hide. When he came up behind Renzo, blew smoke in his ear and told him to bend over the desk, the young footman did not hesitate to obey. Damiens prepared to insert himself without ado. There was no need for the niceties demanded by society ladies or expensive whores. And why deny himself a little rough pleasure? Should a servant not think it right and proper to be taken by his master, and by such a rampant cock?

The old servants stood dumbstruck. They had seen plenty of strange sights, but the English milord was quite the most shameless. And yet, for all their clucking and tittering, they could not prevent their shrivelled loins from stirring at the sight of handsome young Renzo all ready and waiting for a lordly stuffing. His recently thrashed backside stuck up in the air as he lay face down on the papers covering the desktop. With his legs apart, and the back of his slender torso in full view, he made a most appealing sight to Lord Damiens, who drew on his cigar, and went to mount him.

Titus had done his work well. His cock slipped between the cheeks, and met only token resistance at the gate before sliding easily into the interior. Damiens sighed with pure pleasure. He was himself again, and all was well.

Being in no hurry to reach a climax, and knowing the old servants had their duties to attend to, he set himself a moderate pace, driving his cock deep each time, and pulling back until the tip was tickled at the entrance. Having a long course to run, he told Titus to bring the old men forward, one by one, so that he could attend to their business.

Titus stood by with pen and ink, and the old men made their representations, explained which creditors needed paying and which might be made to wait. All the while Damiens rode Renzo with elegant movements. He said little, but drew deep on his cigar, refreshed himself with sips of champagne, and allowed himself the odd groan of satisfaction. The old men did not know whether to laugh or avert their eyes, but when, their business completed, they shuffled out, throwing glances over their shoulders, they were as impressed by their copulating master as they were flustered. Such goings on! These English milords were splendid barbarians.

Damiens could have continued his leisurely fuck all day. With an excellent smoke, and a view of the Grand Canal shimmering in the morning sunshine, and the equally pleasing sight of Renzo sprawled before him, he saw no need to hurry his pleasures. But he was not to be left undisturbed for long. Titus returned with a frown on his face. 'My lord, the servants say they have taken in a boy downstairs.'

'So what, Titus? Can't you see I'm still fucking this one?' Damiens was finally moving towards a climax. To be interrupted was little short of impertinence. If Titus wasn't such a reliable fellow . . .

'They say, sir, that he cannot speak. They think he may be a spy.'

'Do they, indeed?' This news was enough to break Damiens' rhythm. He wanted no trouble with the authorities. He spent enough on bribes as it was. But he knew enough of the Venetian character to feel sure they would admire him if he showed panache in dealing with a spy. He stubbed out his cigar, downed the last of the wine, and set about fucking with a will. 'In which case, Titus, we shall put him to the test.' His breath was short. 'If he is a spy, we will give him a tale to tell his masters about life at the Palazzo Ferri.'

Rob opened his eyes and saw a large woman leaning over him. Her features were coarse and bloated. As their eyes met he shivered. In the cold, the dark and the silence, she loomed as if intent on taking possession of him, body and soul. He tried to speak, but the woman shook her head vigorously and placed a hand over his mouth. There were whispers in the background, and the sound of feet running on stairs.

A man's voice was barking orders, and the woman's face disappeared to be replaced by that of two young men. One stared down with a twisted smile playing on his lips, and the other widened his eyes as if to alarm a child. There was more shouting, and Rob found himself lifted roughly and set on his feet. All at once he felt giddy and his knees buckled. He fell sideways into the arms of one of the attendants, who shook him violently. There was a roaring sound inside his head, and his mouth was horribly dry. His gut tightened into a spasm and released liquid into his bowel.

He struggled to be free, but the ruffian held him tight. Rob managed to point a finger to his belly, and perhaps because the man sensed a crisis, he found himself left to sway on his wobbly legs. Looking round he saw he was in a dark chamber, and surrounded by perhaps a dozen men and women who were staring at him as if he were the strangest sight they had ever seen. Some wore fine livery, but most were dressed as kitchen servants and handymen.

The only light came from a couple of barred openings low on one wall that let in the shimmering glare of sunlight on water. The floor was covered in puddles, and the air was dank and fetid. Cages stuffed with live poultry were stacked in a corner, and the high walls were hung with weaponry. A massive staircase rose along the back wall lit by two flaming torches. Under one of these a tall figure in a blue and gold dressing-gown was standing, hand on hip, looking down at the scene below with an expression of studied distaste.

The young man who had been barking orders strode towards Rob. He carried a riding-whip and spoke slowly in what Rob took to be Italian. As he came close Rob could feel the warmth of his breath.

Rob shook his head in confusion. The man continued to shout in his face and prod him with the whip, until Rob swayed and fell towards his interrogator, who without ado, pushed him away and used a gloved hand to slap him hard across each cheek. 'Keep off, you blackguard.'

Hearing English, Rob cried out in surprise. But he could not speak. Words failed to form. His tongue lolled loosely in his mouth. He wanted to say, 'I'm an Englishman, sir,' but the sound was as distant and indistinct as a drunk muttering in a stupor.

The man stood back. 'I fancy you understand me, young sir,

but if you will play the fool, be assured this is not the place for jokes. Nor will we be beguiled by trickery.'

Rob did his best to stand straight, but he hadn't the strength. He tried a second time to speak, this time to say, 'Able Seaman Weaver, off the *Dawn Treader*, a merchant ship in His Majesty's service,' but the words were as slurred and jumbled as before, and he was quickly overcome with dizziness, and a fresh loosening in his bowel. His vision faded as he fell.

The next he knew he was gasping for breath. Shafts of brilliant light flickered in front of him, and his nostrils and mouth were full of cold water. He was drenched. Suddenly he was aware of laughter, loud and mocking, and as his sight cleared he saw that he was in the same dark chamber but was now seated on a chair. Several men were standing round and looking at him with expressions of frank appraisal. One held an empty, swaying bucket.

To wipe away the liquid still troubling his eyes, and dripping from his nose, he attempted to raise his hands, but found they were tied to the sides of the chair. When he tried to rise he discovered his feet were bound and that a rope fastened him at the waist. All he could do was return the men's stares, and pray they meant him no harm. But he only had to look a couple of them in the eye to know that harm might well be their intention. They stared at him with the steady gaze and sure stance of those who have pleasure and sport in mind.

If only his shirt was not dripping with cold water, his head did not ache and he did not feel so cold and vulnerable, he might have been able to muster sufficient spirit to put up a defence. As it was he was too weak, too disheartened, too confused, lost and alone. He could only lower his eyes and wait to see what they would do to him.

He did not have to wait long.

A swarthy fellow stepped forward. His hands gripped his belt, and his smile revealed gaps among his yellowing teeth. His eyes shone bright with desire. He stood close, and leaned back to push his fly forward, close to Rob's mouth. There was no doubt what he wanted. But Rob was not prepared to give the ruffian such pleasure. Sooner or later he would have to resist, if he were to avoid sucking off all of them, so he might as well do so right from the start. Like an animal that can only defend itself from a predator by revealing its defences, Rob parted his lips and showed off his white teeth. He snapped them together in a fierce bite.

For a moment the man lost heart, and took a step back, but another fellow standing right behind him said something, and pushed his way past. Without ado he unbuttoned his fly and reached in for a large coiling organ, whose wrinkles were rapidly disappearing as it expanded.

The man pushed a finger into Rob's mouth, and laughed. When Rob did not part his teeth, the man withdrew his finger and used his hand to box Rob's ear. Then he tried again, and this time Rob, without realising he had done so, opened his mouth like an obedient patient ready to have his teeth pulled.

The man grabbed him by the crown of his hair and, jerking his head back, used a thrust of his hips to insert his cock into Rob's mouth with all the casual confidence of a man taking a piss.

Rob gagged, and might have tried to close his bite, but his head was too far back, and his mouth too far open. The man took a firmer grip of his hair, and Rob felt the binding ropes cutting. Further resistance was impossible. He could only submit and hope to survive.

The first man was not much longer about his business than if he had indeed been taking a piss. Nor did he produce much spunk. Rob felt a warm, unwelcome dribble run over his tongue, but little else, despite the man's mighty roars which would not have disgraced an ox servicing a cow.

As soon as this first tormentor slunk off, stuffing his flabby stump back into his fly with a smug grin on his face, a second man stepped forward. This one was younger, more businesslike, and the cock he produced was longer and sprang forth from the folds of linen with its head already free of the foreskin and ready for action. He stood over Rob and laughed, bent forward to plant a kiss on his lips. Rob saw that he was really very handsome, with broad shoulders and fine dark hair, his eyes lit as much with intelligence as lust. Not that the fellow was any less inclined to use cruel means: he slapped Rob hard across the mouth he had just kissed and rubbed his stiff cock teasingly against Rob's nostrils. Sensing that this new tormentor was not a man to be denied his pleasure, Rob once again opened his mouth, felt the cock travel inwards until it hit the back of his throat and turned downwards before being pulled back to make a fresh thrust.

This young man was no novice in the arts of love. Although his cock was long, and slid through Rob's mouth to plunge down his throat like a leaping dog, there was a control, a sense of naked animal lust tamed by an intelligence that bore in its wake a certain tenderness. For all the squalor of the occasion, Rob found, as he strove to breathe and to accept the warm length of firm flesh delving into him, that there was something pleasurable in the invasion. Even the smell of his oppressor's sweat was sweet and meaty. Had he not been bound hand and foot he might have reached out and held the stranger close.

The climax came with all the force and spillage of a young man expending himself with passion and energy, and Rob thrust back his head to accept the load without rancour. Whatever the circumstance, he was in no doubt that the man had been making love to him, just as the poor doomed stowaway had when they lay in each other's arms on the *Dawn Treader*. There the love making had been tender, as befitted the yearnings of two lonely young men, while here it had been roughly administered. Nevertheless there had been finesse and feeling in every expert thrust and near-withdrawal.

As the handsome young fellow pulled himself free, and ruffled Rob's hair and muttered, '*Che bei capelli biondi*,' as he swaggered away, there were sounds of approval from those watching.

Rob felt himself shudder. The warmth flooding his insides seemed to turn cold and sticky, and filled him with nausea. He was waking from a pleasant dream into dangerous reality. If he left himself at the mercy of these ruffians, it was unlikely he would find another to equal the fellow at that moment busy squeezing his cock back into his breeches with a smile of frank delight.

Rob had to think quickly. Although his experience of life was limited, he fancied himself an observant fellow, and he remembered how, on the *Dawn Treader*, some of the crew, unable to defend themselves, had found protectors to fight for them. In return they were expected to perform whatever tasks were necessary to retain their defender's favour. Rob had not found such doings seemly, and had despised both the protected and the protectors. But he had been green still in those days, and only now was learning that sooner or later all men come to face the moment when they are forced into the basest calculations and must resort to whatever expediency allows them to survive. No matter how degrading the choice, Rob knew that, in the end, it is better to live than perish.

And so, faced with a line of half a dozen ugly men of low rank, united only by a transparent wish to take advantage of him and use him as their plaything, Rob moved to save himself. He called out to the young fellow whose cock he had just sucked dry, 'Why, sir, will you not linger a while? Is your appetite so shallow you will leave after the first course, when so many others are on offer?'

This time his voice rang out clear and true. He hoped someone might understand. After all, he had heard English spoken in the dungeon before he had passed out.

There was a laugh from the shadows, and the young man with the riding-whip, who had addressed him in English, appeared. He spoke Italian, and was evidently translating what Rob had said because the fellow still adjusting his breeches turned towards Rob with an expression of amused surprise. From the corner of his eye Rob saw also that the eager expressions on the faces of the men waiting their turn were changing from open lust to wary caution. He had chosen the right man as his champion. For the first time since he had been dragged from the canal, Rob allowed himself a moment of pure relief. Already the line of those waiting to enjoy him was melting away, and was now unlikely to be swollen by rumour to include servants from other palazzi, passing tradesmen, footpads, and all the other opportunists on the city streets. It was better by far to surrender to the young man whose cock had recently been plunged down his throat with such finesse.

★

Rob soon discovered that his protector was not a servant of the house. With his hands still bound, he found himself led out of the palazzo's rear entrance, up some steps and across a small walled garden, past crumbling statues and vast decaying urns, towards the gatehouse. There were shouts of derision from onlookers watching from the surrounding windows. Rob felt like a common slave in the sodden remains of his sailor's uniform, but there was nothing he could do except allow himself to be dragged along, roped to a young man of whom he knew nothing, who pranced ahead as if he were the lord of the palazzo.

Rob remained alert, however, and noticed that the garden gate opened on to a narrow street, which led over the dark canal, from which he had been rescued, to disappear among tall buildings. To escape on foot, he told himself, would be better than by water.

The gateman, a thin, bent figure in a torn grey overcoat, with a pair of glasses pressed on his swollen nose, and clutching in his mittens a keyring the size of a dinner plate, cackled into mirth as Rob was pushed in through the gatehouse door. A sharp word made the old man stand back and they passed by into a tiny room half hidden behind a curtain. This was furnished with nothing more than a meagre bed, a shabby chair and a writing desk, on which were piled loose and scrolled papers, books and parchments, quill-pens, inks and guttered candles.

Once the door was shut, the young man's manner softened. He took Rob's hands and used a knife to cut through the rope binding them. A half-smile played on his lips. '*Mi chiamo* Silvio. *E tu?*'

Rob understood, and smiled back. 'And me . . . Robert. To my friends . . . Rob.'

Silvio was still smiling. 'Rob? *Si, bene.*' He frowned with concentration. 'You call me . . . Signore . . . sir.'

Rob nodded. 'Aye-aye, sir.'

Silvio was still frowning. 'Aye-aye . . . What is . . .?'

Knowing he must keep the initiative, Rob fell to his knees. He reached forwards and placed a hand on Silvio's fly. 'This, Signore, is my . . . aye-aye.' He glanced up into Silvio's dark

42

eyes, and saw that they were no longer surrounded by a frown but were the centre of an expression of bewildered delight. 'And this . . .' he leaned forward to kiss where his hand had touched '. . . this is . . . Rob.'

# Eight

Although Silvio was a mere secretary in the service of the Palazzo Ferri's landlord, the better part of his income derived from the reports he laid regularly on the local magistrate's desk. These gave colourful accounts of the milord's doings, the mysterious methods he had used to enrich himself, and of his unusual tastes, the many comings and goings necessary to satisfy them. In this way he had proved himself useful to those whose duty it was to spy on foreigners, and the authorities who must negotiate the fees and permits required of them.

Nevertheless, Silvio felt himself lacking the respect properly due to a man of his learning and abilities. His father was a humble cobbler who had paid for his son's studies at Padua, and after such sacrifice was eager to see evidence of his son's status. If Silvio could contrive to arrive at his father's shop in one of the palazzo's fine gondolas, attended by a young servant with golden locks, the old man might cease his nagging. Besides, Silvio had enjoyed leading the bound young northerner through the garden to his room, and was now captivated by the idea of showing him off to the whole of Venice. Would not every fop lolling on the Rialto envy him as he strode past followed by such a handsome and unusual servant? Would not the whores calculate his worth, and even respectable ladies eye him with interest from behind their masks and fans? In a city where the only sound currencies were gold and human flesh, Silvio knew he had an asset worth more than any magistrate's purse.

He would not give up his prize without a fight.

It had been almost noon before Lord Damiens fell asleep. He left instructions that he was not to be disturbed until seven. With a ball to attend, a dinner beforehand, supper afterwards and a visit to a brothel, if there were winnings at the gaming tables, he needed the rest.

On the lower floors the household returned to a state of bored inactivity. There were too many servants and, given the milord's way of life, there was not enough for them to do during the usual hours of work but often too much at other times.

In the kitchens the maids sat around preparing food for their evening meal, gossiping with the footmen, who were pretending to polish silverware. They passed the time discussing the young foreigner they had dragged in from the canal. Most took the view that he should have been well fucked and thrown back where he had come from: those who could not speak in a civilised tongue were not to be trusted. A more kindly few, however, felt he had been harshly welcomed in a manner that showed them in almost as poor a light as the doings of the milord and his henchmen.

Only the arrival of Titus, his lordship's young valet – his riding-whip, as always, at the ready – put an end to the fruitless debate. Although disliked below stairs, Titus was also feared as a power in the household. As the servants hurried to be seen busying themselves, Titus demanded to know what had happened to the young intruder.

'Silvio has him,' said a footman, whose command of English, learned as a mercenary, did not prevent him from earning a smart cut across his backside for failing to add a respectful 'Signore'.

'Has him? Where?' Titus seemed perplexed.

'In the gatehouse, Signore. The rascal was ravenous . . . Once he'd had a taste of Silvio . . .' the footman shrugged '. . . he was like a dog, begging for more.'

This news displeased Titus. Such a development was not a part of his plan. He had expected to find the foreigner confined in one of the dungeons, and put to use for the general pleasure of

the household. With the stuffing knocked out of him he would
have been full of gratitude when rescued and presented to his
lordship, whose eye he had caught when Damiens had briefly
inspected him from the staircase. Without doubt he would be
eager to fuck him, but he preferred to have his bed kept warm
by the grateful and the willing. Titus did not relish having to tell
his master that the object of his desire had fallen into the hands
of Silvio, a young man whose first loyalties lay elsewhere. In
Venice those with divided loyalties were dangerous.

As Titus left the kitchens he told himself he would have to
choose carefully the moment at which to report this defection to
his master.

Meanwhile, in the small room at the back of the gatehouse, Rob
lay on the narrow bed and pressed himself close against Silvio.
Their clothes lay across the floor and bedding, and a dappled
watery light played across their naked bodies. Both were of the
same height and much the same build, but one had pale skin
while the other's was much darker. Neither had spoken for a
while and, their cocks flaccid once more, each was content
merely to sigh or, now and then, press his lips against the other's
warm flesh.

Their love-making had led them into unexplored territories.
Rob had planned a seduction as a diversion, and as the bold
prelude to his escape, but his nakedness compelled him to
dispense with subtlety. To allay any suspicions Silvio might have
had, he had knelt and closed his mouth over the cock that had
only recently fed him.

Silvio had flattered himself that the pleasure of having a head
covered in soft golden hair offer its mouth at his groin was no
more than due wages for having saved the fellow from the rabble
in the palazzo's kitchen. But as Rob worked delicate miracles
with his tongue and lips, Silvio had found himself overcome, not
merely with urgent lust but also with the desire to show his lover
the man he was. He pulled Rob's head from his crotch and raised
it to kiss the warm lips.

Everything about the Englishman was new to him – the soft
fine hair, the voice, the seaman's hands and feet, skin that smelt

of limes. They fell back on the bed where they writhed together and strained in surrender and conquest. Silvio, used to a chaste, lonely existence, felt himself shedding his skin of aloofness, and detaching himself from the claws of loneliness, which had dug into him so deeply and for so long. Rob, on the other hand, had taken Silvio's passion as a challenge to imitate those bites, kisses, and caresses so liberally expended on him. He engaged in fervid give and take, and showed a calculated wantonness. Their love-making, although born of ambition and deception, eventually melded into the spontaneous union of two souls variously and helplessly voyaging into the unknown.

When they were done, neither thought to move. They were lost in their separate reveries. The silence was broken by the soft rippling of a gondola drifting past, or by the sound of the bell that roused the grumbling gateman from his siesta. Rob's thoughts were no longer of escape, and Silvio no longer felt consumed by any ambition to reduce his lover to mere human bounty. As the light softened and faded, and they drifted towards sleep, they closed their arms around each other as if to offer protection from all the dangers of the world that lay beyond their small domain.

Nothing was done on time in Venice, and when Titus shook his master awake the lamps had already been lit on the landings, and through the deep windows in the great bedchamber swallows could be seen swooping and diving as a silvery twilight spread over the Grand Canal. This was always a fraught moment. If Damiens woke unrefreshed, or with a head still sore from too much hock and brandy, he would greet those serving him with insults and threats.

But on this day, at least, Titus was spared the task of placating his master's sorry moods. Lord Damiens woke with a smile, and bade his valet a good evening as he stretched his long limbs with easy sensuality. He demanded nothing more than a cup of hot chocolate and almond and cinnamon cakes warm from the oven. He gazed around as if delighted that fate had delivered him from his dreams into such magnificence.

Eager not to dampen his high spirits – for he was as moody as any flouncing tart – Titus set out to amuse his master as he dressed him, and thereby keep his mind off thoughts of the intruder. There had been other comings and goings at the palazzo that day which were worthy of recounting. And so, as he powdered Damiens' crotch and armpits and made ready his stockings, he told how a local countess, very much down on her luck after being deserted by her cardinal lover, had arrived on foot with a bedraggled daughter in tow. She had come less to pay her respects than to offer up her offspring, which she had done without finesse and with only a puny runny-nosed page in attendance. Titus had sent the sad party on its way. 'It would seem, my lord, that her churchman has left her without so much as the price of hire for a gondola.'

Damiens laughed. He always enjoyed hearing of his valet's ruthless way with those unworthy to be received at the Palazzo Ferri.

Nor had the unfortunate countess's visit been the only one. While kneeling to ease a pair of freshly perfumed silken under-pants up his master's legs, Titus related how he had sent an impertinent tradesman away with a flea in his ear. The man had dared to demand settlement of an account only six months in arrears. After that, as he used his palm and fingers to ensure his master dressed to the right and before he fastened the buttons on his silver and grey brocade breeches, Titus told of a visit from a young Englishman. This person, of unprepossessing appearance, had presented himself as being on the final leg of a Grand Tour. Titus had interrupted his stuttering explanations to suggest he find himself a guide of decent local pedigree or, at least, one of the Englishmen residing in Venice, who made a living from introducing young men to whatever level of Venetian society was compatible with their status. This unfortunate, too, had been dismissed.

Emboldened by Damiens' laughter, Titus went on merrily, speaking through clenched teeth, which held several pearl-tipped pins, as he made a fifth and successful attempt to tie an acceptable knot in his lordship's cravat. He told of how old Lord Cambrake had turned up in a state of inebriation and had immediately passed out on a chaise on the *piano nobile*. Titus had ordered a bed to be made up on an upper landing, and the fat old man had not stirred when carried up three flights by four sweating footmen. This story delighted Damiens, who told of how the old drunk had once fought with the Duke of Marlborough in the Peninsular War, but had since degenerated so much as to be unwelcome even among the most impoverished Venetian noblemen. The tale allowed Titus time to complete his duties by sprinkling cologne on a lace handkerchief, which he placed in a side pocket of his master's splendid burgundy and gold coat.

But if the valet thought he had distracted his master's attention sufficiently to avoid the topic of the young intruder, he was mistaken. Damiens was as skilful in reading the minds of his servants as they were in reading his moods, and he well knew that Titus's pithy story-telling was a cover to hide news he would rather not mention. It was not his habit to be bested by his servants, nor did he take kindly to being manipulated. As he made to leave, therefore, he paused to choose a nosegay from among a display set beside one of the long mirrors. 'So tell me, Titus, what has become of our young friend?'

Titus knew it would be unwise to play ignorant. 'He is with the landlord's agent, master.'

Damiens glanced up a moment from examining himself. 'You mean that rascal Silvio?'

'Yes, my lord.'

'So one spy has the custody of another.' Damiens did not sound angry, and he resumed his inspection by tugging at his shaggy locks. His wig-master would attend him later, just before the guests arrived, because he preferred to go bare-headed in his own house.

Titus was not fooled. His plan had failed and he would have to face the consequences. 'My lord, the intruder is not, I think, a spy. He is not Venetian – indeed, sir, I very much suspect he is an Englishman, although he has been in no state to tell us who he is.'

For a moment Damiens neither spoke nor lifted his eyes from the mirror. Titus stood still, not daring to move until he knew what his master's reaction was going to be.

'We have dinner guests, do we not?' Damiens still had not moved.

'Yes, my lord, and the ball at the Palazzo Mazzario.'

'Of course.' His voice was barely audible. 'And supper?'

'Here, my lord, or at the gaming house. Wherever you wish, sir.'

'My wishes seem to count for little.'

Titus did not dare reply.

'Remind me, Titus . . . in the morning.' Damiens strode towards the door. His fancy pumps snapped on the polished wooden planks, and he called out, 'Be a good fellow now – and don't forget.'

'Forget, my lord?'

Damiens stopped at the door that had been opened by a footman. Without looking round he said quietly, 'That I must meet our young friend from England . . .'

'Of course, my lord.' An expression of relief spread across Titus's face.

Damiens strode on through the door. 'And offer you a choice.'

'A choice, my lord?' Anxiety returned.

There was a patter of footsteps on the stairs as Damiens disappeared. He called out, 'Between a thrashing and sodomy.'

# Nine

U nder the terms of the landlord's lease Silvio was entitled to a daily meal in the palazzo's kitchen. His recent affluence had not dissolved his taste for economy, and he made a habit of fasting during the hours of daylight before presenting himself at the kitchen door at dusk. He did not care what he ate, so long as his plate and wine jug were full, and he was content to sit by himself in a corner away from the long tables where the servants ate. If there was a lamp to read by, and warm food was served promptly, he made no complaint.

But with Rob in tow such modesty was overtaken by pride. Silvio refused the small table in the corner and called for a larger one. He demanded three courses, instead of his usual two, bottled wine, and silver knives to cut the meat and fruit. When the steward hesitated, Silvio banged his fist on the table and said that if he were denied his full entitlement he would remind Lord Damiens of his obligations.

While this altercation was going on, Rob's fair good looks drew all eyes in the kitchen. Gone was the soaked and ragged uniform: in its place he wore one of Silvio's plain white shirts. This had been left open at the neck, as if ready for love-making, and he was sporting a pair of black breeches that showed off to elegant effect his thighs and calves, and the bulge between his legs.

Silvio, too, had forsaken his shabby coat and stained trousers for a freshly laundered shirt and a pair of yellow breeches that flattered his dark skin and eyes to startling effect.

Although no one dared say so, for fear of being seen to side with those who might be traitors to the house, the two young men made a striking pair, and the young maids who brought their food did so with blushing cheeks and trembling hands.

Since jumping ship Rob had eaten only crusts and drunk water, so the plate of seasoned fish and vegetables, the warm fresh bread, and excellent wine, seemed like the food of the gods. His spirits rose, and he wondered at his luck. Was it not a miracle that a Kentish lad, who had been set upon only recently by scoundrels and left for drowned, should find himself seated in the kitchen of a grand house? And was not the food the finest he had ever eaten, and did not the ruby red wine taste as sourly delicious as life itself?

The kitchen was as busy as the *Dawn Treader*'s decks when all hands were called. The cooks stood over their ovens and fires, stirring steaming pots with giant spoons, and wiping away sweat from their faces with their sleeves. Two fat butchers hacked at some game amid swirling feathers. Bare-armed maids rushed back and forth from the scullery, and liveried footmen lined up to carry food to the diners upstairs. The double doors leading to the back stairs swung to and fro as they hurried out with massive platters, painted in gaudy colours, and silver dishes, encrusted with decoration, held high over their heads, while others came crashing back in to take their place in the queue once more. Everyone was shouting and cursing, at one another or themselves.

Snatches of music could be heard from upstairs, and overhead the pitter-patter of leather soles and the low roar of conversation penetrated the thick floors.

Rob felt dazzled. 'This must be the grandest house in Venice.' He reached into his mouth to retrieve a large fish bone and, holding it up for inspection, smiled at Silvio, who replied in rapid Italian. Rob did not bother to try to understand. He cared only for the movement and the excitement all around. His senses were swimming.

Silvio reached across and touched Rob on the forearm. 'The milord . . . he is not . . . good man.'

Rob was startled. He had not expected to be addressed in English. 'Who?' His attention was already drifting away. One of the footmen had winked at him, and Rob was eager to wink back. Despite his unfriendly welcome earlier in the day, there was no denying that some of the fellows looked perfectly splendid. Everyone, he decided, should wear livery. It seemed a pity to have to sit in silence with Silvio, who was always frowning and shaking his head, when Rob could have joined in the fun.

But Silvio was determined to have his say. He struggled on in English. 'Bad here . . . much bad here. Do you understand?'

Rob did not – neither did he want to. The footman had winked a second time, then said something to the fellow standing beside him, who looked Rob up and down with open interest.

Silvio touched his arm again. 'I shall help you . . . go.'

Rob glanced across at Silvio, who was still staring at him intently. His saviour he may have been but, now that his belly was full, Rob felt able to stand on his own two feet. He needed no help from any gloomy scholar eager to play nurse. 'Go? Go where?'

'Here . . . much danger.' Silvio pointed a finger towards Rob, who shrugged and turned back to see what the footmen were doing. What danger could there be among such handsome fellows?

When their meal was over, Silvio did not wait around. He rose and stood over Rob to make sure he did not linger. Rob saw no reason to hurry back to the secretary's dingy room when he might be enjoying himself in more lively company. But Silvio insisted, and in the end lifted Rob to his feet and took him by the arm as he led the way.

Outside it was dark, and a soft evening breeze disturbed the trees overhead. As soon as the kitchen door closed behind them, Rob freed himself from Silvio's grasp. Their love-making earlier in the day may have been sweet, but Silvio had since lost his charm. The idea of spending the evening with him, of being pawed by him and sighed over while being lectured in Italian, was insufferable.

With the food and wine fresh in his system, Rob was in a mood to be reckless and, glancing round to make sure he and Silvio were alone in the garden, he decided to make a break for it. The *Dawn Treader* might still be in port, and ready to set sail to other cities where other adventures would be waiting. And even if it wasn't, Rob was sure it was better to be a free man roaming the city. Venice would favour the brave.

He ran towards the gate, but even in the darkness he could see that it was locked. A light was on in the gatehouse, and he could envisage the old man sitting there clutching his ring of keys. Dodging to his right, and ignoring Silvio's cries of alarm, Rob made towards the high fencing that bordered the narrow canal at the rear of the palazzo. Again, it was clear that there was no way of escape: the fence was high and spiked – if he tried to climb it he would find himself impaled.

He could hear Silvio calling his name, laughing, and when he looked round Rob saw him standing on the path, hands on hips, like a patient mother waiting for a child. He must know there was no way out. For a moment Rob thought he might flee back to the kitchen and follow the serving stairs up to the *piano nobile*, and from there jump into the Grand Canal. It was a brave thought, but a silly one. Rob could not swim, and he remembered again that the water was foul with the plague.

'*Vieni, bello . . . vieni.*' Silvio was almost cooing. No doubt he had in mind some punishment and was enjoying coaxing his captive back to face it.

But Rob had never been one to give up. There was still one way out of the garden and into the city.

He ran towards the gatehouse and flung himself against the door so that it burst open. The old gatekeeper was sitting on a stool beside a table. A lamp shed a soft glow, which illuminated the huge keyring hanging from the front of his belt. With a single stride Rob was close enough to take hold of the ring and wrench it free. It came away with a loud click. The old man remained where he was, staring up at Rob with an expression more pitying than alarmed.

Rob turned to make for the gate. With the keys in his hand he was more than half-way to freedom. Silvio was standing just outside the doorway, shaking his head. Rather than trying to stop the runaway he stood to one side and let Rob pass.

Perhaps, Rob thought, the Italian had decided to let him go rather than face a pair of English fists.

The gate was in two parts: the first, carved from dark wood, was merely decorative and opened at the lightest touch, but behind that the palazzo fronted the city with two sheer sheets of metal, which overlapped at the centre to provide space for a large lock.

There was enough light from the gatehouse for Rob to see that the largest key on the ring would fit the main lock. Looking over his shoulder to make sure that neither Silvio nor the gateman was about to foil him, he inserted the large key. Its way was blocked. Rob tried again, with no more success. He peered down to get a better look, and saw that a bolt had been shot across the keyhole. With a sinking feeling, and aware that the two men standing close behind him were showing no concern, he took a closer, longer look at the lock. He cursed.

He had been expecting to find a device such as there would have been in England, where a lock could be released simply by turning a key in it. But Venice was not England, and such simplicity was alien to its nature. Here the lock was in its turn locked by any one of a dozen other locks, arranged in a circle and charged with flat bolts that shot across the main keyhole. To open this subsidiary lock Rob would have to find the right key among the dozen on the ring. His first choice was unlikely to be the right one. Nor the second.

Rob let the keyring drop. He knew he was defeated. In a city as full of trickery as it was of water, he should have known better.

Silvio nodded to the gateman, who rang the alarm bell hanging inside the gate. Lights flickered in the palazzo's lower windows, and the doors opened. Men were running towards them. Silvio stood close and whispered in Rob's ear. 'Much danger . . . I say you . . . much danger.'

But Rob was not listening. It was too late for advice, or second thoughts.

★

Five men took Rob to a dungeon close beside the Grand Canal and chained him to the wall in a cell no more than half his height. They stripped him of Silvio's clothes and left him naked. One of them, a fat man whose belly bulged from beneath his black jerkin and sported leggings made from strips of leather, beat him with a truncheon. Rob shielded himself as best he could, but as the blows fell he felt as lost and bereft as any orphan. Afterwards he lay, shivering uncontrollably, until amid many taunts and much laughter, a blind man was led forward. With a fixed grin on his ruddy face, he dropped his breeches and allowed a bystander to take his prick and direct a stream of warm piss over Rob.

The puddles on the floor steamed. As the men left, one threw Rob a threadbare, foul-smelling cloak. He sat in the dark, aching with cold and from his bruises, and passed the time, like many chained there before him, praying for deliverance.

For a while there was no sound other than dripping water, but then Rob became aware of distant merriment. It was, he decided, the milord and his guests taking to the gondolas on the Grand Canal as they set off for their evening's pleasures. The sound came to him as an echo across water, both faint and clear, and he wondered whether his compatriot knew whom he was keeping in such misery. His father had told him that the rich never spare the poor, and that a man might as well hope a dog would not bark in the night as expect a lord to think twice about the suffering he inflicted. Perhaps, Rob thought, as tears brimmed in his eyes, he should have listened to his father more often.

In the end sleep came, albeit fitfully, and with the cloak pulled tight round him, he found the warmth to persuade himself he would survive the night. Sometimes he was disturbed by the sound of water lapping in the wash of some vessel on the Grand Canal, sometimes by the clanking of loose chains in other cells, and the sinister screeching of rats. But mostly he slept, and dreamt of other places and better times.

And then he was wide awake.

There had been a thud, and a muffled shout, then silence. And it was the silence – so dense and absolute, when it should have been woven from a thousand tiny sounds – that sent shivers down Rob's back. He strained to hear something, anything, but could not. And yet the water still lapped, and the chains clanked. But such noises, already familiar, were not part of the dreadful invading silence in the background that overwhelmed Rob. It was not the natural silence of empty stillness, rather that born of humanity – a concoction of held breath, rigid muscles and the fear of death.

It could not last . . . and it did not. There was a terrible grating roar, shouts, the rattle of chains, the crack and thud of whips, curses, desperate pleas and cries of agony. Light flashed across the vaulted ceiling and cast shadows that flickered into shapes quite as grotesque as the protests of the damned.

Rob pushed himself further into the corner of his cell and pulled up the cloak round his face. The lights were getting brighter, and the ghastly sounds drew closer. He could hear the crunch of boots on stonework, the rhythmic crack of whips, and the curious shuddering splash of the lash meeting flesh. A terrible procession was making its way through the dungeon, and was about to pass the open entrance to Rob's cell. He buried his head in his cloak, but could not govern his horrified curiosity, which demanded he look up at the savage parade.

And a terrible spectacle it was. Led by two masked men carrying flaming torches, more than a dozen men walked past enveloped in black, hooded cloaks. They were followed by others carrying flares, and after them came several fellows with oiled hair and bare arms dressed in leather tunics and armed with whips. These they cracked in slow time as they marched. Finally there was a pathetic troop of prisoners. Stooping and chained, muttering in diverse tongues, dressed only in rags, bearded, joined one to another at the collar, and with backs criss-crossed with stripes, these desperate men staggered past in single file, driven on by curses and the tormenting whips.

Not one had looked into Rob's cell and seen him crouching in terror.

# Ten

---

$R$ob was woken from uneasy sleep by the arrival of Titus, accompanied by two strutting footmen. While one knelt to release Rob's ankle from the chain, Titus announced, with the formality of an English butler, that it would please Lord Damiens to receive his prisoner in his bedchamber. Unless there was an objection, it would be his honour to convey Rob there forthwith.

Too dazed and numb to consider the motives behind, or the consequences of, such an invitation, Rob struggled to his feet. He drew the sodden cloak around him, and stepped out of the cell into the dark passage through which the ghastly procession had recently passed. He straightened his back, relieved to be standing once more like a man rather than some lower form of life. 'Why, sir, have I been kept prisoner?'

'Your discourtesy last night, sir, aroused our just suspicion. But today you are the guest of Lord Damiens.'

'And who were those wretched creatures in the night?'

Titus widened his eyes, less in surprise than mock-distress. 'Wretched creatures? Your mind must have wandered.'

'I think not. Perhaps your master will –'

Titus took a step closer. His eyes narrowed. 'You will not mention any such thing to Lord Damiens . . . What you may have seen, or imagine you saw, is of no consequence. Forget last night, if you value your life.' He turned away, and nodded to the footmen to follow him. 'Believe me, *you* may hold life dear, but in Venice it is cheap.'

The journey from the squalid dungeon to the magnificence of the palazzo's upper floors was short. Rob was led up a narrow flight to a small landing, and on through a low doorway to emerge at the side of the great entrance hall. He blinked in the airy brightness. This was a separate world, yet how close it was to the darkness he had just left. Did life on these upper floors somehow depend on the wretchedness below?

Such thoughts were quickly banished as Rob followed Titus up the broad stone staircase leading to the *piano nobile*. He had heard of the magnificence in which the wealthy lived, but in his mind's eye he had always seen luxury as no more than an inflated version of the comforts he had himself experienced. He was not prepared for the sight which greeted him on the first landing.

Titus led the way into an immense chamber. Beneath a high, timbered ceiling the room ran the whole length and width of the palazzo, from the open doors and balconies at the front, through which could be seen the Grand Canal in its morning glory, to the thickly leaded windows at the rear, which overlooked the garden. Two impossibly elaborate chandeliers had been lowered for servants to replace the candles, and the walls were hung with tapestries. In each corner loomed larger than life statues of male figures wrestling, and several vast oil paintings depicting Venetian scenes were displayed on easels. What little furniture there was had been somewhat haphazardly stacked along the walls.

Rob stared around, aware of his filthy condition, for he was still covered by nothing more than a shabby cloak. At the far end of the room some bewigged ladies were taking hot chocolate and chattering, while a young man with sleek black hair, wearing a turquoise coat with a scarlet sash, sat playing a spinet. One lady looked round, but seeing only footmen, the milord's valet and a stranger in a dark cloak, turned back with the unfeigned indifference of those free of any inclination to consort with servants.

Titus whispered in Italian and went out, leaving Rob in the custody of the footmen, who once again assumed the role of jailers. One held him by the arm, while the other took a small gilt chair and set it for him. After the cold and the horrors of the night, he was happy enough just to sit in such an airy room, filled with sunlight and sweet music. Whatever lay in store could be no worse than what he had already endured. He closed his eyes, inhaled the briny air and smell of hot chocolate, and felt himself as close to heaven as he had recently been to hell.

By the time Titus reappeared and announced that his master would receive his guest, Rob had fully recovered his wits, and was of a mind to demand to know why he had been kept a prisoner. Venice might be ruled by tyrants, but he was an Englishman, in the house of an Englishman, and he would demand an Englishman's rights.

Even so, he could not help but notice the cold look in Titus's eye, and the nimble way his fingers toyed with his riding-whip. He would save his anger for the milord.

Titus dismissed the footmen, and led the way up a further wide staircase, this one built along the palazzo's outside wall, with deep narrow windows on each step. These provided an ever more astonishing view. First there was the ancient city around the Friary, its red brick bathed in morning sunshine, and after turning a right angle, Rob found himself looking out over the Grand Canal as it stretched towards the Rialto. The movement and colour, the scale and spectacle, seemed to weave itself into a backdrop too dazzling to comprehend, and Rob had to lower his eyes to gather his thoughts before meeting the master of the extraordinary household.

On the landing a small crowd had gathered outside a massive oak door guarded by two liveried footmen. Seeing Titus these servants immediately opened the double doors, and moved to hold back those waiting to gain entry. Titus went ahead, without acknowledging the various bows and greetings, and Rob followed.

Unwashed, undressed and quite unprepared, Rob found himself in a great bedchamber. As he looked around, he was lost for words as he tried to make sense of the scene before him. His imagination had remained the child of his innocence and inexperience: it had provided him with no means to measure the luxury and extravagance that will always, as surely as whores follow an army, attach to wealth and power.

Unlike the *piano nobile*, which had been bathed in morning light, the bedchamber was filled with a soft glow of sunshine filtered through dark blinds lowered over the open windows. But it was not that contrast, or the splendid furnishings that aroused Rob's amazement. Rather it was the variety of activities under way that astonished him as no mere view of the Grand Canal ever could.

The great bed had been stripped of its sheets and covers, but not of the two young men who were idly fornicating among its pillows. They were watched and encouraged by a couple of fops, who were attempting to excite themselves by rubbing their cocks, which hung limply from their breeches. An intense-looking young man with spectacles was peering at the act of intercourse as if he were engaged on a scientific investigation. Over by the largest window, a whore had arranged herself and her dress on a small gilt chair so as to show off her lips, nipples and labia. Rob noticed that each had been painted a different shade. A young man, wearing nothing but a nightshirt and garters, was kneeling between her open legs and sniffing smelling salts while swigging brandy in an evident attempt to summon the courage to pleasure her with his mouth. Another fellow, rather older, naked, and without either a wig or hair of his own, was being soundly and noisily chastised by a second whore. This energetic lady, also bare-breasted, was applying a switch to shoulders that had already bled a few trickles and seemed pleased enough with her work to have ordered another devotee to his knees to perform the act already being enjoyed by her companion in trade.

Damiens himself sat in the centre of all this at a dressing-table on which two monkeys were gambolling. One was keen to show off a red bottom, the other a stiff prick, ambitions shared by two young men dressed as Greek athletes whose poses and embraces made the subjects for an emaciated artist, who was struggling with shaking hands to catch their likeness. As Rob watched, Damiens demanded to see the sketching pad. After examining the smudges and lines drawn in red chalk, he shook his head and let it slip to the floor. Much distressed, the artist bent to retrieve it, and received a lordly boot up the backside.

When Titus approached his master and whispered in his ear, Damiens immediately turned on his stool and pushed back his gown of blue, gold and red silk to place a hand on his hip. As he did this, Rob could not help noticing that he showed off not only a fine dangling cock but also one side of a muscular torso, with its nipple erect, and below a flat stomach, a well-made thigh and calf. Having expected to be patronised by a cissy, Rob was disconcerted by the nobleman's flaunting of his taut masculinity.

Damiens smiled, beckoned Rob with his forefinger then clapped his hands. '*Grazie per tutti . . . e basta. Domani . . . forze . . .*' He turned to Titus and tossed him a purse. 'Show them all out, and reward them as they deserve.'

Without ado one of the young men on the bed dismounted the other with practised grace. They both slid off the mattress and, suddenly coy, protected themselves with their hands as they tiptoed to their clothes piled nearby. The seated whore dropped her dress and used a hand to replace her breasts inside her dress, as did her strict companion, who threw away her switch. The men with whom they had been dallying began to search for their clothes as they might along a riverbank after swimming, and the athletes did the same, while the artist promptly gathered up his materials and his monkeys and was the first in line to receive his tip. The others were not far behind. And in no time they had all dressed, been paid, and had taken their leave with flourishes as elaborate as they were insincere.

Lord Damiens watched this comedy of departure with an expression of amused distaste until the doors finally closed behind the last of the hirelings. 'Thank heaven they've gone. Why *do* I invite them?' He turned to Titus. 'In future you must restrain me. I am too generous . . . It's the air here, it undermines the will, and softens the brain.' He gave Rob a flirtatious smile. 'Why, sir, how elegant your garb!'

Rob bowed, taking care to hold his robe across his front. 'I must beg your pardon sir, for my own clothes have been destroyed.'

Damiens shook his head in mock despair. 'These things only

happen in Venice. It is quite the worst place in the world. I've been here for less than a year and have lost more than I can tell you.' With a last glance at himself in the mirror, he stood up and motioned to the footmen to remove the dressing-table. He was a couple of inches taller than Rob, and for all his fancy manners was built like a man in his prime. 'I expect you have been cruelly treated. It's the way here – you must not mind.' As he spoke he moved closer to Rob, and did not trouble to close his dressing-gown, which hung open to reveal his knob standing at half-mast.

'I have been made your prisoner, sir.'

'Does it not take more than a ball and chain to imprison an Englishman? Nevertheless I apologise to you, sir. I shall make it my task to see that you are rewarded for the injustice done you.'

The apology took Rob by surprise. He had been intending to pursue his complaint, and to demand to know what was going on in the house, but Damiens' graceful good manners left him at a loss. Furthermore there was the hint of a reward, and after so much discomfort he felt inclined to accept any that came his way. He therefore held his tongue and merely bowed.

This clearly pleased Damiens, who smiled and stepped close enough to take hold of Rob by both shoulders. 'It is good to meet an Englishman.' A catch in his voice made him pause to clear his throat. Then he continued, 'Judging by your accent, sir, my guess would be that you are a man of Kent.'

Their eyes met, and Rob, hearing himself spoken of so accurately and in such unexpected circumstances, was unable to restrain himself from falling into the nobleman's arms. 'I am indeed, sir, and most grateful I am, sir, for your kindness in noticing it.'

For a moment the two men held one another tightly, but such intimacy could not long survive because Rob was in no fit state to be touched. Sensing this he drew back and muttered an apology. Damiens smiled but did not try to disguise his distaste for the stink that had invaded his nostrils.

He called for a nosegay. 'My dear sir, we need a tub, hot water and plenty of it. Also salts, a barber and clothing.' He glanced at Titus, who gestured to the two footmen. The three withdrew.

The two young men stood facing one another, the one in a

robe of finest silk patterned in rich colours, the other wrapped in a cloak of coarse threadbare, fabric saturated with brine, dirt and urine, yet neither felt the need to cover himself, nor to avoid each other's eye. They met as countrymen far from home, and they met as equals. Despite the hubbub on the canal below, there was a stillness in the room. Rob tried to think of something to say, but no words came, and he gave up. If his lordship was content with silence, why should he not be?

After a moment Rob felt a sharp quickening, and looking down he saw that his cock was sticking up, as was another half hidden among folds of rich silk.

A tub lined with fresh linen was carried in and set in the centre of the room. Kitchen maids and footmen came up the long flights of stairs laden with buckets of hot water that sent up clouds of steam when tipped into the tub. Titus barked orders, and used his whip to swipe any passing backside, while he hurried to find powders, salts and perfumes. An elderly tailor of effeminate appearance came staggering in with a measuring-stick. Having lost his breath on the stairs, he collapsed to his knees before Rob, who had tossed off his cloak and stood naked, legs apart and hands on hips. The old man wheezed loudly as he set about ascertaining the length of Rob's inside leg, and called out his findings to a younger but scarcely more masculine assistant, who noted them on his sleeve with a piece of crayon. When the old fellow struggled to his feet to take the width of Rob's chest, he found his breath returning, and with it his sense of smell. He stumbled back with an anguished shriek and produced an orange silk handkerchief that he held to his nose. Having apologised for his condition to Lord Damiens, Rob saw no reason to do the same for any underling, so he stood his ground as the poor fellow did his best to complete his work without drawing air through his nose.

Damiens, meanwhile, was choosing clothes for his handsome guest. As news of each measurement reached Titus, he ordered up fitting garments from the trunks in which the milord stored his wardrobe. These were piled to the ceiling in a closet off the bedchamber, and Titus stood by the narrow doorway whispering threats to those rummaging within.

With the measuring done, and sufficient hot water brought, it was time for Rob's bath. Footmen stripped to their shirts and with rolled-up sleeves stood grinning with sponges dripping in their hands. As Rob strode towards them the air was thickening with the vapours of the oils and essences that had been tossed into the tub. The steaming water was boiling with dissolving salts, and linen towels were piled close by. Everything was ready for a toilet that was likely to prove as much unlike any Rob had previously experienced as the Palazzo Ferri was to his family's humble Kentish cottage.

Before the footmen would allow him to enter the tub, Rob had to stand on a sheet of marble to be sponged down. As he felt the warm water cleansing his skin's caked, slimy surface, his spirits rose and he wondered at the changes in his fortunes. Two days before he had been a sailor, worth no more than the labour of his callused hands, then a deserter, the plaything of cut-throats, then a prisoner, and now the honoured guest of a man of wealth and noble birth. What was the point of looking to the future when the present tumbled all around him in such confusion?

Rob looked around and breathed in the warm fresh air. A midday wind was troubling the blinds, and he could hear the calls of the gondoliers on the canal far below. The tub stood filled with invigorating solutions, and the footmen were smiling at him, ready to wash away the last of the dirt. Nearby Lord Damiens sat on a gold-backed chair, with Titus at his feet. They, too, were smiling as they waited for their guest to step into the water. Rob made to lift his left leg and test the water with his toes, but his heart seemed to miss a beat, and for a moment the world stopped still. He closed his eyes to savour it, and knew that all the elements of his being were in balance, his soul reconciled to being encased in human clay. Then he stepped in.

The footmen gave him a good drubbing, disguising the energy of their attack with shouts of merriment amid the steam and sloshing water. Rob did not mind. His body was used to rough handling, and he made no complaint when scrubbed and ducked. His limbs were twisted, his balls squeezed and his hair pulled.

They turned him over and spread his cheeks to wash his hole, they pulled back his foreskin and painted his knob with thick oil. They anointed his feet with soothing unguents, rubbed alcohol on his nipples, and pummelled his back with knuckles bound in rags that had been saturated with the juice of fermented figs. When he stood they rubbed a sweet-smelling ointment into his hair, poured astringent down his torso and legs, and beat him with willow twigs. They washed out his mouth and nose with salted hot water, and straightened his fair pubic hair with fine combs until it hung round his cock like a collar.

He lay back to let them do their best and worst. Whatever happened, he would emerge clean and refreshed, and he knew that when he stood and shook the water off himself, and the footmen wrapped him in towels, Lord Damiens would be watching.

# Eleven

The footmen's method of drying Rob was no less robust. They delved between his toes, and explored the patch between scrotum and back passage with much determined rubbing of towels. A fat barber in a starched white apron appeared through a cloud of powder to snap his scissors over Rob's blond locks in a frenzy of small cuts. He doused Rob's hair in warm oil and combed it to a glossy sheen. This Rob quickly tousled, while the barber stooped to pay attention to Rob's pubic hair, which he trimmed and powdered. His work done, he withdrew to make way for an apothecary in a black coat carrying a leather casket from which he took two phials, one blue and one green. The blue he sprinkled over Rob's hair, explaining that it was a rare elixir purchased that very morning from a Syrian selling his wares on the Zattere. The green one contained a colourless liquid, which he spread over Rob's chest, and rubbed into his nipples until they burnt. Finally a tall and effete-looking young man with his shirt hanging out and enormous silver buckles on his shoes hurried in with a wooden bowl, a ladle and some laundered rags. Without so much as a by-your-leave he pulled Rob to his feet, turned him round, grabbed his arse and ordered him to bend forward and part his legs. Too startled not to obey, Rob found his crack being painted with a gluey substance.

'I grease all the holes for his lordship . . . just in case.' The man lisped and had a London accent. 'Once it melts you won't feel a thing.' There was a smack across Rob's buttocks. 'Up you get – All done! No touching now.'

Rob felt he might as well have been a piece of furniture in need of beeswax. He glowered, but there was no point: the young man was already bobbing and curtsying to Damiens as he made his way out.

By the time the experts were all gone there was not an inch of Rob that had not been powdered, massaged or subjected to some form of close attention. When one of the footmen, himself drenched in sweat and water spilled from the tub, held out a robe of palest green silk trimmed with dark pink, Rob was content to be enveloped in the cool, soft material. He let out a purring sigh and snuggled into it, as golden slippers were placed on his feet.

Lord Damiens, seeing that his underlings had done their work, ordered a collation be brought and dismissed the servants. They went laden with towels, perfumes, buckets and piles of unwanted garments, while four sturdy fellows appeared to remove the bath, under whose weight they staggered like stage comedians.

As one group of servants left, another hurried in with a table and chairs, trays of food and drink, and all the trappings required for a meal. When they, too, were gone the room was quiet. Only the distant commotion of the Grand Canal broke the silence. Damiens was clearly irritated to see Titus still lurking by the windows, pretending to change the angle of the blinds. He told his valet to leave. The servant, usually so upright and cocksure, made his way to the door with bowed head. Even his riding-whip drooped. Damiens cursed him and called him a dog. For good measure he threw a glass goblet after the man, but even with splinters in his tail the cur did not hurry. He took his time, and reproached his master with a jealous stare, before pulling the door behind him with a fearful clatter.

Damiens sighed. 'Well, now, young sir, shall we . . . take refreshment before we dally?'

Neither of them moved. Instead, they stood looking into one another's eyes – one pair as truly blue as the sky on a summer's morning, the other the colour of horse-chestnuts when lovingly polished in a schoolboy's pocket. There was no need for words, and when Rob felt Damiens' hand grip his cock, he felt no surprise.

Damiens broke the spell with a playful tug and went to the table. Rob did not follow, but stood watching as the milord picked a fig from a silver plate, split it, tilted back his head and squeezed the fruit from its skin so that it slithered on to his tongue. He beckoned Rob to his side and pointed to the table where shellfish, game and cheeses jostled for space with loaves, sweetmeats and delicate fruits of the south. But Rob had no appetite for food. In touching him, Damiens had lit a small fire in his loins that would not easily be extinguished.

Rob did not think of himself as one to make advances. Since leaving England he had been the object of many men's desires, and had been put to use often enough, but only the gentle stowaway on the *Dawn Treader* had provoked in him any fierce urge to take physical possession of another. So he surprised himself when he knelt and kissed the inside of the milord's thigh, and nestled his head between the strong legs. Perhaps the pleasure of being well scrubbed and set down in such magnificence had made him bold after being kept prisoner in such squalor and amid such horror. Or was the impulse nothing more than the spontaneous after-effect of Damiens' grip and tug on his cock? Whatever its cause, the kiss had no less an effect upon its recipient. The milord choked on a piece of shellfish. Rob felt a hand playing with his hair, disturbing the crown where the apothecary, only minutes before, had scattered a perfumed tincture from the Levant.

Damiens sighed and lifted Rob to his feet. He parted Rob's elegant robe and, with a connoisseur's eye, studied the figure within before stooping to plant a kiss on Rob's left nipple. He used his teeth to sear it a little, and then soothed it with moistened lips.

A shaft of quickening pleasure ran through Rob, and he felt a jolt behind his cock. Damiens bit again, more lightly, although no less determinedly, before moving his attention to the other nipple. This, too, he awarded a fierce nip.

Rob was not used to the pink buttons on his chest receiving such attention. His mother may have played with them when he was a lad in her arms, and there had been a schoolteacher whose fingertips often chanced to find them when leaning close to supervise. But the pair of rosy circles, with tight hillocks at their centre, that decorated his chest seemed a curious place from which to launch a seduction. Even so, the bites, nibbles and soothing licks, applied so soon after the apothecary had rubbed in the burning lotion, set Rob's whole torso alight, and ensured that his cock stood up and stuck out between the folds of his gown.

Damiens took hold of Rob's shoulders and pushed him to his knees. He used no force, or words of command, but there was no doubt of what he had in mind. Rob, seeing the milord's thick length of flesh growing fast, sensed there was nothing to be gained by resistance: Damiens was used to having his way. So Rob prepared himself for the long haul. He guessed Damiens would not spill himself early, but neither would he allow his sucker back on his feet before he had released his flood.

By showing willingness, Rob hoped to win the milord's approval, which he would surely need if he were ever to get out of the palazzo. He looked up to see whether Damiens might already be showing pleasure.

What Rob saw chilled him. Damiens was staring down with an expression that was as intense as it was unfathomable. Dark curls framed his face, and brown eyes shone brightly under jutting brows. His skin had grown pale and was drawn tight over his cheeks, while his mouth, wide enough to hint at an agreeable sensuality, was shaped by thin, sneering lips. It was, Rob thought, a face to entice and intrigue, to lure astray, even to die for. It invited him to squander himself, and discover himself, but gave no promise of comfort or satisfaction. It faced the world with pride and appetite, and held its secrets to itself.

Rob lowered his eyes to his task. Between folds of finest silk, the cock loomed before him buttressed by swollen blue veins. It rose into the light like an outcrop dominating a chasm full of dark undergrowth in which were hidden two vast boulders. As Rob went close it grew still larger, until the purple helmet broke free of its cover. A droplet quivered on its tip – nectar to attract any passing bird of paradise. Rob flicked his tongue to catch it, and closed his lips over the warm wet skin as the lactic scent of the milord's groin flooded into his nostrils.

The cock was of unusual length, and in sucking on it Rob soon discovered its head was pressing against the back of his throat. He had always supposed a mouth and a cock to be of equal length, but this one was barely half in and already he was gagging. By the skilful use of his tongue Rob was able to keep Damiens groaning with pleasure, but it would not be long before he demanded full entrance.

Rob had made love to men only a few times, but he had seen enough of life in the palazzo to guess that Damiens took his pleasure with cock or arse every day. There had been men on the *Dawn Treader* with large cocks who had grown used to having others kneel to worship them. They had shown little tolerance for any fresh-faced newcomer who, beguiled by size or lured by encouraging words, knelt to offer satisfaction without being possessed of the skills for the job. Those standing over them often grew angry, grabbed the poor supplicant by the scruff of the neck and thrust his face against them so as to force a climax. Rob had seen others cuffed and cursed until, exhausted and half dazed, their mouths gaped and they fell sideways to the floor. He was determined not to suffer such humiliation.

Action being better than anxious anticipation, Rob pulled back until his lips were playing with the very tip of the cock. Taking hold of the large hairy balls, he played with them, and then squeezed until, glancing up, he saw that he had the milord's full attention. Rob let go of the cock, and still tightly grasping the heavy balls, cleared his throat and asked, in as polite a manner as he could muster, if they might retire to the bed, which would provide a more comfortable setting for their exercise.

Damiens hesitated. Rob knew that he was taking a risk because the milord was not used to taking orders. But Rob guessed that if he held the hairy bag of balls securely, and kept his face close to the large cock with his mouth shut, Damiens would be in a mood to agree. Whatever the airs he assumed, he would want a quick resumption.

'Must we?' Damiens might have been disturbed while reading a book. 'I suppose the bed might . . .'

'It is love's playing-field, my lord.'

Damiens snorted, but pulled his gown across him and walked over to the bed. This was still strewn with the disorderly sheets upon which the young show-offs from the male brothel had sported earlier. Damiens lifted the corner of a sheet with an expression of distaste, hesitated, then shrugged. 'Very well. I haven't all day, so make haste, and for God's sake, man, let's see some spirit in your work.'

The milord lay back on the bed, Rob opened his gown and applied his mouth once more to the cock, which had lost a little of its stiffness. But his tongue soon restored its vigour, and another squeeze on the sack ensured that Damiens was once more as taut at the groin as he was relaxed elsewhere.

Rob went to work. Not for nothing was he a yeoman's son. He knew that if he were to bring matters to a swift climax he must apply himself to the task with daring. If that meant innovation, and taking a risk, so be it.

He pulled back from the cock and quickly shed his own gown. Damiens let out a cry of displeasure at the first act, but quickly sounded his approval at the second. With lithe grace Rob moved up the bed so that he shared it equally with the milord, rather than kneeling at its edge like a supplicant. He turned and spread his knees far apart, then settled himself across Damiens' chest, and bent forward so that his arse was in the milord's face, and his mouth once more close to the stiff cock. He began to suck and push. The long knob of flesh moved unhindered through his mouth. When the tip hit the back of his throat, Rob halted its progress to stifle his gagging. Once the involuntary contraction was gone Rob impaled himself further on the pulsating cock, until all of it was taken. For a moment Rob felt as if the whole of his being would rebel, and reject the oversized intruder, but he kept his nerve, and as he pulled back, and forced air in through his nose, the crisis passed. He plunged a second time, and more forcefully, and heard Damiens let out an involuntary cry. As he pulled back, and made ready to dive again, he knew that his gamble was going to pay off.

But even so, a voice within Rob told him that Damiens would not let him off lightly. He would withhold his climax to savour the sensations, and would cling to the summit for as long as possible. After all, a proud man will want to show self-control at the critical moment, and Damiens did not strike Rob as one to let himself down.

As Rob pulled back, and briefly let go of the cock to take in breath, he told himself to keep to an even pace and not to hurry. For a second he felt himself rebel, and was overtaken by an intense urge to rid himself of the loaded shaft waiting to flood his insides. But he caught hold of himself and, like a thrown rider remounting without hesitation, pressed his lips round the cock and continued the chase, ready to ride hard and far.

He was spurred on by Damiens, who found his face only inches from Rob's arse. The firm muscular buttocks, each covered in a light down, rose and fell before him with virile precision. Rob's legs were stretched wide so that the hole, propitiously greased, glistened invitingly. When Rob's grinding movement brought the hole to within an inch of Damiens face, it was not surprising that the milord should take it upon himself to stick out his tongue at the passing orifice. Despite the sting of the ointment, there was enough natural saltiness to delight the tastebuds, and the mildest whiff of shoreline decay.

Feeling the devil's lick on his behind, Rob had to master an urge to clench. But it was not the moment to worry about a minor raid on the back entrance – not while the battle raged at the front. Nor was Rob surprised when he felt a hand clamp itself on his balls, its fingers divide them then use them for play in the hand as one might before a game of billiards. Indeed, he welcomed the seepage of pure sensation from his groin, which added much-needed fuel to his desire to master the cock in his mouth as it writhed towards its climax.

He drove on. Already he had achieved what only minutes earlier he would have thought impossible. Not only was the whole cock in his mouth, and reaching half way down his throat, it was slipping in and out with all the ease of one of the new-fangled piston rods on the threshing machines he had seen demonstrated at the Ashford Fayre. Did he dare believe he might bewitch the milord by such expense of energy? If he did win his approval he might soon be able to ask for his freedom. For the first time since his attempted escape, Rob allowed himself to imagine the palazzo gates opening. By nightfall he might be walking the streets of Venice.

It is always dangerous to allow the mind to wander when coupling with a determined man. Rob's dreams of escape were interrupted by the sharp sensation of a thumb slipping through his sphincter. He protested, but Damiens simply cursed him for being an uppity whore, and threatened to have him whipped. Rob felt a finger probing alongside the thumb to widen the slick slippery opening. No wonder the servants had known to take care with their soaps and towels when rubbing his arse.

Still spirited enough to answer the invasion, Rob took hold of the milord's balls and gave them a clenching squeeze. But if he hoped to punish he was to be disappointed, for Damiens cried out with the guttural delight of a true rake, and told Rob to press harder. As Rob pulled and pummelled the balls, and slid the cock in and out of his mouth, and up and down his throat, he wondered how long he could keep up the pace.

And then, without warning, Rob found the cock pulled from his mouth like a cork from a bottle. He was shoved from behind and fell forward over Damiens' legs to end up with his mouth pressing against the milord's toes. For a moment Rob lay still, not sure what to do next. His mouth ached and his throat was on fire.

Fingers were probing his arse again. He heard Damiens whisper, 'Suck them, you little tart, suck 'em . . . for your life's worth.'

Having never thought to suck anyone's feet, let alone that of a hairy-legged man, Rob hesitated, but the sensation of a finger scratching his arse's inside made him obedient. He stuck his tongue out and ran it down the instep.

Damiens sighed, and told him to do the same to each toe. Rob had done many strange things in his life, and thought of many more, but showering affection on a row of toes had not been one of them. But, diligent as ever, and encouraged by the increasingly pleasurable sensations spreading out from his arsehole, he went to work, spreading his saliva over the toes like a snail's trail. Certainly it was easy work after the labours demanded by the milord's cock.

Too easy, perhaps. Damiens sat up and pulled his legs from under Rob. Before he knew what was happening Rob found himself pushed further along the bed until he slipped off the end. He lay with his face pressed against the floorboards and his backside stuck up over the end of the bed. With a sense of the inevitable, Rob saw Damiens get to his feet, and slip out of his gown. He threw it over Rob's head. Its soft warmth surprised him and he breathed in its special perfume, a mix of fine cologne and sweat.

'This has all become most tedious. I think, sir, stern measures are in order.' Damiens clapped his hands. 'You shall not be a dull dog.' He pinched Rob's thigh and ran a hand down over his backside. There was a clatter of footsteps. 'Ah, Titus, we need some assistance here . . . some twine . . . a gag, perhaps . . . a handkerchief will do . . . and your whip.'

'Of course, my lord, at once.' Titus was running for the door even as he spoke.

Rob tried to use his hand to remove the gown, but it was not easy, and when Damiens saw what he was doing, he told him sharply to lie still.

He was happy to obey. To be lying half off the bed, face down, with his backside in the air, might not be dignified, but the novelty, and sense of helplessness, were not altogether disagreeable. Was not love-making a duet of give and take, of leading and being led?

Hurrying footsteps announced Titus's return. Rob heard whispers, then his hands were roughly seized, drawn together behind his back and tied with cord at the wrists. The robe was stripped off him and Damiens knelt beside him to open his mouth and force inside a linen handkerchief. A length of black silk was wound round his face, masking both his mouth and eyes. Only his ears were left uncovered.

Titus used his whip to lay a dozen cuts across Rob's arse. Damiens thanked him for this service, and told him to stand by in case further punishment was required. Rob squirmed but knew complaints were useless. He lay and waited.

Before long he felt his legs being parted and his arse cheeks pulled apart. Rob heard Damiens mutter his approval, and felt a finger delving in the crack. With his arse up in the air there was nothing he could do to influence his fate, so he mustered his common sense and prepared himself to make the best of whatever ordeal lay ahead. Even so, he felt the prick of injustice. Why should a milord be able to truss him, and powder and grease him like a bird for the oven? It was not fair, even if — and the small voice of honesty spoke again — the adventure was as likely to prove pleasurable as it was painful.

# Twelve

L ord Damiens knew what he wanted. Rob felt the milord's knees pressing into his sides, a hand grasped his cock and balls and pulled them to hoist his arse higher into the air.

'I'll teach a fellow who shows me his arse while sucking.' Damiens gave the balls an extra pull and let go. 'I'll be damned if I don't ride this cockhorse topsy-turvy.'

Rob felt a light tickling sensation around his hole. He could not see, and heard nothing more than Damiens' breath and the nearby scrape of Titus's shoes on the floorboards. Far away a boatman was singing on the Grand Canal, and a violin played.

'Let's see if we can open this door with a simple key.' Damiens spoke in a hoarse whisper.

Again there was pure sensation around Rob's hole. For a moment he thought it must be a finger gently used. But hot breath gave the game away. It was no common tickling stick that toyed and jumped, probed and licked: it had to be the milord's tongue, used with expertise. It delved and moistened, then curled into a soft but sinewy rod to test the hole's defences. After that it withdrew between lips that kissed and blew warmth, and sucked, until the rim felt as easy and relaxed as a cat basking in sunshine. Then again the dancing tongue came forth to pirouette and leap, landing in every sensitive spot, only to prance on to the next.

With such a coquette at his rear entrance, Rob could not hope to resist. And when the invader brought his machines of war to bear . . . but Rob would spare no thought for that. The present was enough.

'I'll warrant, sir, you're quite the prettiest fellow in the hind-quarters. I've not tasted so sweet a raisin, nor one so neat and tight.' Damiens' voice was gravelly with desire. 'Shall we play a man's game?'

Rob was pulled forward over the edge of the bed so that the whole of his torso fell down the side, leaving the arse more vulnerable than ever. Then his legs were shifted further apart and, without warning, Rob felt the milord's cock pushing at his hole. In no position to clench his buttocks, and resigned to playing no active role, Rob let the cock slip in. Whereas his mouth had not been large enough to take its length, his arse had room enough. Rob felt its width as it took possession and drove home its advantage by thrusting and dragging in the void.

Rob had been fucked before, but this was different. He had always been taken by men who pressed their chests to his back, cock to arse, and legs against legs. This time Damiens stood over him, his feet planted on either side of his head, legs braced against his torso, so that the cock entered him upside down, and drove itself along the base of the back passage.

There was pain, but with the quality of pleasure purring at its centre. There were sore patches, and aches, and the nagging sense of being possessed, but always in the background currents of pure feeling. These flowed through Rob carrying prickles and stabs of delight fierce enough to induce a sense of abandon. His cock strained against the soft sheets and left them wet. His nipples were burning again, while the cock sliding in and out soothed the fiery itch around his hole like a balm from heaven.

But Damiens was evidently beyond such troubling thoughts. A man to enjoy a fuck, pure and simple, he was, Rob guessed, more likely to be thinking of what he would eat when he was done, and of the sleep he would need to be fresh for the rigours of the evening. As Rob lay face down, gagged and blindfolded, beaten and fucked, still not a free man, and at the mercy of a household whose cellars resounded to the cries of prisoners, he wondered why he did not feel more wretched. Pleasure kept breaking through his doubts. Damiens rode him with his cock plunging through the hole so that his hairy scrotum was rammed against the underside of Rob's torso. There was something elemental about the expenditure of so much energy on a ride to nowhere. Pleasure spread through his limbs.

Damiens was warming to his task, and employing an accelerating rhythm that demanded he rise and fall along with his cock. But just as the move from canter to gallop can never be seamless, so he soon had to bridge the gap between an orderly progress and a dash to the finish. He took hold of Rob's legs by the ankles, and spread them far apart so as to gain fuller and easier entry for his bursting organ. What before had been a carefully developed ride between mind, stamina and cock, became a disorderly plunging and rearing, as his mind lost control and the steep climb reached its summit. For a few seconds he rammed his cock as deep as he could, oblivious to the world and the heavens, tied only to the warm enveloping void he had conquered which would now receive the spurting juices of his manhood.

With a cry forceful enough to be heard by the gondoliers plying their trade far below, and to distract any midday bird flying overhead, Damiens let himself go, and slumped forward between Rob's legs, which were still stuck up in the air like tent pegs.

Rob, in his blind and mute state, was aware only of the purity of the sensations spinning through his system. He felt Damiens relaxing at his climax, and half regretted the ending of both ordeal and pleasure. But he had failed to notice that he, too, had been journeying towards a climax. The sensations pouring through him were not being dissipated. His straining cock was drenching the sheets, while the milord's was jerking and convulsing at the far end of Rob's sore back passage.

As his climax approached, Rob began to emit involuntary shouts of delight that Damiens mistook for cries of anguish and sobs of distress. He pulled himself from Rob, and signalled to Titus to help him rip away the blindfold and gags, and release the bound arms.

As the pair worked, Rob came to the moment of no return, and began his heady descent towards satisfaction. But such was the intensity of the sensations rippling in his system, and so tight and strained his cock and balls, relief came not in the form of a series of ejaculations, each slightly less than its predecessor, but rather as a single and all-encompassing moment. He did not know who he was or where, or why. He existed only in purest ecstasy, undiluted by thought or prayer.

A second wave of sensation juddered through him. This reached his loins with a sudden, obliterating crescendo, and erupted into an ejaculation at the very moment that Lord Damiens, alarmed by the sight of Rob groaning and twisting at his feet as if in death-throes, bent forward to lift him to his feet. A stream of hot thick come, well brewed and stewed, rose in an elegant arc into whose pathway the milord moved with open mouth. It splattered against his lips, and chin, and flooded into his nostrils, but most shot into his gaping mouth to settle on shining teeth and slick tongue, its warmth and consistency a delight to the palate of any gourmet.

# Thirteen

Damiens stared down at the fountain showering him, while Titus, seeing his chance, moved closer with his whip at the ready. But Rob was already laughing. He took hold of his cock to direct the stream, pushing it lower so that the globs splattered over the milord's chest and nipples. Damiens made as if to complain, but Rob merely aimed lower still towards the dripping cock, which so recently had deposited scarcely less of a load up his own backside.

By then Damiens was laughing too. He had the sour enticing taste of the cream on his tongue, and tested its warmth and consistency between his fingers. He rubbed it into his hair and neck, and smeared it over his nipples and cock. And he laughed.

Titus scowled, but he knew it was useless to protest. His master had found a new favourite. It would do him no good to be seen spoiling the fun. With a shrug of the shoulders, and muttering a promise of revenge, he strode from the room.

The two lovers did not hear him go. Neither did they hear the gondoliers' songs, the swallows flying high over the canal, or the midday cannon fire at San Marco. They heard only each other's laughter, saw only the light shining in one another's eyes, and felt only the warmth of an early summer's day against their naked, sated bodies.

They drank hot chocolate, and ate freshly baked bread smeared with preserves, then filled glasses with a light frothing wine and devoured shellfish and fruit. They lay on the bed with pillows behind their heads, and stuffed one another's mouths, and called for the doors to be left open, so that the cooling afternoon breezes might blow over them. They heard the spinet playing on the floor below, and the servants running on their errands, the calls of nearby orphan children at their play and the melancholy song of a blind beggar rowing himself towards the Rialto.

Rob had always slept after coming. Sometimes, on a long summer's evening in Kent, he had jerked himself empty simply to get to sleep, or had found himself drowsy after a bout with his cock in his father's orchards, when he should have been working. But that afternoon he was fully awake. His body was content to rest, but his mind was on fire. When he looked round at the palazzo's splendour he was no longer dazzled by the confusion of riches. Instead, he saw how colour and shape, space and scale were all combined in unison and absolute clarity. It was as if he had been sleepwalking all his life, and had woken to see with someone else's eyes, to feel with someone else's senses.

But the routines of the household could not be held at bay for long. Even a new lover must take his place in the order of things, and with the bedchamber doors left open, and the afternoon nearly over, those with business to attend to were becoming impatient. A motley group had gathered on the landing below – musicians for hire, cooks with menus, creditors, opportunists, panders and schemers, and the usual variety of friends, whether true, false or fair-weather. At first patient, they grew less so as others pressed around them. With Titus in no mood to scold, they were soon bold enough to make their way up the stairs, and before long were huddling on the landing. They peered into the immense chamber and, not being prudes, were more intrigued than startled to see the milord dallying on the great bed with his fair-haired friend. They watched as Damiens planted a kiss upon his companion's lips, and stroked his slumbering cock like a favourite cat. Some exchanged gleeful smiles, and others used signs of hand and eye to convey their amusement.

Then there was a rumpus. Stirred by the hand on his cock,

Rob moved to put his arms around Damiens, and draw him into a full embrace. But this ambition was too much for those waiting outside. Driven by a common will they entered and made for the bed.

Damiens might have attempted to stop them, but Rob was already upon him, and his broad yeoman's arse was raised up for all to admire.

Some intruders lost their nerve and fell back when confronted by this muscular form rearing before them, but others were made of rougher mettle, and gathered round the bed regardless. At first Rob did not believe that city folk could be so immodest as to burst in upon a scene of love-making. But hearing the commotion, he glanced round and saw that he was indeed kissing and fondling the milord before an audience of at least twenty citizens of the Republic.

He fell back on the pillows with a groan, and lay there, legs apart. He scowled at the busybodies gathered around. Lord Damiens took his time but he, too, conceded defeat, swung his feet off the bed and called for his slippers and gown. Titus came forward with a smirk on his face. Like any servant long in service he did not have to put his message into words as he knelt and placed slippers on his master's feet.

Provided with a robe of Oriental silk to restore his modesty, Damiens strode over to the table where the food was still displayed, and with a graceful bow and motion of the hand indicated that everyone should tuck in. This caused a stampede that left Rob alone on the bed, with only a solitary companion. This was an old man, his face scarcely less powdered than his wig, who sat on the edge of the bed and looked down at Rob's cock with rodent eyes. He winked, and licked his painted lips. When Rob glanced away he immediately felt his cock disturbed. Looking down he saw that the old devil was using the nails of thumb and forefinger to lift and examine the organ like an object for sale in the market. Rob brushed away the man's hand, and noticed with revulsion that the fingernails were inches long, and as filthy on the underside as they were thickly varnished in purple on top.

The old man arched his eyebrows, and smiled to reveal a

mouth full of blackened stumps. '*Poverino* . . .' his voice was as high as a choirboy's '. . . poor boy . . . *in questa casa* . . . this house . . .' With a merry shrug he drew a fingernail like a knife across his throat, and let his head droop to one side as if it were about to fall off. Then he rested his gnarled hand on Rob's thigh, and scratched the fair skin lightly with fingernails as long as coffee spoons, and beckoned a servant for the use of an arm to lever himself upright. With a final wink he wobbled off to join the rest of the party.

For Rob to have appeared naked in public might not have offended the Venetians – most of whom had more pressing concerns than bedroom decorum, while others were beyond scandal – but Rob felt that by their intrusion they had forfeited any right to decency. His modest upbringing asserted itself and, beset by thoughts of self-respect, he decided the time had come to cover himself, and not merely with soiled sheets or a skimpy robe. He might have lost his sailor's uniform, and the fine shirt he had bought, but the tailor had measured him from neck to feet. If he were a little shorter than the milord, he was an inch taller than Titus, and in so much as his measurements seemed to coincide nicely with his rank in the house there would surely be clothes to fit him.

And, as if to prove true the fallacy that lovers' thoughts run close together, Lord Damiens left the throng by the table and came over to the bed. Rob looked up at the handsome face, which scowled down with loving mock-severity, and could not prevent himself from sighing at the sheer delight of being in the favour of one so powerful.

Rob had never got anything he wanted in life without making payment in one way or another, but with Damiens, each languorous pose struck, every toss of the head or shot of the hip, flick of the wrist and curl of the lip, was eloquent of a character formed by the obedience of others to his every wish. Rob lay basking in the warmth of this noble being's approval, and allowed himself to fancy that Damiens was a god whom he had met in Venice.

'You must have clothes, Robbie. I'll not have you made public property.' Damiens turned to Titus who, ever the running dog, was hurrying to his master's side. 'Find that lazy tailor, and have him bring clothes fit for a fellow who will stand at my side. And if he is already drunk tell him I shall see him whipped.'

Titus ran a cool eye over Rob as if to make an appraisal more realistic than his master's. Rob noticed the insolence, but Damiens did not for Titus knew his master too well to linger.

Damiens sat on the edge of the bed, and placed a hand on Rob's thigh close to where the old man had recently rested his. Rob trembled at the change, and Damiens smiled. 'We shall see you in satin and bows, Robbie, like the young prince you are.'

'I am a sailor, my lord. I deserve no more than plain covering.'

'Nonsense.' Damiens looked away towards a troupe of dancers, who were accompanied by violin and trumpet players. They had entered unnoticed and stood waiting for permission to perform. 'We are not in England, Robbie.' His words were faint, and Rob supposed he was talking as much to himself as to him. 'In this house lords are as likely to be beggars as an orphan boy. If you are to be at my side you must dress the part.'

Rob felt an urge to reach out and touch the milord, who was still looking away, but at that moment the musicians struck up. The room was filled with the richness of the violins, and the brilliance of the trumpets. The dancers threw off their dark cloaks and revealed themselves dressed as the characters of Venetian comedy. They set off on a stately sarabande, amid much applause from those still eating their fill on the other side of the chamber.

The music was slow and melancholy, and the dancers went through their paces with a graceful artifice, but Rob found the noise and distraction intolerable. He was still naked in circumstances that were becoming ever more public. For a house that had proved impossible to escape, it was remarkable how many strangers seemed able to gain entry for no better reason than to make an exhibition.

Rob used the bed-sheets to cover himself as best he could, but many eyes were on him, no doubt speculating as to his origin, purpose and future. And to make matters worse two dancers approached Damiens and invited him to join them. As soon as he was on his feet the tempo changed to allow a sprightly lilting tune, and with all the grace of his breeding and build, Damiens

85

tripped off across the floor to become the centrepoint of the ballet.

A woman climbed on the bed beside Rob. She was young and shapely and said something, but was unable to make herself heard over the music. Rob could smell her musk as she pulled a breast from its cover, and stroked it invitingly as if it were a small animal in need of comfort. Rob noticed the nipple was painted a silvery green except for the stem that was bright red. Uncomfortable at finding himself approached so openly, Rob looked away and was relieved to see Titus leading the tailor towards him.

An explosion on the dance floor made Rob start. The girl beside him screamed with laughter and others joined in. A buffoon hidden among the dancers had lowered his bright yellow breeches and ignited a firecracker inserted between his buttocks. This had caused not only a loud report, but also released a cloud of foul-smelling gas.

In the confusion Rob slipped off the bed. The tailor was bowing and talking fast, but Rob had no idea what he was saying. Titus shoved Rob from behind, and Rob turned on him. There might have been a fight had there not been another explosion, this time from the other side of the room where a second firecracker had gone off in the depths of a girl's cleavage. There was renewed laughter.

Titus was at his side. The valet flicked his whip lightly across Rob's naked hide to encourage him towards the corner where the tailor was waiting. Two screens were being erected to provide privacy. With all the dignity he could muster, Rob walked the few steps as the music started up once more. It was, he decided, a relief that at a time when all eyes might be drawn to him, there were many other sights to be seen quite as diverting as that of a fair-haired young Englishman without his clothes.

Behind the screen there was as much frenzy as in an anthill. The tailor stood dabbing himself with cologne, while Titus looked on with his usual disdain, and at every opportunity laid his whip across the arses of two footmen deputed to act as dressers. These unfortunates were rummaging for suitable items among the contents of two large travelling trunks. Whenever they held up a garment either Titus or the tailor would shake his head, and when Rob expressed approval of a fine pair of dark blue breeches, Titus told him it was no business of his to decide what he might wear. Rob felt affronted at this treatment, but did not care enough to make anything of the insult.

There were further explosions on the dance floor – these emitting sweeter perfumes – and more laughter, and the sound of fresh arrivals eager for enjoyment. Only half an hour before, a drowsy afternoon peace had permeated the great bedchamber and nurtured Rob's new-found happiness. Now an atmosphere of heady pleasure and near riot had taken hold. The music and dancing grew faster and wilder amid shrieks of delight, the clatter of shoes, and a mix of perfumes made heavy by the warmth and press of swirling bodies.

One man had opened his fly to reveal a large artificial member, which gyrated in time with the music, and two ladies stood facing one another with their skirts lifted pleasuring themselves with pieces of fresh fruit. Two fops were kissing each other by the open window close by an elderly Scottish laird, who was exerting himself by thrashing an ancient whore whose shrieks made hard competition for the band.

In the tight confines behind the screens Rob was becoming impatient. He had half a mind to abandon Titus and the fussy tailor, and the sweating footmen, and march forth to join in the dance. His nakedness would seem no more than honest abandon amid such licentiousness.

Perhaps sensing the danger, and the milord's wrath, Titus quickly approved a pair of well-cut grey and black breeches with stockings to match, and a plain white shirt prettily edged in lace. The tailor picked a coat finished in pure white silk that flattered Rob's lean build. To this was added linen underwear, a cravat of adequate simplicity, and dark shoes with fine silver buckles. By contrast the wig chosen was modest enough in size and weave to cast doubt on the wearer's rightful position in the social order.

A mirror was brought and Rob found himself well pleased with the figure of manhood it reflected.

Had Titus and the tailor completed their task in similar good faith all might have been well. But they were undone by the pleasure they had found in making the choice of wig, and were unable to resist further cleverness. They therefore tied Rob's cravat with a knot loose to the point of vulgarity. Worse, the pin they used to secure it had at its end a ruby too large to adorn any true gentleman's neck.

Ignorant of such malice, Rob took a last look in the mirror, and decided that the time had come to make his entrance. He would no longer be a figure of fun, to be displayed naked as if fit only for pleasure between the sheets but, rather, the handsome fellow the mirror showed him to be. Would he not look like a prince when he stood beside his milord?

# Fourteen

---

At that moment the music came to an end and, with much
fluttering of fans and handkerchiefs, the revellers ceased
dancing. Some settled into conversation, while those engaged in
other activities rested where they were, or moved towards the
table where the servants were laying out refreshments.

Clearly ignorant of any reason why others should not share
his high opinion of his appearance, Rob was making his way to
the centre of the room where Lord Damiens stood talking to
an elderly contessa. This elegant soul, although wearing only
a simple day dress, was devoid neither of fortune nor the
remnants of beauty. Furthermore, she had wits enough to
require no more than the evidence of the corner of her eye to
note that the fair-haired young fellow approaching was more
bumpkin than any debutant of her own class. Always alert to the
pitfalls of social embarrassment, she curtseyed to her host and
withdrew.

Unused to being snubbed, Lord Damiens turned and, seeing
Rob coming his way, immediately understood the cause of the
contessa's departure. Although raised among rakes, and at home
with the dissolute, Damiens was fastidious in his distaste for the
awkward or inappropriate. He might carouse with thieves and
desperados, and find amusement in brothels and gaming houses,
but his easy ways and manners were deceptive when it came to

distinctions of rank and dress. He could be as prickly in such matters as any princeling.

Taking his undressed state as an excuse to leave the floor, Damiens made a sign to his steward that the room should be cleared. Without pausing to make his farewells, Damiens took Rob by the sleeve of his white silken coat, and leading him away from the throng, whispered, 'I think we shall have a word with young Titus.'

Expecting compliments, and perplexed that his arrival should be the excuse to end the revels, Rob was in no mood to return to the screens. If he had drawn eyes while naked, who could tell what tributes he might provoke clothed? But Damiens was not to be defied. He marched the young sailor back to the screens, behind which the tailor sat sharing a jug of wine with Titus. The two footmen knelt before them to polish their boots. A little tipsy, and deafened by the clatter of the departing guests and entertainers, the small group did not notice their master's arrival. They continued with their gossiping and tippling until Damiens took hold of Titus's riding-whip and laid it smartly across its owner's shoulders.

The group struggled to their feet, and braced themselves for a show of displeasure.

Damiens pushed Rob among them, and used the whip to point to the cravat and pin. 'What is the meaning of this? Do you have it in mind to make this fellow a buffoon?'

Rob's cheeks coloured. There was a silence, broken by Titus. 'My lord, you bade us dress him. That we did.'

'And left him looking fit only to attend a rat-catcher's wedding. How dare you put him in fancy things, then knot his cravat as tight as a counting-house clerk's. And what is that?' He struck the ruby pin with the tip of the whip. 'You make him look like a tart ready to peddle his arse. And as for this abomination –' With a flick of the crop he sent Rob's wig flying.

Rob protested, and reached down to retrieve it. His cheeks were almost as red as the ruby at his neck. 'You are unfair, my lord. I saw in the looking glass . . . Never have I seen myself so . . .'

Damiens sighed. 'You do not understand, Robbie.'

Rob stared round at Titus and the tailor. The former met his eye boldly, but the tailor stared down with pursed lips. The two footmen were trying to extricate themselves by inching their way backwards.

'No, I don't.' Rob's cheeks were burning, and thick teardrops of humiliation were gathering on his eyelashes. 'What have I done wrong?' His voice rose with emotion and he used the back of his hand to wipe his eyes. A lock of yellow hair fell across his brow, and his lips were quivering. A feeling of uncertainty such as he had never before known was creeping through him, and melting his proud manhood.

Damiens took Rob's hand and kissed it gently on the palm. 'Don't upset yourself, Robbie. You have done no wrong. Titus here thought to make sport of you rather than obey his master. That is all. You are as true a fellow, Robbie, as he is false, and just as I will punish him, I shall reward you.'

Rob tried to smile as he blinked back the tears. 'I thought . . . when I saw myself . . . what a fool I am.'

Damiens lifted his knee and snapped the riding-whip over it. He handed the pieces back to Titus who, his spirit broken along with his stick, took them with cowering meekness.

Then, as the sound of the departing revellers faded, Damiens led Rob back to the centre of the bedchamber. Holding Rob at arm's length he looked him up and down and, eyes mastered by love rather than the niceties of upbringing and rank, he found himself overcome by the desire to possess and keep the young sailor.

He did not care what adventures brought Rob to his house, or what secret motives he might harbour. What did it matter if he looked a little absurd in his Italian finery? What Englishman would not, unless a nobleman such as himself?

It had been two years since Damiens had been in England, and during that time he had wandered the wastelands of the Continent. The only Englishmen he had met were those such as himself, black sheep sent into exile, and he had found no comfort among them. Of course, there had been others – servants, mercenaries, and sundry adventurers – whose company had provided amusement for an hour or two, but there had been no one to counter the ever-present and ever-growing feeling that those less disdainful would have known to call homesickness.

As he looked at Rob he felt his loneliness turning to hope, and his lust to generosity. The young man was so handsome, so without artifice. His blue eyes shone with nothing more complicated than a longing for love. Earlier, when they had coupled, Damiens had been overwhelmed by desire. He had lost himself among strong arms and legs, a chest and belly as smooth and flat as the buttocks were round and warm, a cock as restless as any jumping salmon, and a face fresh and open like a fine summer's morning. But in return for such gifts he had offered Rob nothing more of himself than his open mouth and the shaft of his cock. He, too, experienced a prick of uncertainty. Could the feeling be shame?

Damiens pulled Rob close. 'I have treated you badly.'

'You have not, my lord.'

'I'll make it up. Come . . .' With his arm around Rob's shoulder, Damiens led the way to the door. '. . . I've something to show you. This way.'

The treasury was a small, windowless room along a narrow passageway running off the main staircase. The steward brought the key in a silver box that rested on a golden cushion. This box could only be unlocked by another key, hidden in a silk purse sewn into the cushion. On entering the small treasure house the steward fixed a torch on the wall, and withdrew with the solemnity of one leaving a sacred place.

If there were a divinity present, however, it was not one recognised by any God-fearing folk, but rather by that pagan master who quickens the hearts of those who find themselves in the presence of great riches.

Rob stared around open-mouthed. Boxes were piled one on top of another over the whole of one wall, while a massive cedar chest took up most of the remaining space. In the flickering light Damiens opened this chest, and bent forward to delve among the contents. Rob stood behind him transfixed. In the corner of the chest, lying in a loose mound as if casually poured there, were gold coins. These Rob knew to be Spanish dollars – he had seen them change hands below decks on the *Dawn Treader*. The rest of the chest was filled with boxes of various shapes and designs, and it was among these that Damiens was rummaging.

'Ah, look, Robbie, here we have it.' Damiens held up a small box to the light. Inside, resting on black velvet, lay a pin with a colourless stone at its head. 'It's a diamond of rare quality.' He held it close. 'See how she dances in the light.'

With a flick of his wrist Damiens pulled the ruby from Rob's cravat, and tossed it on the floor. He leaned closer to brush his lips against Rob's. 'This will look better . . . Let me push it through . . . Ah, there! I must not prick . . . must I?'

Rob stood still, but thrust his Adam's apple forward a little. Was he, Damiens wondered, half hoping the milord hand would slip and pierce him? The idea was tempting. If he were to open a vein in the young sailor's neck, how would it be to see a little blood flowing from the prick of so fine a needle?

Small bubbles of sweat were forming along Rob's upper lip. The room was hot, and the torch shed a lurid, uncertain light. Damiens felt a pressure at his groin, and Rob's warm, fresh breath seemed to stroke the skin on his face and neck. He arranged the pin just so, and took a step back to judge his handiwork. It could not be faulted, and neither could Rob, whose fair hair fell in tousled locks over his brow and whose blue eyes shone in the semi-darkness. His smile revealed pearly teeth, and small dimples on either side of his mouth.

Damiens had not noticed these before. Perhaps it was a trick of the light. But, then, neither had he noticed the brave width of the shoulders, and the way the folds of the shirt lay loosely over his flat stomach. He could not resist running a hand over the soft linen covering the hard ridges beneath. There was nothing, Damiens decided, soft about his Robbie. He might have been tearful earlier, but the body spoke of rough training and the hard life, and Damiens was still young enough, and athlete enough, to admire that. And to desire it.

Despite the cock standing up out of his dressing-gown, Damiens decided he should not yet give way to his returning lust. If the young fellow deserved rewards, and he did, then he should be given them without delay or condition. It would not be seemly to be thought to want anything in return for his gifts.

Damiens bent once more to search among the boxes and coins. He thought he might try a ring his father had won in battle in Germany; one he remembered as having emeralds set among sapphires and garnets. It would nicely set off Rob's colour. But, in the flickering light, the box was hard to find among so many. Although his gown was open at the front, the rich silk was heavy enough to make him sweat in the close atmosphere, and when he first felt a light pressure on his flank he thought nothing of it. Having found the box, and used his fingernails to force it open, he realised that it must have been Rob's hand on his hip.

He took the ring from its tiny box and held it up to the light. He smiled as he watched Rob straining to get a good look, and the way in which his expression softened into warm delight as he saw the stones sparkling.

Damiens took Rob's right hand and slid the ring on to his forefinger. 'It suits you well, my lad.' Damiens kissed the hand and let it go to allow Rob to study it more closely.

'It's a . . . fine thing . . . my lord. More than I deserve.'

'I am the judge of that . . . but, yes, it is handsome on you.'

Rob held out his hand at arm's length, and splayed the fingers so that they could both admire the jewels. For a moment Damiens thought he saw a flaw in the emerald. Without thinking he reached out and pulled the hand close.

He stared hard at the green stone, and saw that it truly reflected and refracted the light from the torch burning on the wall behind him. 'I must have been mistaken. It has no flaw. It is true.'

'As am I.' Rob's voice was soft.

'No man can be as hard or true as stone. It's not the way God made us.'

'But I am, my lord, harder than this stone, and truer than its light, more loyal even than its worth.' Rob was staring into Damien's eyes.

'Then fill your pockets with gold, Robbie, and may you prove to be what you say you are.' Damiens bent to scoop up the Spanish pieces, which he poured into Rob's coat pockets. Then he bent again, and poured them down the front of his breeches.

After that he held handfuls high overhead and let them run down over Rob in a golden shower.

Rob did not protest, as Damiens hoped he would not. Only the weak complain over a lover's gifts, and every god must expect sacrifice and offerings.

When every one of his pockets was full, and his shirt-front bulged like a glutton's, and his hair was woven with gold, Rob fell to his knees, and pressed his head into Damiens' groin.

But Damiens was not in a mood to be sucked. After giving so much away he preferred to take his reimbursement with a straightforward fuck. He had found Rob's arse and hole much to his liking, and after so much gentle feeling and sentiment he was ready to be himself again, and reassert his rights as lord of the house.

He met no resistance. He told Rob to unlace and drop his breeches, and it was quickly done. The fine linen underwear came as a surprise – Titus had not stinted in dressing the young sailor – and aroused an already burning aggression. Damiens half tore the silken white coat from the sturdy back, and pushed up the loose shirting. He pointed to the side of the cedar chest, and was pleased to see Rob go over as eagerly as a hawk diving for a mouse, spread his legs and wait.

Damiens could have taken his time. As a rule he enjoyed bringing a certain languor to his fucking. But his cock was up and straining. It was ready to enter whatever dark, humid territory its owner might wish it to conquer, and rather than call for a servant to bring grease to smooth the way into Rob's fine hole, he contented himself with spit on his hands. He slid them all the way along the downy crack, and made sure the entrance was moist.

After that, and without ado, he shook off his robe, and while the torch began to gutter, the air stifled and his slippers trod loose gold underfoot, the milord took hold of his cock. Without warning he dug it into his young friend's backside, and set about riding him at a fair canter.

It was not his most elegant fuck, nor his most long-lasting, but there was directness and a hint of the savage about it that Damiens liked to think Rob would appreciate. Although they had roused each other's fine feelings, Damiens did not want Rob to forget that he was the master, and that just as a yeoman will find hard fucking in the fields and barns of Kent, so he will find it in a Venetian palazzo. He drove himself on, pumping with all the ferocity of a farmer's lad eager to raise water at a well.

Not that he struck any pose that was not as elegant as his manners. While Rob lay over the side of the open chest, with his head down among the gold coins, Damiens rode him from behind with his hands placed lightly on his hips. With the rhythm and depth of his thrust set, he had time to look around at the treasure house, and allow himself a moment's pleasure at the sight of so much wealth.

It was the common ambition of Venetians to ensure that, while English visitors might arrive rich, they should leave poor. But Damiens had seen too much of the ebb and flow of wealth, the slow ruin of those perpetually on the move and the larceny of those that fed off them. He had made it his business in Venice to gather as well as to spend, and to employ his wits in enterprise as well as dissoluteness. He meant to return to England rich, and he was willing to employ all the means necessary to ensure that outcome. But in the meantime, with his treasury full and a fresh-faced young lover to fuck, the world, for all its tedium and callow ways, was a fine place.

Damiens returned his thoughts to the job in hand, and with renewed vigour set about making the fucking as memorable a rogering as any young man inclined to sodomy could wish for.

His climax came as Rob's low grunts were echoing in the bottom of the chest. Damiens wrenched his cock from Rob's arsehole, and let his come spurt and stream over the treasure chest. At the same time the torch went out, and Rob, sensing the emptiness inside him, grabbed hold of his own cock, raised himself upright and let his load course through the darkness to splatter over the coins so promiscuously scattered on the floor.

That night, after the pair had feasted alone, they went up to the great bedchamber. The bed had been made up, and scattered with sweet-smelling flowers and herbs to encourage easy sleep. It was not long before Rob was dreaming that he was at home in

Kent tending the lambs beneath a sky full of scurrying white clouds. He did not hear the gondoliers singing, or the revellers returning from the Rialto. The bell at San Tome tolled the hour, but did not disturb the fair-haired young man lying in the arms of the English milord.

And then he was awake. The bed felt cool, and the breeze from the canal was chilly. Somewhere cats were fighting, and there was a piercing scream in the far distance.

Was he alone?

He whispered, 'My lord, are you there?' but there was no reply.

The doors were ajar, and a dim light was coming from the stairs. A figure was standing on the landing, looking in. Rob could tell it was too short to be the milord. Was it a servant? If so, why, at so late an hour?

The figure stepped forward and entered the room. It was Titus. Without his whip Rob had not recognised him.

'Where is Lord Damiens?'

Titus did not reply, but walked over to one of the windows overlooking the Grand Canal.

'This is the best time. Venice is herself at night.' Titus turned and beckoned Rob. 'Come, I'll show you something.'

Rob slid off the immense bed and walked over to where Titus stood looking out into the night. 'I asked you where his lordship is.'

'Look at the canal. Are you looking? Now answer me this. Is the canal empty, or full of traffic?'

'It's empty, Titus, any fool can see that. Now answer my —'

'Look again, take your time. Do as I say.'

Rob looked down at the black mass of water, which glittered here and there where the breeze or a passing craft disturbed it. In the far distance he could see the Rialto Bridge at the canal's bend, and gondolas, their lanterns lit, were clustering round a landing where people were leaving a palazzo. As Rob watched he saw what Titus meant. The canal was not empty: it was crowded with gondolas and other craft, with all the traffic of Venice, and scarcely less so than during the day.

'You are right, Titus. But where is Lord Damiens?'

Titus took a couple of steps back from the window and turned to look Rob up and down. 'The Palazzo Ferri is like Venice. It may seem full of life during the day, but its business is done by night. So go to bed, sir, and mind you sleep till morning. By then his lordship will be safely back at your side.'

With a smile Titus patted Rob's shoulder and wandered away.

When Rob woke to daylight the milord was indeed back at his side, and sleeping deeply. Rob shook him awake, and asked where he had gone in the night. Damiens pretended to be too drowsy to reply. Rob pressed him, but then, as he drank his hot chocolate and waited for a reply, Damiens reared up beside him. His face was pale with rage. He grabbed Rob by both shoulders, sending the cup and saucer flying. Not caring that he spat in Rob's face with every word, he said, 'What business is it of yours? Are you sent here to spy? Is that why you simper and flutter your eyes at me? Let me promise you one thing, Robbie, if you ever dare ask such a question again, I'll have you whipped until the flesh is stripped from your back.'

The two young men stared at one another until, with a weary sigh, Damiens fell back among the pillows and closed his eyes. 'Leave me, Robbie, before I say or do worse.'

# Fifteen

On the Piazza San Marco, under the Campanile where coffee and hot biscuits were sold, a row of sedan chairs had been set down. Tough bearers stood behind, while inside each chair sat a lady with a fan, staring ahead as if waiting for her future to arrive and release her.

Further along towards the landing-stages outside the Palazzo Ducale, a crowd had gathered. Word was spreading that a British man-of-war was at anchor out in the bay, waiting for permission to land an ambassador and his party. The morning mist hung as heavy as a laundered sheet – even the island of San Giorgio was shrouded – and no one was sure whether they might soon see a great spectacle, or find that they had wasted their time.

And if time was to be wasted, these were the people to do it. A few looked as if they might be on business – clerics easily distracted from their hurry, errand-boys with their pushcarts, clerks laden with briefs, truant apprentices in their aprons, guards sweating in heavy uniforms, perplexed tourists with their venal guides. But most were there because they always were. There were street merchants and acrobats, beggars and fire-eaters, fops and tarts, urchins galore, pedlars and men for hire, and those who stood alone, or leaned against a wall, as watchful as dogs, and as sure their day would come.

At midday, as the cannon fired and the first rays of sunshine glistened against San Marco's rearing horses, those who had been staring out over the water received their reward. Two craft were approaching across the bay, both freshly painted and with the British ensign and the Lion of Venice flying on their masts. Their oars rose and dipped in a unison to rival that of any local oarsmen, and on the stern stood officers in uniforms whose cut and economy might have been designed to reprimand the weary extravagance of the local officials' garb.

Choirboys clad all in red stood on the landing-stage and raised an anthem in praise of God, the city and the sea. Trumpeters came marching from San Marco, and several platoons of guards fell in. Representatives of the city's six districts stood in the heat with expressions of haughty pride, while the dense crowd parted willingly to allow through a group of magistrates, with two torturers and an executioner in tow. Guildmen paraded, as did other dignitaries, and when the craft drew close to the landing-stage, and raised oars, the crowd pressed forward with cheers mixed with sharp comment, laughter and jeers.

The officers disembarked and, unused to firm ground, swayed as they stretched their legs.

But soon the spectators were shielding their eyes against the sun as another craft was spotted further out in the bay. This one was larger, with a deck raised above the ranks of oarsmen. A sailor stood proudly on the prow in defiance of the choppy waters, and others stood guard at each gangway. On deck there was a group whose only uniform was excess. Wigs rose into the air, and garters fluttered, as did gaily coloured handkerchiefs. Frilly lace frothed at every wrist and neck, and sashes of blue and white were as dazzling as the sky. Coats were cut to reveal bulging bellies and groins, and had as many buttons of silver and gold as their wearers had seen summers. While some of the faces were as rouged and painted as a tragedy queen's, others were powdered to a deathly pallor, which sent a shock through the crowd who were familiar with the plague's ravages.

As this astonishing vessel approached, a cacophony went up that drowned even the carillon from the Campanile. The trumpeters played a great fanfare, and the choirboys strained their voices higher until their cheeks were as red as their caps. The guards' drummers beat out a rhythm all of their own, and the mob cheered and whistled, and let off fire-crackers until even the seabirds left their perches.

The ambassador was first to step ashore. He wore an immense hat decorated with black feathers over a wig powdered to a pale blue. His coat was also blue and decorated with medals, his breeches were skin-tight, and his black shoes shone in the sunlight. A murmur of approval went up at the sight of an elderly fellow so ramrod straight. He walked forward to the empty dais where the Doge would soon take his place. Behind him came three young men, rather more extravagantly dressed but still well within the bounds of convention and dignity. After them came the curious crew who had attracted the crowd's eyes while still far out in the bay. Closer to they were no less strange. As haughty as peacocks, only their youth kept them from grotesquerie.

After another lengthy fanfare, the Doge appeared. So old and infirm that many believed the rumour that he was a corpse manoeuvred by dwarfs secreted among the swathes of his cloak, he gave no sign of being alive as he was carried to the dais, where a second throne awaited him beneath a gold and purple canopy.

As attendants edged him into place, and his entourage huddled round, the British party strutted with elegant disdain while local noblemen jostled for position

When all was ready, and the hubbub had subsided, the ambassador took a step forward. He removed his hat, and swept it along the ground in front of him as he adopted an elaborate pose of respect. He handed a letter to an officer of the Republic, and proceeded to deliver a speech in Latin. This was met with impassivity.

There followed an expectant pause during which an attendant whispered in the part of the Doge's ear not covered by a bejewelled headdress. When there was no reaction from the throne, a gentleman standing close by clapped his hands, at which the trumpeters sounded another fanfare and the choirboys set off once more in praise of Venice, God and the sea. The crowd cheered, and up on the dais there was much mutual doffing of hats, and bowing low, which showed off many arses of differing shapes and sizes. More poses were struck, many hands on hips that drew back coats to allow judgement of the size and efficacy of the bulges revealed.

Before long the Doge was raised up once more for the journey back to the palace. With final bows the ambassador's party began to descend from the dais to mingle with the common crowd. The guards made way for them, which allowed one of the ambassador's trio of equerries, a young fellow fresh from England by the name of Lucian Parry, the opportunity to cast an eye over a group of idle Venetian youths. He noted with satisfaction that everything he had heard about the city's attractions seemed likely to be proved true.

The trumpeters led the way towards the piazza, and Lucian saw how the magistrates stood back and bowed with smiles as thin as the paper they used when condemning a man to torture or death.

When they reached the piazza the group stopped to take their first refreshment of coffee and cakes, and to be introduced to the ladies who had been waiting with such patience in their sedan chairs. Each as noble as she was destitute, the pimps had considered it neither safe nor proper that such ladies should be seen plying their trade alongside those who lacked their advantages of birth. Some were pretty, others were not, but as far as Lucian was concerned the woman soon snuggling against his chest, and muttering French doggerel, could just as well have been a gargoyle as the new Cleopatra. His eyes were elsewhere.

Two of the chair bearers were as sturdy a couple of young ruffians as Lucian had seen since he had last strolled along Cheapside, and he was determined to make their acquaintance. Accordingly he winked at one, who nudged the other. A sigh on his chest told him that his lady had received the same message, and as she withdrew she made a sign whose meaning was as unambiguous as it was close to Lucian's thoughts.

In coming to Venice Lucian had two ambitions. The first was to serve his dear cousin the ambassador. The second was to fuck as many young men as he could lay his hands on. He had heard that his old companion in debauchery, Charles Damiens, had fled to Venice after running up debts and gambling away four estates one sultry June night. In the clubs along Pall Mall it was held that he had been wise to go, if only because destitution was less wearisome in Venice and the fucking cheaper.

Not much cheaper, however. An impertinent pimp pocketed a ducat before he would consider putting two of his whores in the same sedan, and then demanded several more for the hire of the two bearers for the afternoon. Lucian agreed because he was keen for a fuck, and it would have been unseemly to argue in such circumstances, but he promised himself he would take a stiffer line the next time a pander became greedy.

Nevertheless, as that afternoon wore on in a squalid room behind the granaries, Lucian found himself less inclined to grumble over his treatment. Having been educated at the second best school in England, he was used to rough buggery, and service in a good regiment had taught him how to deal with brutes. After two weeks at sea with only fops for company, and a crew cowering under the command of an ardent flogger, Lucian was ready for action with no holds barred. Entertaining two at a time was a challenge, nevertheless, but once the initial horseplay was over, and the pair had spilled their first loads, the sequence of dominance and submission progressed with smooth logic, and left Lucian satisfied his money had been well spent.

For their part, the two ruffians were tamed by their expenditures and exertions, and were afterwards able to offer the young Englishman sound advice as to where further pleasures might be found. They accepted their tip with no more ingratitude than convention demanded, and bade their guest farewell with thanks not devoid of sincerity.

Daylight was already fading as Lucian made his way to his lodgings. The route took him through the Piazza San Marco. The lights were being lit, and the square was filled with honest souls on their way to Mass. A gypsy boy handed Lucian a nosegay of herbs, and when he fumbled for some coins, the boy smiled impishly and ran off.

Lucian stood a while to take in the scene. There was a sense of excitement in the air, of life lived with daring and for the moment. He had grown weary of London – had almost grown weary of himself. In Venice, far from home, he would find himself again. The long journey had been tedious, but he was glad he had made it.

Just after midnight Lucian left his lodging, where he had been provided with an excellent meal and a room overlooking a quiet square, and made his way towards the Rialto Bridge. The streets were empty and, the wind being chilly, the few people he passed were well wrapped up inside their cloaks. Only as he approached the Rialto did the streets grow crowded. He noticed how the young men of Venice gathered in groups to lounge around and show off their legs, buttocks and groins. On the highest part of the bridge several were leaning over the wall with their backsides stuck out at inviting angles. Used to London, where young men drew attention to themselves by more circumspect means, it was only with difficulty that Lucian managed to prevent himself from running a hand over those shapely globes, or even giving the more provocative a firm smack. But he reminded himself that where fops gathered cut-throats often lurked in the shadows.

Once over the bridge Lucian found himself alone as he walked through the deserted market, and on beside a narrow canal. He stopped to take out the directions the ruffians had given him, and then continued until he reached a bridge, across which there ran a low unlit passage under a building. Emerging on the far side he found himself in a small piazza with a church in one corner and a house with a walled garden beside it. Opposite this stood a shuttered building, whose only inviting feature was a small lamp burning by its main door. This was shaded by green glass and shed a lurid light.

Ill at ease at finding himself in such a remote part of the city, Lucian went over to the door and pulled the bell. There was a tinkling somewhere inside, and a shout, followed by a dog barking, and a bellow of deep laughter. Then there was silence, until the spy hole on the door was opened and Lucian found himself staring at a pair of shrewd eyes magnified by spectacles.

'Are you receiving this evening?' Lucian knew always to use English when entering a brothel.

'Si, si . . . Signore. You are most welcome.'

The door opened and Lucian stepped inside to find himself in a wide passageway leading to a courtyard. The doorman led the way past two gondolas on stilts, a pile of barrels, and the remains of a bonfire. A dog barked until cursed at, then whimpered. The only light came from the doorman's lamp, and as he was hurrying forward Lucian found himself forced to make his way though the debris as best he could. His fine leather shoes squelched in the mud surrounding a fountain. He had not been expecting a palace, but neither had he thought that on his first night in Venice he would have to ruin his shoes simply to reach a house of pleasure.

The doorman stopped at the foot of a narrow flight of stairs, which ran up the side of the building to the second floor. When Lucian caught up, the man invited him to go ahead up the stairs. But as he began the climb the bell rang again, and with excuses, the doorman set off to answer it.

Cursing himself for his misplaced sense of adventure, Lucian made his way to the top of the stairs where there was a small balcony. He paused to get his breath, and looked back, hoping to see the doorman returning but all was quiet. There was a door on the balcony, but it was unpromising, being low and made of plain wood. The windows on either side were dark. Unable to think what else to do, Lucian rapped on the door. At first nothing happened, but then the door swung open.

Somewhere a mandoline was playing, and there was a rush of air carrying the scent of jasmine and orange blossom. Four young men stood around a porcelain bowl of exquisite design. They must have been brothers because each was rather short, with oiled curly black hair and a pretty girlish face. Naked except for girdles of flowers strung around their waists, and binding their wrists and ankles, they were idly masturbating, as if hoping to contribute to whatever was in the bowl. Behind them, bound to small gilt chairs, were two large black men, both gagged and with silk scarves tied across their faces. Their long cocks dangled idly between their open legs. The room was circular, and well lit by four candelabra sculpted in the form of Nubian slaves holding torches. On a sofa to one side an elderly man was being energetically spanked across the knee of a young man in the costume of a Roman legionnaire. Opposite him a very fat young fellow was having his arsehole probed by a long tube attached to a hookah through which a gentleman of obvious refinement was drawing breath.

Lucian, who was not so naïve as to be distracted by such displays, walked straight past and up a flight of stairs that led to double doors with coloured glass panels of the most elaborate design. He pushed them open and entered a second reception room. This one had a more leisurely air in that it contained several young men on their knees attending to the genital needs of various gentlemen who were taking their ease while their pink pricks stuck up from their breeches. A youth with black hair and Oriental eyes sat playing the mandoline, and the air was filled with the scent of Turkish cigarettes.

Seeing Lucian in the doorway, one of the gentlemen pointed him towards an alcove curtained off by heavy drapes. Lucian went through and found himself in a smaller, softly lit room dominated by a table covered in gold damask. Over this was strewn in higgledy-piggledy fashion the remains of a meal, some wine bottles and drinking glasses, scattered papers, a money-box, used napkins, a whip and several ledgers. Reclining alongside on a chaise was a slim man in a red-dressing gown who was digging at his back teeth with a silver pick. His height was exaggerated by a steep wig, decorated at the front with a fine jewel, and his shoes had raised soles.

Lucian explained that he was an equerry to the new ambassador, and expressed the hope that, if the goods on offer were to his taste, his would become a regular face. The man removed the pick from his mouth and tossed it on the table, but otherwise did not move.

Lucian felt his patience begin to ebb. 'Do you understand me, sir? My Italian is sadly lacking.'

'Of course I do. Tell me, Englishman, what you want?'

'I've a will to fuck a tight-fitting hole.'

The man shrugged as if disappointed. 'We have many of those.' He clapped his hands.

A door to one side opened and a troupe of perhaps a dozen young men came in. They were naked and seemingly picked to contrast with each other. A fellow who sported short black hair was followed by one with long locks the colour of marmalade. A tall one stood next to a short one, and a skinny fellow held hands with a muscular youth. A stumpy cock nestling in a bed of thick black hair was placed next to a long slender one. Skinny legs stood beside thick thighs, and a smiling beauty was placed beside a scowling rogue with an unkempt beard. As they formed themselves into a line, firm buttocks rubbed against a droopy backside, as did a hairy chest against one as smooth as polished leather.

Lucian congratulated the master of the house on the range of his goods, but was unable to hide his disappointment. He had been hoping for something exceptional, something to quicken the heart and loins, while ravishing the eye and stimulating the mind. He had been lucky in the past. Would he ever forget the Frenchman with two cocks he had discovered in a house in Bristol? Or the five young Arabs who had delighted him in Spitalfields? There had been a fellow from Saxony who entertained in a hovel outside Clerkenwell, and whose eyes were so pale they shone like pure light, and a Russian in Rochester with the stamina of a bull.

There was nothing to equal them among the figures lined up before him. They were decent whores, no doubt, and would work hard for their money but, like so much reasonably priced merchandise, they would make for a dull evening.

The master of the house must have read Lucian's mind because he stirred himself to rise and dismiss all but one – a young man with a smooth, bronzed body, dark brown hair and a cheeky smile. 'See how you find him, sir. He is newly arrived . . . from the Euganean Hills, and may still need some taming, but I'll wager his spirit will amuse you.'

Lucian studied the young man closely and had to contain a sigh. He was pretty enough, and had a merry glint in his eye, but there was nothing exceptional about him, nothing to take away the breath. Suddenly bored, but with a sufficient itch behind his balls to need a fuck, Lucian tossed some coins on the table and nodded to the young man to lead the way.

He was expecting to fuck in a bed, and was surprised to find himself led along a narrow corridor and into a grand sitting room decorated in the French style. The walls were panelled in white wood edged in gilt, and double curtains were elaborately gathered over the window. The densely woven carpet depicted fruit and flowers. A large mirror dominated one wall, and candles lit in its ornate frame shed a flattering light. Elegant sofas, armchairs, and footstools were scattered around. Lucian's spirits rose. It was a fine setting in which to exercise the rights of hire over a sweet-faced young man. That afternoon he had been on the receiving end of two cocks. Now he would turn the tables. Perhaps he would enjoy himself, after all.

But the fellow proved hard to pin down. He had the lithe body of someone ten years younger, and the spirit to go with it. Not that he was coy: he grabbed his cock and played with it until it stuck up, then pranced around as if engaged in a priapic dance. Lucian thought to sit and watch, but no sooner had he sat than the fellow was draping himself across his knee to invite a well-deserved spanking. But that, too, was not to be, for as Lucian raised his hand the proffered bottom slid away, and was soon being thrust this way and that as the crazy dance continued.

A waiter appeared with wine and cakes and, perhaps sensing Lucian's frustration, managed in leaving to land a smack fair and square on the cheeky bottom. This discipline had a most remarkable effect. The gleeful expression was gone in a flash and in its place came one of pouting regret. For a moment it seemed that tears might flow, but it was not to be, for like a chastened dog the fellow came slinking over and knelt before his master.

Amused by the pantomime Lucian rewarded him with a kiss and, then without further ado, took him by the hand and led him to the sofa over which he had the fellow bend with his legs wide apart. It was, Lucian told himself, high time he had his fuck. He loosened his breeches, and used a hand to rummage in his fly and release his cock. With a surging sense that all was well with himself and the world, he grabbed it, peeled back the skin from its helmet and, after planting a good-luck kiss upon his fingertips, transferred the blessed touch to the very tip of his prick. He closed his eyes as he might if diving into deep water, let himself fall forward, and added his weight to the lucky aim of the libertine as he plunged his cock through the rectal gates deep into the unknown caverns beyond.

A frenzy seized him. Just as a good rider will betray his talent the moment he takes the reins, so a good fuck manifests himself the second the ramrod enters the guts. So it took no more than an initial thrust for Lucian to realise he had been given the pride of the litter, and with a cry of delight he sent himself deeper to do justice to the magnificent creature he was riding. It would be a long fuck, and a sweaty one, one to remember, certainly, but a challenge to any man, and Lucian was determined that he should not, in thirty years' time, be sitting in his club and feel the cold shivers of regret that one evening, just arrived in Venice, he had been given the ride of a lifetime only to find himself dismounted in the field.

# Sixteen

There were not many male whorehouses in Venice, despite brisk demand, and most were infested with the pox. But there was one Lord Damiens believed to be the equal of any in Europe, and that was to be found along the Rio della Pergola. It was run not by some retired merchant seaman with rouged cheeks, but by a gentleman of genuine mystery. Where he came from nobody knew, and his name, Old Pic, gave no clue. He was as tall and elegant as any Englishman, and spoke all the civilised tongues, and he brought to his profession that easy and spirited competence that will inspire a client to return quite as much as a pretty face or bottom.

It followed, therefore, that having had harsh words with Rob that morning, Lord Damiens should bring his new friend to the house on the Rio della Pergola. Their gondola arrived a little before midnight and, as always, Old Pic was on the landing stage to usher the milord inside with bows and promises of novelties and proven pleasures. They took the main staircase and passed by rooms in which varying scenes of depravity were in progress to reach the alcove where Old Pic did his business. He sat by the table, which was covered in gold damask, while Lord Damiens and Rob sat on gilt chairs. Several young men of the house stood in attendance, with their shirts and flies unbuttoned to reveal their charms.

It was apparent that Damiens was in no mood for anything mundane. He waved away the attentions of several provocative young men, and dismissed Old Pic's suggestion that he try one or two of the less usual pleasures on offer. Rob sat in silence, watched closely by Old Pic from the corner of his eye.

'The truth is I'm fatigued.' Lord Damiens slumped as far as the chair would allow, which caused two of the attendants to giggle.

Old Pic glanced their way and gave the handle of his whip a warning caress. 'I must take that as a criticism of the house, my lord.' He shook his head in sorrow. A turquoise jewel sewn into the front of his wig shone like a third eye. 'I shall endeavour to redeem my reputation.'

'Nothing energetic, I beg you. I still remember those Cossacks . . . too exhausting.'

'A mistake based upon a misunderstanding, my lord.' Old Pic beckoned an attendant and whispered in his ear. 'I've an inspiration, my lord . . . rather a naughty one . . .' As the attendant hurried out, Old Pic invited his clients to rise and follow him.

At the end of a short corridor a door stood open. Old Pic led the way and Damiens and Rob found themselves in a small room containing little but a bed draped in Turkish rugs, and piled with cushions. Small tables set with refreshments were being placed on either side. A scarlet wall hanging with a Pompeian scene embroidered in gold covered one wall, lit by shaded candles, but elsewhere the room was in darkness.

At Old Pic's invitation Rob and Damiens made themselves comfortable on the bed, while attendants removed their boots and wigs and loosened their clothes. When all was ready the candles were extinguished. There was a rustling as the hanging parted at its centre to reveal a large gilt-framed window. On the far side, and lit as dramatically as any painting by an old master, there was being enacted a scene that made Rob sit bolt upright, and even caught the milord's full attention.

A young man was bending over the side of a chaise with his legs spread to be rogered by another standing over him. This fellow was thrusting and pulling his cock with the utmost vigour.

'I assure you they cannot see us,' whispered Old Pic. 'It is a device of the glass . . .'

111

Rob laughed, and the milord chuckled as he congratulated Old Pic. 'How ingenious . . . I'll wager there's nothing like it in London. And how well that fellow shafts. May we toss him a coin in appreciation?' Damiens laughed and called out to encourage the players.

Old Pic shushed him. 'I beseech you, my lord, no demonstrations.' He sounded quite alarmed. 'What you see is not a piece of theatre. They are pleasing themselves.'

'You dirty dog, Pic. What do you make of it, Robbie?'

'Excellent, my lord.' Rob took a gulp of wine, but without looking away from the mirror. Some of it trickled down his chin.

Damiens wiped the red dribble with the back of his sleeve. 'And which of those two fine young animals would you choose to be, Robbie?'

'The yeoman must bend before the lord, mustn't he?'

'Indeed he must.' Damiens reached over and placed a hand on Rob's loins. He squeezed them until Rob murmured a complaint. Out of the gloom an attendant emerged to untie Rob's fly. The ever-ready cock stood up among the linen foliage.

'But sometimes a lord must himself . . . bow . . .' Damiens leaned across and closed his mouth gently over the expectant cock.

As the milord sucked, Rob lay back, content to feel the warmth enveloping his cock, and the old itch stirring inside him. He watched the mirror and the energetic fucking on the far side. While he could not judge the young man with his arse in the air, the man doing the shafting was devilishly handsome. Although not tall, he had a fine body, with broad shoulders and a sinewy flat stomach. His features were refined, despite the distortions caused by the effort of fucking, and there hung about him an aura of cruel sensitivity. The hair was luxuriant and black, and hung on his shoulders like a libertine's mane, but his eyes were the coldest shade of blue. The skin was pale, except for boyish rosy cheeks, and he fucked with the abandon of a Bulgar.

After a while Damiens evidently grew tired of sucking, because he pulled away and rested his head sideways on Rob's groin. He, too, watched the mirror.

There was silence in the room, during which Old Pic took out his timepiece and, affecting surprise at the hour, withdrew. As the door-latch clicked, Damiens sat up and yawned. 'The trick wears thin, as tricks always do. Shall we . . .? I know a gaming house.'

He slid forward to the end of the bed and sat staring through the mirror while an attendant hurried forward with his boots. For a moment he did not move. Then, with a low cry, he stood up and pressed his face to the mirror.

The attendant moved to restrain him, but was pushed away. 'By all the lords of hell, I know that fellow.'

'Which one, my lord?' Rob was at his side. Closer to, the scene was no less diverting. His cock was rampant.

'Curse you, Robbie, the fellow in the saddle.'

Rob glanced sideways, and saw on Damiens' face an expression of great feeling. Was he jealous of some pretty-faced whore? 'Who is he, my lord?'

'I'll wager fifty Spanish dollars that's Lucian Parry. But what on earth is he doing here?'

Old Pic was beside himself with embarrassment. He could find the words neither to apologise, nor to explain. All he could say, and he said it over and over, was that fate had played a trick. 'The chances must be a million to one or more. Truly, coincidence is the devil's magic wand . . . but a million to one or more.'

Rob could see that neither Lucian nor Damiens was in the least upset. A man who will fuck his servants in full view of his household was not likely to be offended by the sight of a friend similarly engaged in a whorehouse. And although Lucian feigned sufficient anger to ensure he was given back his ducats, with a few added as compensation, only a fool could have failed to see that he was far more pleased to have found his old friend than humiliated by the circumstances.

They were in Old Pic's alcove. While the proprietor sat beside his table muttering apologies, Rob and the two reunited friends stood smiling at one another as they drank the very good wine that had been rushed up from the cellars. For Rob, however, the occasion generated mixed feelings.

Only that morning he had seen the vicious anger that Lord Damiens would direct at anyone who crossed him. Rob was not used to such sudden changes of mood: in his family a loving brother was steady in his affection, just as a bullying neighbour was always a bully. A fellow was what he was. In the life he had known, there had been no trap-doors through which the unsuspecting might fall to injury. To find Damiens suddenly enraptured to discover an old friend further undermined Rob's sense of security. And a closer examination of Lucian gave him no cause for confidence.

If Rob had found Damiens dashing with his chestnut hair and aristocratic manners, Lucian was even more the young master. If Damiens affected languor and a sultry lustfulness to mask his true self, Lucian was like a coiled spring with a loose lock. Rob could not deny that he was attractive, just as he could see a ruthless will and a lack of conscience. If only, Rob thought, Damiens could be content to be all his, it would not matter who his friends were or what they shared. But knowing that he was condemned to use his cunning to keep in the milord's affections, he could not avoid the evidence of his stirring loins – the proof of Lucian's appeal.

He did not, therefore, look away when his eye met Lucian's, but rather held it, until both understood the other's intentions.

Damiens was keen that the three of them should return to the Palazzo Ferri. There was much to talk about, he declared, and drinking to be done, and if anyone felt the need of a fuck there were plenty of obedient footmen to choose from.

Old Pic permitted himself a shudder at this suggestion, and warned of the paradox of whorehouses being governed by privacy while any palazzo will be the hotbed of gossip and scandalous rumour. But Damiens was not one to listen to such homely advice. He ordered that the gondola be brought and, without bothering to replace his wig, prepared to leave.

Rob noticed that Old Pic allowed himself a smile of satisfaction, and did not bother to rise when the milord and his friend took their leave. Knowing the pair to be in deep conversation, and oblivious to all others, Rob paused briefly before following.

Old Pic sat back on his sofa, and let a hand play with the jewel in his wig. He gave Rob a shrewd sideways glance and sighed. 'Why do you stay?' His voice was weary.

'I am curious, sir. Was it only chance that Mr Parry was in the mirrored room when his lordship . . .?'

Old Pic silenced him with an impatient flick of his wrist. 'Go, you wretched boy. You have a Venetian's suspicious mind.'

Rob did not linger, but ran along the corridor and through rooms in which the smell of opium drifted like a graveyard mist, down the stairs and out on to the landing-stage. Damiens and Lucian were waiting for him, both standing in the gondola with their cloaks up round their necks and the hoods over their heads. Rob jumped in beside them, aware that he wore no coat and that his golden hair blew in the breeze. His sailor's sense of balance allowed him to land hard but without rocking the boat, and he smiled at Lucian, who smiled back, before shaking his head and turning away.

Damiens cursed him for keeping them waiting, but Lucian was full of praise for his athleticism, and as they journeyed down the Grand Canal the talk was of the hard life at sea and all the good it will do a lad.

# Seventeen

---

The night was no longer young, but the two friends wished to talk. Chairs were set on the *piano nobile* so as to give a view of the Grand Canal. A sharp wind was rattling the windows and disturbing the water below. To counter the bleakness Damiens had a flute player woken and brought in to run through some simple melodies. But the wine tasted sour after the fine vintage Old Pic had provided, and the conversation did not flow easily.

Rob had gone up to the bedchamber after Damiens had told him he looked pale and in need of sleep. But his absence only made more obvious the spell he had cast over the two aristocrats. They did their best to talk of friends and foes, of the ups and downs of reputations and the general flux of life, but Damiens was aware that Lucian was distracted by more immediate thoughts. Nor could he put the young sailor from his own mind.

In the end they gave up the pretence, and spoke with candour. Lucian stood by the window and looked down at the waters, whose turbulence seemed to match his own. 'I've come to Venice bored with life. I need novelty, Charles. My duties here will not be burdensome, and I intend to educate myself, so that my years of manhood will not be lived at second hand or wasted in cheap pursuits. This morning I saw the young men by San Marco, so confident and elegant in their finery . . . and I thought, Here I can be myself, after all the lingering doubts in London.' He sighed and let out a short, bitter laugh. 'And what bewitches me here in Venice? The fair hair and honest eyes of an Englishman. Am I gone mad?' He turned from the window and looked down at Damiens, who was watching him while sipping wine.

'There is more to Venice than young men. And you're right, it's a city where a man can find himself . . . or be himself . . . enrich himself.'

'You have prospered here.'

'Mightily. I came with nothing.' Damiens shrugged. 'Now I have all a man could wish for. But I cannot deny my Robbie is desirable cargo.'

'Nor should you. He is yours, after all.' Lucian strode from the window to refill his glass, but did not drink at once and instead stood staring down into it. 'He lies in your bed, does he not, waiting for you?'

With a wave of the hand Damiens dismissed the flute player. 'What is mine, Lucian, is yours.' In the silence Damiens barely spoke above a whisper. 'Besides, I hardly know him, except to fuck. Have him, if you want.'

'He would not have me.'

Damiens stood up and went to the window. It was his turn to look down at the dark churning waters. 'My dear fellow, how little you know of Venice. Your manhood will need no fetters here. You will not hear rehearsed the dainty thoughts of Monsieur Voltaire, nor the fine piffle of Monsieur Rousseau. Venice is the world as it has always been, and should always be. And as for Robbie, for as long as he is in this house – and it is not my intention that he should leave it – he will be had by whomsoever I say. I am the master here.'

Lucian was at his side. Together they watched a craft, propelled by a dozen oarsmen, making its way towards the Rialto. The steersman kept time with a melancholy call.

Lucian drained his glass. 'You may be right, Charles, but one thing I know already. I've had arses in Antwerp, in Riga, in every part of London, along country lanes, in barrack rooms, stables, manor houses, royal palaces – and always for lust – but never, ever, have I set eyes on the likes of your Robbie.' With great force he threw his glass into the fireplace. 'He is a god come to earth as a clod-hopper.'

Damiens laughed. 'I'll warrant you he's a very pretty fellow, but I think not a god.'

'Then you have not looked into his eyes.'

'I have, but with my own eyes not yours.' Damiens clapped a hand on his friend's shoulder. 'Go to him, Lucian, make him yours for as long as you want. If I feel the itch, I'll fuck a footman. They may not be gods, but they know how to spread their legs.'

Lucian did not wait for second thoughts but went towards the doors where a servant was waiting with a light to lead the way up the flight of stairs.

Damiens watched him go, then turned back to the window. The waters in the canal were as dark and disturbed as before.

Rob was asleep. In dreams he was not to remember he was back on board the *Dawn Treader* as she ploughed through the Bay of Biscay one bright gusty morning. At his side stood not the young stowaway but his old friend Angus, still as sturdy and strong as on the day they had parted. His dark hair was tousled and shiny with brine, and his feet were as brown as the deck. Overhead the thick web of ropes creaked and grumbled all the way up to the masthead. When the order came to go aloft Angus was first away, his body almost doubled up as his hands and feet raced upwards. When Rob felt the sting of the rope's end, and heard the quartermaster's curse, he reached for a firm grip, looked up and saw Angus far above. How good it would be, Rob thought, if just the pair of them could stay aloft for ever, with only the wind and the sea to disturb them. He saw that Angus was already half-way to the masthead, sprawled against the rigging, with the sun directly above him, shining down like a fiery hunter's eye.

And then Rob was awake. There was light in the room and a footman was reaching under the bedclothes to rub oil between his buttocks. He turned and saw a figure being undressed by a valet. He lay back and muttered a blasphemous prayer of thanks. A wave of joyful anticipation ran through him. For the remainder of the night he would share the milord's bed with Lucian rather than its owner.

Lucian had candles set around the bed, ordered the shutters closed and dismissed all the servants. Although he wore a long robe of dark blue and silver, it hung loosely from his shoulders as he came to the bed. With a single glance Rob took in and judged the torso, groin and legs. It was not a yeoman's body, like his own, which had been developed by hard labour and exercise but, rather one that had remained entirely unblemished, and had the limber grace and poise that only horsemanship and training with weapons will bring. The firm legs met where the cock hung tautly from a bed of black hair. Everything about the man was well-knit, in proportion, and ready for action.

As Lucian leaned forward to kiss him lightly on the lips, Rob smelt the fresh sweat under his armpits, and the yeasty scent rising from his groin. The combination tickled his nostrils. A hand had his cock in a firm grip, and squeezed. Another toyed with his right nipple, tugged at the stem, and caressed the surround until his whole chest rippled with pure sensation.

Rob lay back to allow Lucian to move on top of him and continue the kissing. His thick black hair smothered Rob's face, while the tongue played inside his mouth until that, too, was filled with sensations like echoes in a cave.

Surely, Rob thought, no pleasure known to man could match that of being made love to by a handsome young devil.

But the devil may have in mind gratification less simple than a kiss or caress. For every pleasure a man can share or negotiate, there are ten he must take for himself, like fruit plucked from a tree.

Rob saw Lucian pull a length of cord from his robe's pocket. Was he to be beaten? But Lucian was soon on top of him again, and kissing him on the neck and shoulders. The sensations were as exquisite as any jewel, and as clear and hard. How easy, Rob thought, to allow the pleasure to wash over him until he drowned. There was nothing to do except surrender to its tyranny.

When Lucian turned him over so that he lay on his stomach, Rob assumed he was about to be fucked. And indeed, with his body already roused, he was a fortress open and ready to be entered. However, it was not to be. Instead Lucian grabbed his ankles and, with speed and skill, tied them tightly. Nor was that the only use for the cord. With no less agility Lucian bound Rob's wrists, then drew the cord tight until his feet and hands met behind his back. He had been trussed like a chicken made ready for roasting.

Rob was about to complain that the cord was too tight when he saw Lucian produce a large white handkerchief. This he folded carefully into a loose wad. He came close, and Rob saw his determined expression. Whatever the task Lucian had set himself, Rob knew he would see it through.

Lucian turned Rob over so that he lay face up. He saw how Lucian held the handkerchief against the palm of his hand, using his middle finger. He loomed over Rob, who tried to move his head out of the way as Lucian used his thumb and forefinger to squeeze his nostrils together. The other hand prised open Rob's mouth. He tried to complain but a finger on his tongue prevented speech. The handkerchief was slowly and meticulously stuffed into his mouth, and poked deftly into every corner and cranny so that neither air nor sound could pass.

Rob could not breathe, and panic was building in his chest. But Lucian released his nostrils so that he could draw breath. Rob tried to cry out, but the soft wad made a mockery of his cries. Deprived of speech, or the ability to move his limbs, Rob felt his senses sharpening. Every nerve ending was alert, and when Lucian's silk robe brushed against his chest, it felt as if a cat had clawed his skin. Despite the darkness he could make out every detail of Lucian's face as he bent close to make sure the gag was in place. Then he secured it with a cord run around the back of Rob's head and knotted over the gaping mouth.

Although he could not speak, or make any sound beyond a muffled cry, Rob heard everything, even the wash of passing craft slapping the side of the palazzo. And he could see, and feel, as never before. A mass of sensitive tissue and sinew, he was at the mercy of Lucian, who stood over him, hands on hips, with his lips drawn into a cold smile.

Lucian ran a finger lightly over Rob's chest and down towards his belly. Rob felt his muscles contract under the touch, which sent ripples of pleasure through his torso. His cock was growing, and he could feel the blood pumping at its base. It would not be long before it strained against his belly, where Lucian's finger had come to rest, like a fox waiting for its prey.

It did not take Rob's cock long to reach up to his belly. The helmet stood free of its cover, and juice dribbled from the slit as it rubbed against Lucian's finger. Rob felt Lucian's hand encircling the helmet. The sensation was too much and, despite the gag, Rob let out a muffled roar of agonised excitement. This earned him a sudden squeeze and a sharp tug on the cock, which began to shudder as a phantom orgasm dissipated the sensations.

Lucian must have felt the cock judder, however, because he moved his hand down to form a cup for Rob's balls. These he manipulated roughly, then dug into the scrotum with his fingers to separate them. He massaged each in turn until the scrotum relaxed and became as soft to the touch as the silky skin around a nipple. Unable to do more than writhe and strain, Rob prayed that Lucian would soon be satisfied, and release him before he lost all feeling in his ankles and wrists.

But Rob knew it was likely that Lucian had other torments in mind. He was not surprised therefore when Lucian tickled the sides of his ribcage, and used his fingernails to scratch at his nipples, nor when Lucian ran his tongue down his neck, and played with his Adam's apple. He smoothed down Rob's fair pubic hair, and twisted a few of the longer strands round his forefinger, and pulled, as if picking daisies. Finally he formed a circle with thumb and forefinger and ran it down the length of Rob's cock until it came to rest at the base. He tightened it, then slowly pressed down to generate fresh feeling in Rob's groin, and put his head close to the helmet so that he might use his tongue to slide up and down the length of hard, purple flesh.

When Rob could stand no more, he could only twist his bound torso this way and that, let out muffled cries for mercy, and strain against the cord binding him. But Lucian had no concern except for his own pleasure, and it was only when Rob began to choke, and felt himself slipping into unconsciousness, that he stopped his torments and untied the cord around Rob's mouth. Then, as casually as if pulling it from his coat pocket, he removed the handkerchief from Rob's mouth, and tossed it away.

Rob lay gasping, and demanded loudly that he be untied. Lucian smiled and shook his head. His expression of confident disdain told Rob that his ordeal was far from over. Yet there was nothing he could do but protest and hope.

Worse was to follow. Lucian picked him up off the bed, as if he were a parcel, and carried him over to a sturdy table strewn with the milord's clothes and effects. Rob felt himself put down close to the edge, face up so that his head hung down over the side.

Without ado Lucian parted his robe and took hold of his slim but by no means small cock. When Rob felt his mouth being forced open he let out his fiercest protest, but again strong fingers entered his mouth and squashed his tongue so that his words were lost.

Lucian bent low and spoke into Rob's ear. 'Be a good fellow and suck. If you bite or spit, I'll have you whipped and left trussed for a week.'

The cock was slipping into his mouth. It was warm and its sides were as soft as it was hard. It did not pause on its way, and Rob gagged as its tip hit the back of his throat. Lucian completed his arrival with a thrust just strong enough to force Rob's jaw open, and his head down, until a straight path ran between lips and upper throat.

Once again Rob could not breathe – but only for a moment because, with a pelvic jerk, Lucian removed himself with the same precision as he had entered.

Rob heard Lucian close to his ear. His voice was soft and coaxing, but with enough menace to chill a summer's day. 'You're not doing your work, my lad. My cock must have a clear path. Are we to be here 'til Michaelmas?' A hand slapped Rob's cheek lightly, but with the playfulness of a whip used to caress.

'Aye-aye, sir.' Rob could no more than whisper.

'That's my lad.' Rob felt Lucian's hand against his lips and jaw, massaging them open, and tilting his head down until his neck felt ready to snap.

When the cock slid in a second time, Rob found he could do

as Lucian had urged, and by forcing his jaw open and his head back, he could take the full length of sleek gristle. As dense pubic hair enveloped Rob's nostrils, he heard Lucian grunt with pleasure. The cock slid back, and instead of coming in again, was removed so as to allow Lucian's sack of balls to dangle over Rob's open jaw. These were lowered into the mouth so as to make a second and more hairy gag.

'Suck on them.' Lucian's instructions were as cool and calm as if he were ordering afternoon refreshments. 'Now chew.'

Rob did as he was told, and munched the scrotum as if preparing to bite the balls off. With his recent practice from the handkerchief, he had no trouble breathing through his nose, and he used the movements of tongue, jaw and teeth to exercise the balls until they were bobbing this way and that. It was an energetic revenge, and Rob enjoyed himself.

So did Lucian, who was writhing around in such a state of abandon he tried to pull the hair from Rob's skull. When he told Rob to go harder, Rob was pleased to obey, and used his teeth to isolate first one ball and then the other. He placed one between his back teeth and his cheek, then sucked the scrotum tight until the pressure was such the ball popped back between the jagged molars, causing Lucian to cry out in a spasm of painful pleasure.

When this game was done, Rob let the balls go almost with regret. Although he demanded once again to be unbound and set free, he did not care too deeply when Lucian smacked his face for his insolence, and told him there were further tasks to be undertaken before the shift could end.

So Rob lay, trussed on the desk like a present waiting to be unwrapped, with his head hanging down. What further use could Lucian have for him? Out of the corner of his eye he saw Lucian standing with his legs apart and his cock sticking up while he used both hands to rub his balls.

From then on, however, Rob found himself used in more conventional acts. He had to receive Lucian's cock in his mouth, and allow it free and open passage. It drove in and out in an attempt to stimulate jaded senses. When that failed, Lucian untied Rob's feet and hands and led him back to the bed to be fucked in a straightforward manner. But as Lucian found his rhythm Rob sensed that the two of them were setting off along a path that would twist this way and that before leading eventually to a climax. Rob lay face down on the bed and let the easy sensations in his arse scatter through his body like mice let out of a cage. It was now his turn to remain calm and savour the effect a cock will have on a tight hole, while Lucian seemed to fall into the grip of a passion that mocked his earlier self-control. Rob laughed when Lucian cursed him, as well as his own mother, all the gods, the devil and his ancestors. Rob felt him digging deeper with each thrust, and could not help thinking that his recent tormentor sounded more like a madman shouting on a street corner than a man of the world taking his pleasure.

The fuck continued, as the clock on the landing ticked away the minutes of the night, and the candles set round the bed guttered. On the floor below Lord Damiens stood staring out at the early traffic on the Grand Canal. In an hour it would be light.

Rob's relief at having to do nothing more than take a cock up his arse gradually began to give way to the hope that Lucian would soon reach his long-delayed climax. The shafts and shudders of sensation still ran from Rob's backside to spread along every nerve and artery, but he was aware of a growing intensity inside himself, a slow crescendo in his mind that had nothing to do with pleasure or pain, or the invasion of his body. More it was the reawakening of long-forgotten desires and satisfactions, as if in being plundered by so efficient and relentless a cock, layers of memory were being peeled away. In an instant he was a boy again. Snatches of lullabies drifted from an open window, and he felt suddenly as warm as when the sun came out on a spring morning. Did a dog bark? Was that the laughter of brothers and sisters playing? Did his mother call, and could that be the smell of mutton boiling, of apples being baked with cloves? Was that his father's hand on his shoulder?

Despite his sensual nature Rob was a sensible fellow who knew that all the couplings that the body can make, and all the pleasures it offers, are of small importance compared to clear thought, decent feelings and a good heart. Being tied and gagged had been no more than a mature imitation of those childhood games played long ago in the fields and orchards of Kent. And just as those who took part in those early contests and rituals showed the character and temper of the men they were to become, so Lucian's cock was opening up those long blocked routes back to that pristine world, where the seeds of Rob's manhood had first been sown.

The relentless energy of Lucian's cock, as it drove in and out, gradually stripped away all the accretions that had gathered during Rob's journey to manhood and left him raw and alone. All he could feel was the cock making use of him, and just as a whore will accept her pimp's hand in anger as evidence of his protection, so Rob took his fucking as proof that only Lucian would defend him.

By the simple and expert application of his cock, in the time-honoured fashion, the ambassador's aide was winning the Kentish sailor.

When Lucian's climax came, Rob was ready with his. They rose to the moment together, like athletes jumping for a ball. They held themselves still at the apex, then let themselves go, and in their embraces spread and mingled their come like saliva on kissed lips. And then they fell back on the bed, and lay together on the wet sheets.

In a few moments they were both asleep.

# Eighteen

Lord Damiens sat in the dark. A servant who brought fresh candles was sent away. There was no need for light. He had much to think about. And he would be seeing things soon enough . . . sights best endured with rested eyes and a clear mind.

That was the thing. A clear mind. So long as he held true to his plans, and saw them through to fruition, it did not matter what sights might pass before him or what the pitying parts of him might feel. He told himself that he must not falter, not when so much had been achieved and he was so close to the goal.

There was a thud and a muffled cry from the bedchamber. No doubt the young sailor was discovering that there are disciplines on dry land quite as demanding as those ruling life at sea. Even so he felt a certain regret that it was Lucian who was doing the buggering. But the idea of interrupting was too dangerous. Sooner or later he would need the goodwill of Lucian, and more particularly the ambassador. When that time came they might make all the difference. To surrender a night's pleasure to insure the future was no more than plain prudence. And yet . . . those blue eyes . . . and the damp lips that parted into a smile . . . those warm rough hands that gripped his cock . . . perhaps after all, he might . . .

There was a clatter in the doorway. It was Titus. A dark cloak was tossed over his shoulder, and he had another over his arm. 'My lord, it is time?'

'Of course.' Damiens rose wearily. 'Is everything in order?' He walked towards Titus, who held out the cloak for his master.

'Yes, my lord. They have arrived.'

'I heard nothing.'

'There is a fresh wind tonight.'

The stairs were only lit on the turns, and the night air was cold and damp. Damiens was glad of his cloak and pulled it close round him. When they reached the ground floor, Titus went ahead to a small door in a corner. He unlocked it with a key attached to a ring on his belt. When the door opened, Damiens went through and made his way down a steep, curling flight of steps. At the bottom he stood in the darkness while Titus came down behind, bringing light and shadow to the bleak scene.

Ahead ran a short wide corridor that ended with a blank wall topped by a grimy window against which the outline of a gondola could be seen, bobbing in the canal. The other way, a narrower corridor stretched back under the palazzo, with storerooms opening off on either side.

Titus led the way along this passage. The light from his torch danced in the cold dank air. At the end there was an oak door, framed with iron rods, which was also locked. Damiens held the light while Titus bent forward to find the key. Apart from the sound of scraping in the lock, there was silence. For a moment Damiens was overcome by an urge to retrace his steps, and leave the task ahead until the next night, or have it done without him. But the door was already opening, and warmer air rushed past as if to escape some infernal source of heat.

Ahead lay another, broader but low-ceilinged, passageway, which soon turned to the right. Torches shimmering on the walls shed a coppery light. Nearby a man's voice rang out in anguish before subsiding into forlorn sobs.

Titus led on, making sure he walked in the centre of the passage. He did not look to the left or right, and Damiens, treading in his steps, kept his eyes firmly on the back of his servant's cloak.

For a few steps all was quiet, but their boots thudded on the stone, and their shadows flickered past the small openings on the bolted doors lining either side. This provoked a mournful chorus from those imprisoned within, who were moaning like beasts of burden. They were calling for what had been taken away, and would never be returned.

Damiens stared ahead and tried to put from his mind the fate awaiting the wretches, who could expect nothing better than a final release into death after a life lived under the lash without a glimmer of hope or peace.

Men in black uniforms came hurrying to quell the noise. Their black leather belts, gloves and boots gleamed as they passed by, cracking their whips and shouting curses and threats. It was not far to the end of the passage, where two men stood waiting on the far side of an iron grille, but Titus was not hurrying, and behind him Damiens heard doors being unbolted. There were more curses and pleas as the whips did their work, and the moans turned to cries of pain.

That evening, after a dinner of roast pheasant and fruit, Rob stood before Lord Damiens on the *piano nobile* as he pinned a jewel on Rob's coat. It sparkled under the chandeliers, but Rob could manage nothing more than muttered thanks as he glanced down at the glittering stone. His heart was heavy, even as he felt his loins stir. All day, since Lucian had left him, his mind had been in confusion while his body sang in praise of his new lover.

To be in Venice, and living in splendour at the beck and call of a milord, might not seem a bad outcome after his sufferings on the *Dawn Treader*. But such was Rob's sense of liberty, that he sensed the confinement lurking beneath all the gifts of jewels, perfumes and fine clothes. He had heard stories about the harems of the Levant, and the losses endured by those men who served there. He did not want to wake one morning to find his balls had been cut off. Better to escape and try to make his way home, even starve on the streets or freeze on a snowy Alpine pass, than live as the milord's eunuch.

And yet, there were such pleasures. If his mind was in turmoil, his body was aflame with desire. Every part of him yearned for sensations undreamed of until he had fallen into the hands of

Damiens and Lucian. Even the light touch of the milord's fingers, as the pin was pressed through Rob's coat's soft fabric, sent a sweet shudder through him and stirred his cock from its raw, aching slumber.

'There, Robbie, how well it looks.'

'More than I deserve, my lord.'

'I want you at my side, Robbie, when we go to play at the tables or amuse ourselves at Old Pic's.'

'I have no fine manners, my lord.'

'You'll bring nature's fresh air to the perfumed salons of Venice.' Damiens grasped the back of Rob's head with both hands, and drew him close to plant a kiss on his lips.

Rob was expecting playfulness and affection, and was surprised when the milord pressed a rough tongue between his teeth and drove it hither and thither, until the pleasure spread through his mouth like a creeper over a wall.

'You are mine, Robbie. All mine. I gave you to my friend last night as a precious gift. But now you are mine again.'

Sometime later, nearer dawn than midnight, Rob stood on the landing-stage outside a gaming house. The canal was narrow and crowded with gondolas waiting for hire as the house began to empty. Those leaving had to pass Rob, who wore no wig so that his golden hair fell in thick locks, and his blue eyes complemented the jewel on his chest. Barely a man or woman failed to look him up and down, while more than a few smiled or otherwise signalled their interest.

When the Palazzo Ferri's gondola appeared, Lord Damiens, who had been gossiping in the entrance, came forward and clapped a hand on Rob's shoulder. 'I am rather drunk, Robbie. You must help me.'

Eager to obey, Rob said nothing but jumped down into the gondola and turned to offer his hand to the unsteady milord. As he did so he saw, out of the corner of his eye, a gondola approaching. Standing in it, for all the world like a Venetian born and bred, was Lucian. His cloak was wrapped tight round him, and he wore absurd green and red feathers in his hat, but Rob's heart leapt at the sight. Ignoring his duty he forgot to offer his assistance to Lord Damiens until he felt the other man clutch at his hand, then let go as he lost his balance. For a moment it seemed the milord might topple into the water, but the gondolier moved quickly to save him. The crisis passed, and Damiens stumbled in beside Rob, whom he greeted with a curse and two stinging slaps across his cheeks.

Just then, as those watching from the landing-stage gasped at such public correction, Lucian stepped out of his gondola. As he paused to toss the oarsman a coin, he noticed Damiens and bowed, then smiled at Rob – as so many had that night. But it was no ordinary smile, rather the contortion of a desire intense enough to curl his lip and narrow his eyes.

Damiens returned the bow. 'The tables are dull tonight, Lucian. Come back with us.' The gondola rocked a little.

'I feel luck at my elbow. Perhaps later, Charles, when I return with my winnings . . .' He ran his eye over Rob once more, causing some of those watching to laugh and whisper comments. 'If the refreshment is as last night's . . .'

'The menu changes.'

'Then I must resist . . . such rare game . . . two nights running . . .' He shook his head. 'Bad for body and soul.'

'But the sport's the same.'

Lucian gave Rob a last look, and bowed once more. 'Keep him for yourself, Charles. He is not for hunting by the common herd.'

Damiens laughed and told the gondolier to cast off. With amused farewells from the spectators, the milord made his way unsteadily to his covered seat. Rob stood and watched as Lucian went up the crowded steps. He looked back before disappearing into the gaming house.

With a sigh Rob turned, expecting to be called to the milord's side, but when their eyes met, Damiens looked away and Rob found himself compelled to stand all the way back to the palazzo.

At first light Damiens fucked Rob. After being made to wait on the landing for an hour he was called to the great bedchamber. Two footmen went ahead of him. While a servant painted his hole with grease, Damiens stood with his back to Rob, drinking hot chocolate while chatting to Titus. In the end he turned, and snapped his fingers in the direction of the bed. When Rob went to lie on the sheets he was told to strip and bend over the side ready for easy taking.

As he fucked, Damiens had no words for Rob, no whispered endearments, only grunts and coarse curses. Rob held his tongue, and closed his eyes to feign suffering. In truth, he did feel the pangs of shame, and feared what his master's displeasure might mean for him, but neither could he deny to himself the madness of the pleasure he felt. It was as if Damiens, in both humiliating and possessing him, had found the key to his deepest, most secret self.

Damiens thrust himself up Rob's back passage with a weary vigour that allowed nothing for finesse and rhythm. Rob heard him emit strange hissing sounds and loud farts. Sharp pangs of raw sensation ran through him as his master bent first one knee then the other to vary his thrust. Fingernails were dug into his back, and drawn along as if the welts might make a picture.

He did not care. Rough treatment was no more than he deserved. What man worthy of the name could pledge his allegiance to a new master, and the very next day submit to the passion of another? If he was treated like a whore, who was to say he was not?

Had he hated being fucked as much as he hated himself, he could have felt he was receiving just punishment. But he rejoiced in every harsh thrust up him, every excruciating line drawn across his back, every squeeze on his balls and jerk on his stiff straining cock. He was intoxicated by the smell of manly sweat, combined with rich perfume and the sour odours left by the footmen. Rob felt the strength of the body that reared over him, and he sensed the energy and pride that gave his master the will to fuck three men in the hour before dawn.

But even as he rejoiced in the milord's mastery of him, a voice within was calmly calculating the odds that within hours he would be in Lucian's arms.

Rob knew Lucian would come. A man does not look at another as Lucian had looked at him unless he is prepared to take a risk. And for all the humiliation he had suffered, Rob knew his worth.

Lucian arrived just after noon. The entrance hall and *piano nobile* were already crowded with those hoping for an audience with the milord, who was still asleep and unlikely to be woken for an hour or more. The servants hurried up from the kitchens with refreshments, and Titus was on the prowl, a new whip in hand, to ensure everything was in order.

The hired gondola carrying a solitary passenger drew little attention, and only Rob, watching from the half-landing, saw that it was Lucian who stepped on to the landing-stage. Rob ran down the stairs and moved forward to intercept him, but Lucian made a sign to him to be discreet and turned to make himself known to a group of French ladies, who were being shown round by a dandified young nobleman. Rob stood in the centre of the hall, at a loss to know what to do next, aware of Titus lounging nearby.

A voice behind him made Rob start. '*La scala . . . subito . . . va.*' Silvio, the landlord's agent, was standing close with his shoulder almost touching Rob's. His agitated manner and drab clerk's garb made him look out of place. Rob noticed that his oily black hair was dishevelled and that his beard needed trimming.

'I don't understand.' Rob did not want to be pestered by the wretched man when Lucian might be watching. But just as he was about to move away he felt something being placed in his hand. He looked down and saw a key.

Silvio winked. 'At the top . . . a room . . . you . . .' He glanced over towards Lucian. 'Your friend.'

Rob clutched the key and wondered if Titus had seen, but he was engaged in conversation with two elderly English clerics, who were using a magnifying glass to admire the genitalia of a large nude warrior carved in marble.

At that moment Lucian approached.

Rob bowed. 'The room at the very top . . . I have the key.' He spoke in a half-whisper, but quickly added in full voice, 'His lordship will be asleep yet awhile.'

They exchanged a few words more, and then, pretending to see someone he knew on the half-landing, Rob walked past Titus to the stairs. There was nothing to be gained by delay, so he took the steps two at a time and, once out of sight, ran up to the *piano nobile*, then on up to the landing outside the great bedchamber. To his relief this was empty, except for some maids carrying piles of linen. Their cheeks turned pink at the sight of him, and they burst into giggles.

The last flight of stairs was much narrower, and dark, and Rob nearly tripped as he made his way up to the top landing. This, too, was more modestly proportioned than those below, although the view from the small window was not. But Rob had no time to admire the splendour of Venice, and inserted the key into the lock of the first of three rooms. When it did not fit he cursed out loud, and tried the second. This too did not fit.

Had Silvio played a cruel trick? Rob turned to the last door, smaller than the others, and inserted the key. It turned easily, and the door swung open to reveal a short flight of circular stairs. Rob ran up and found himself at the topmost point of the Palazzo Ferri, a square tower open on each side under a tiled roof. Flustered birds flew from their perches.

Venice lay before him. He breathed in the fresh air and raised a hand to shield his eyes against the brilliance. Above the rooftops he could see the lagoon shimmering on the horizon, and all the other islands. To the north, in the far distance, were the glimmering mountains with snowy peaks. Everywhere water sparkled in the sunshine, and all the traffic and casual splendour of Venice was in full view. Rob stood awestruck.

When Lucian appeared, he looked as if dazed until he saw Rob. Then his lips curled into the familiar smile. From then on he did not take his eyes off Rob until he closed them as their lips met.

It was as if the glories beyond no longer existed.

# Nineteen

Shirt-tails flapped in the breeze. Between them Lucian's pink cock stood out resplendent, its purple helmet drying in the sunshine even as it was moistened by juice dribbling from the tip. Rob smelt its warm musk as he knelt, and pressed his head against Lucian's firm flat stomach. He ran his hands up the back of Lucian's legs, and delighted in fingering the fine black hair that ended abruptly at the sweet ridge where leg gave way to taut buttock. Flesh hardened by muscles eased into that as smooth and warm as polished leather left in the sun, and as firm as ripening fruit.

Lucian stood looking out over the city, his clothing undisturbed above the waist, while he ruffled Rob's fair hair. On the long journey from England he had passed the time dreaming of the adventures that might await him in Venice. Even in the wildest dreams he had not conjured anything as dazzling as the scene below, or pleasures to match those provided by the young Englishman, who was just then beginning to lick his straining rod.

For Rob a man's cock, if stood up, was as much a challenge as a pair of clenched fists. Only a coward would turn away. So he went to work with a zeal made the more keen by the suspicion that if he left Lucian unsatisfied he might find himself betrayed, despite all Lucian's passion and yearning glances. A man of his class would no more fear for his honour in doing such a thing than he would when destroying a lame mount.

So he took the long, upright cock, and used the roof of his mouth to lever it downwards to increase the pressure. At the same time he fondled, squeezed, and divided the hefty balls, while forcing his other hand between the legs to reach round between the cheeks and use his forefinger to find the hole. With the daring of one who knows he is working well, he pressed his finger hard against the tightly closed ring, until with a sigh of agonised relief, its owner relaxed and let the intruder through the gate.

Rob did not let up. He tugged the balls, and he curled his tongue around the plunging cock. Now and then he pulled back and used his teeth to nibble the tip. A second finger got through the hole, and then a third, to reconnoitre the space within. Lucian began to buckle and twist as one fierce sensation was piled on another.

Rob felt Lucian falling backwards but still did not let up. Even when Lucian landed on his rump with a thud that pressed Rob's finger further into the arsehole, he kept the rhythm going with his mouth, and kneaded the balls. In truth, nothing could have prevented him from continuing the heady business of bringing Lucian to his climax.

He did not notice, therefore, that their exertions were providing a spectacle for two figures who had emerged from the stairs. One was drably dressed, and beneath his oily locks wore an expression that might have been a smile if it had not lacked both humour and goodwill. The other was snapping a whip against his thigh and frowning with a disciplinarian's satisfaction.

The first Rob knew of them was when he heard Titus say, 'Pray do not disturb yourself, sir. We shall remove this monkey and see that he is dealt with.' His voice was as matter-of-fact as it was obsequious.

Before Rob had time to react, he felt Lucian's hand on the back of his neck, pushing him down on to the cock. 'I beg you, sirs, stand aside to leave this scallywag to finish his business.' Lucian, although his voice was strained, sounded unperturbed.

Reckoning there was nothing to be done except to continue as he was told, Rob went back to work, and edged himself further up so that he could get more of the prick in his mouth. He drew on it hard to get saliva, and at the same time plunged his fingers further up the back passage. If he kept it up, Lucien would soon spurt his come.

But he had not considered the effect his energetic labours would have on the two young spectators. Titus was the first to make a move. He raised his whip and laid it firmly across Rob's backside. Rob felt the cut, and jerked his arse, but otherwise let the pain give fresh impetus to his efforts. A second stroke added more fuel, which set Lucian gasping from the sensations forced upon him. Then Rob heard Silvio's voice, its hoarse whine eloquent of sinister intent. Glancing back Rob saw a small knife in the agent's hand as he knelt behind him.

For a moment Rob feared for his safety, but Silvio soon made clear what he was about. There was a sudden loosening around Rob's rump, and he felt fresh air on his backside. His breeches had been cut away at the arse to expose his backside to both the air and whatever scheme the pair might have in mind.

Rob heard Titus laughing. Then, with a curse, the valet began to lay into Rob's bare backside with the whip, landing each stroke with the force and precision of one for whom the duty to chastise was both a privilege and a boon. Rob took the blows with stoicism. So many sensations were running through his mouth that, a little violence at his other end was almost welcome. A flogging may act to stimulate as well as to punish, and he remembered how Silvio's fine cock had risen at the sight of him being mistreated in the palazzo's kitchens. It was idle to believe it would not be stirring again. When Titus tired, Silvio would be certain to make his presence felt.

So Rob was ready when Silvio made his move. The beating over, Titus had delivered some routine words about the need for modesty in a great man's house, and then gone below. Silvio, seeing Rob's bare, protruding arse, took the opportunity to have a second helping of what he had feasted upon one afternoon not long before. He lost no time in untying his breeches, and settled himself on his knees directly behind Rob. His long, thick prick stuck out in front of him, and he used both hands to aim its firm head at Rob's crack. As it met the warm firm flesh it quivered, as did its owner, who was overcome by the heady pleasure of taking possession of the young sailor once more.

Rob welcomed the thief at his rear on the principle that a stuffing is preferable to a thrashing, no matter how expertly delivered. He relaxed, therefore, and allowed himself the pure pleasure of knowing that the thrust would leave no wound no matter how many times it stabbed.

With a rhythm to keep at both ends, Rob knew he would be stretched to achieve satisfaction for both his customers, but he was glad to try, because it was his nature to please any man with a fine cock on the rampage. No one would entirely blame a man who was earnestly sucking one fellow while being well fucked by another.

With Silvio and Lucian face to face as the one fucked and the other lay back to be sucked, Rob knew that neither man would cede the tiniest measure of pleasure. He was their field of battle, and each was set upon victory – would cry havoc rather than give ground.

The going was tough. Rob's mouth seemed to have been made a passageway for an engine as relentless as the motions of the earth. No longer did he add any small refinements to add flavour to the pounding; it was all a matter of endurance as Lucian struggled not to bring himself to his climax ahead of Silvio. He, in his turn, had evidently learned as a scholar that the weak link in a chain is he who first lets go of himself. So Silvio thrust deep and true, but with deliberation and a mind disciplined by loneliness. There was, Rob sensed, no chance that he would come unexpectedly. It was more a game of chess than a race to the line.

But if stalemate had been in sight, the impasse was to be broken by the arrival at the scene of the master of the house. A word in Lord Damiens' ear as Titus woke him, hinting of the sport up in the tower, was enough to make the lord leap from his bed. With a robe of purple and black wrapped around him, and gold slippers on his feet, he called for attendants as he made his way towards the stairs. Titus was left to wonder whether he had been too hasty in making his report.

The scene that greeted Damiens as he emerged on to the small square tower would, in almost all other circumstances, have amused and delighted him. He approved of team effort, and any chain where the fellow in the middle was the most attractive would have his approval. But the trio huffing and puffing on the floor before him was ill matched. The sight of Silvio fucking his own favourite was particularly offensive, but the man's impertinence so exceeded his worth as to make him appear more jester than rival. And he was the landlord's agent. Perhaps all that was needed was to make sure that Silvio's punishment fitted his ambition rather than his rank.

But Lucian was a different matter. To come upon an old friend lying naked below the waist while being sucked off was certainly a strange turn of events, but one that might be turned to advantage. Damiens did not wish to compromise his influence with the ambassador, or alienate an agreeable compatriot and companion in exile. Besides which Lucian occupied by reason of birth that altitude of the social order where misdeeds could be forgiven that would certainly merit the scourge lower down.

So it was appropriate that a whipping boy was to hand. And as Damiens watched Rob suck one cock while taking another up his backside, he decided there had never been a candidate more suited to that uncomfortable role.

But the most immediate problem was how to bring the small orgy to a quick conclusion without offending Lucian. Deciding that bold action would be preferable to discretion, Damiens pulled back his right leg, took aim with the sharp point of his gold slipper, and delivered a swift kick to Silvio's lean but shapely backside that added impetus to a thrust the agent was making up Rob's back passage. This sent a shaft of pure feeling through Rob's system that made him bite the cock just then lingering at the back of his throat. This in turn caused a moment's panic that destroyed Lucian's hitherto faultless delay, and lit the fuse that would tip him over the brink. He cried out in pain as the climax took hold, and reared up with an expression that in any other circumstances would have had Damiens calling for a doctor. Silvio, too, was at the point of no return and, sensing a draw where defeat had seemed inevitable, let himself fall free into the ecstasy that is the reward for long climbs.

All at once Lucian's come was spurting in Rob's mouth, its frothy flavour as delicious as the soup of any French kitchen, while he felt the stiff rod at his rear shuddering and jerking as it, too, sent its essence deep into him. While these unlikely wet-nurses delivered their milk, Damiens stood in astonishment and in the grip of something close to awe at the sight of two healthy young men simultaneously emptying themselves into an improbable vessel.

Of the three, Rob disengaged himself with least fuss. He swallowed hard and frequently, and waited patiently while Silvio went about pulling his long slither from his arse, an action that caused much jerking about, and cries of discomfort. Lucian, on the other hand, was either exhausted or embarrassed. He lay back and covered his face with his hands.

But Rob's efficiency did nothing to ease his distress at discovering the milord had been witness to the final stages of the orgy. His lust had undone him, and he knew he would be punished. He got to his feet with as much dignity as he could muster, considering his breeches hung in tatters round his knees, and his cock would not stand down.

He turned to face Lord Damiens.

'Your breeches are in shreds.' The milord spoke with cold disdain. 'It's a pity your arse was more tenderly dealt with.'

'Yes, my lord.' Rob was looking at the floor, but glanced up in the hope of seeing something of the warmth he had only recently generated in Damiens' eyes.

'We shall remedy that.' He turned to the footmen smirking in the doorway, and used a motion of the hand to indicate that they should take Rob down and need not handle him gently.

Nor did they. Rob found himself held by the scruff of his neck and pushed down the narrow flight of steps. On the landing a boot up his recently breached and still uncovered arse sent him stumbling towards the next flight. He tripped and fell. Another boot went into his stomach, and another was aimed at his backside.

Too proud to cry out, or beg for mercy, Rob got to his feet and turned to spit at his tormentors, but the two ruffians in fancy clothes were too quick, and one landed the back of his hand across Rob's face before he had had time to gather spit. Rob fell against the wall and, tasting blood on his lip, put a hand to his face. As he did so, one of the footmen stepped forward, grabbed him by the balls, then led the way down the next flight of stairs.

The pain was excruciating, but when Rob moaned, the footman tightened his grip and drew Rob closer, so that he lost his balance, and had to be pulled harder until he regained it. Nor was the agony made any more bearable by the knowledge that as they turned the corner on the stairs, they would come in full view of those gathered outside the milord's bedroom, waiting for the daily audience to begin.

And so it was that a crowd of twenty or more patient souls were able to enjoy the spectacle of a liveried footman coming down the flight of stairs with one hand stretched behind him. This gripped the balls of a broad-shouldered young man, whose exceptional good looks were in no way compromised by his stumbling along while naked below the waist. His golden hair fell in thick locks over his brow, and into blue eyes, from which tears fell over cheeks reddened by embarrassment. His long cock hung down over the hand holding the balls, and as the strange procession passed by those watching were able to admire a fine pair of buttocks, freshly criss-crossed with red marks. A second footman, smiling broadly, brought up the rear.

A cardinal from Bavaria, who had urgent business with Lord Damiens, had to rearrange his underwear. Two painted Scottish lairds, who had been holding hands and petting one another, simply stood and stared, but a prince of the Bukovina saw nothing out of the ordinary. However, several young ladies from a convent school in the Dolomites found their expectations of life raised, as was the disappointment of the nuns escorting them.

One raffish fellow clapped his hands, and several joined in with hearty laughter.

Although the landing on the *piano nobile* was empty, as was the entrance hall except for a scattering of servants, the procession's arrival in the servants' quarters presented the footmen with another opportunity to humiliate their captive. Rob found himself forced to stand on the long table in the centre of the kitchen, while footmen, maids, chefs, boatmen, tradesmen, delivery-boys, and sundry riff-raff gathered to watch the sport. The lamp-lighter, an agile youth whose pretty face belied a mean character, sprang up beside Rob and used a length of cord to tie his hands to a metal hook driven into the ceiling. Two burly fellows stood below and fingered their broad leather belts to ensure Rob did not object.

The sport was such as might be found in the lower chambers of any great house. The barber took a razor to Rob's groin and shaved away the fair hair, bootblack was melted and rubbed over his balls, and stems of celery were shoved up his backside. The chef covered his cock with a sweet sauce so that some slatterns might lick it off, while the older servants enjoyed themselves by teasing his face with dusting sticks. One enterprising young man went to some trouble to raise Rob's shirt and tickle his nipples, and was much gratified to see their stalks standing erect. The naked buttocks attracted a fair number of admiring strokes, pinches and slaps, and the golden hair was tugged and run between the fingers of those curious enough to stand on the table.

Throughout the ordeal Rob stood with bowed head. He had been raised in a world where there were few choices, and loyalty to the squire was taken for granted, no matter how villainous the fellow might be. His betrayal of Lord Damiens, therefore, demanded punishment: both the present entertainment and the flogging that would follow, were nothing more than simple justice. He had seen others subjected to worse trials, and had not objected. So he took his punishment with a passivity and acceptance that helped to make it bearable. He would not complain, nor would he refrain from weeping. A display of contrition might stir sympathy once the fun began to pall. But even as he stood, with tears dribbling from the end of his nose, his balls black, his half-stirred cock well-licked, his arse well reddened, and his hands and arms numb, he knew that he had been in the grip of a tyrannous lust. He would have to suffer whatever martyrdom it demanded. Indeed, even as a delivery boy tugged on his cock in the pretence it was a doorbell, his body was set alight with the hope that, come the night, Lord Damiens would send for him.

# Twenty

A s it happened, Lord Damiens had more urgent matters on
his mind than any further punishment. It was enough that
Rob had been taught a rough lesson, and that the young man
continued to demonstrate his charms when they lay together.
The milord was willing to forgive.

For Lucian the embarrassment was less that of being discovered
with his cock in Rob's mouth than in having entered the palazzo
in so secretive a fashion. But, again, Damiens was of a mind to
make light of the incident. He assured Lucian that so trivial an
indiscretion could not possibly dent their firm friendship.

But for Rob the aftermath was less comfortable. He was not
flogged as he had feared, and he was still called to the milord's
bed each night. But he went there with a heavy heart. Since
coming to Venice he had suffered every humiliation, but had also
caught his first glimpses of love. He knew that he wanted love,
but was now sure he would not find it with either the milord or
Lucian. For while they had set his loins alight, and shown him
the broad avenues of pleasure that lead to love's temples, they
had not breached his innermost self. That lay, like a wild beast,
dozing, half watchful, half lost in dreams, as it waited for the
moment to wake, stretch, and go hunting. Until then he would
submit as he must, but he would not expend himself. Every
orifice might lie open, and he would assume any position required

for them to be stuffed, but he would hold himself back from his masters. He would not fuck them. He would not spill himself inside them. For much as it startled him to think such a thing, he was not willing to shed his seed in such low places.

One overcast morning, as Rob sat naked on the floor in the great bedchamber while Titus and two footmen attended Lord Damiens in his tub, the conversation, which had until then failed to lighten the morning's leaden mood, turned to a visit expected later that day. It seemed a certain Polish prince had taken a palazzo near the Ca' d'Oro. This nobleman had let it be known that it was his ambition to make himself the envy of Venice but had recently staged a ball that, for all its magnificence, had pleased only that small part of society eager to be thought God-fearing. Rumour now had it that he was intending to redeem his position with another ball, this one masked, to which those previously excluded for reasons of reputation would be invited.

Lord Damiens was perplexed. 'I am not familiar with the manners of Vilna or Warsaw.' He rose from the tub. 'We may find ourselves ambushed.'

Titus placed a towel on his shoulders 'They say, my lord, that the Prince is most dashing.' He bent to use a comb on his master's pubic hair.

'You shall come, Robbie.'

Rob looked up with a frown. 'My lord, I know nothing of the fine ways of society.'

'I doubt that fine ways is what the Prince has in mind, for all his dash.' He lifted a foot from the water and shook it in Rob's face. 'Besides, Robbie, it's time you made a splash.'

Rob managed a smile. 'Will we use disguises, my lord?'

The barber set a stool in the tub so that the milord might sit. He dipped his razor in the warm water, while Titus rubbed olive oil on his master's cheeks. With deft strokes the barber shaved the skin to a sleek shine.

'Surely, Robbie, your fair features are disguise enough?'

'I fear so, my lord.' Thinking he may have spoken too frankly, Rob lowered his head as if in grief.

But Lord Damiens was not in the mood to examine such melancholy. He stepped from the tub and ruffled Rob's fair hair as he passed by. 'Dress now, Robbie, or our Prince of the Poles will get the wrong idea.'

The days dragged. All Rob's hints that he might be allowed out to roam the streets were met with evasions. He was still a prisoner. Nor was escape possible, with the gatehouse well guarded and water on every other side. In Venice every house was its own island, and captivity more the norm than freedom.

But just as the prisoner will find his cell has become a whole world, so the palazzo seemed to expand the more familiar Rob became with its many rooms and dark corners. Sometimes he would walk in the garden and, with nothing better to do than sit and stare, he would look up at the windows on the palazzo's back wall and try to remember which window opened into which room. There were always a few he could not place, just as on passing through the kitchens he would often see faces he had not seen before. Were these the desperate souls he had seen paraded in the dungeon? And, if not, what had become of those wretches?

There were other mysteries. Every day lighters came to the landing-stage at the rear of the palazzo where weeks before Rob had been found floating. Tradesmen would unload barrels, sacks and wooden chests, which would be piled in a storeroom reached down steps beside the kitchen entrance. What were these supplies that required replenishment every day? Although the household was large, and the milord extravagant, day-to-day needs were covered by the many delivery-boys who came running from the market each afternoon.

Occasionally, when Lord Damiens dined where male bedfellows were not welcome – no matter how handsome – Rob was left to roam the palazzo. No longer a novelty in the household, he was not pestered and aroused no suspicions. He took to exploring small rooms up the tiny passages that led this way and that, behind and between the grand rooms.

One evening, as he stood at the window on the *piano nobile* looking down at the traffic on the Grand Canal, he noticed two lighters approaching. He recognised them as those that regularly brought supplies, and watched as the lights on board were extinguished. The two craft disappeared into the narrow side canal and were lost in the darkness.

Rob walked to the other end of the room, and waited to see the lighters moor at the rear landing-stage. But they did not appear. Curious, Rob decided to use a recently discovered passage and flight of stairs to reach the side of the palazzo that overlooked the narrow canal.

The passage was to the side of the main landing, and as no one was about Rob quickly pushed aside the heavy drapes blocking the entrance. It was dark and he had no light, but his memory was good enough to see him safely to the stairwell. He trod with care for the steps were steep, but after a while a light from below began to show the way. When he reached the narrow landing he found that a naked torch had been left burning. The passage leading to the side of the building was ahead, but Rob noticed that the stairs did not end as he had thought but continued down. Intrigued, because he had no recollection of their existence, he made his way down the tight spiral. Dank air blew up, there was no light, and at the foot of the stairs he bumped into a door that opened at his touch.

He was near the end of a broad passage. High on the end wall one of the lighter craft could be seen through a dirty window. In the other direction the passage ran back under the palazzo, past a staircase where a torch burned and on to a metal-framed door. Unable to get a clear view of the lighter, but satisfied that it was unloading goods for the palazzo, Rob walked towards the staircase, think he would use it to return to the upper floors. He had, he decided, done enough exploring for one evening. The lower floors would always remind him of his degradation on the first night he spent in the palazzo and the dreadful procession he had seen.

At the foot of the stairs, Rob looked back to see whether the outline of the lighter was still to be seen through the window. Seeing that it was, he placed a foot on the first step but stopped immediately.

Someone was coming down the stairs. Rob stepped back and pressed himself against the wall. He was not hidden, but stood in the dark; if he stood still, there was a good chance he would not be seen.

Whoever was coming down the stairs knew the flight well because the footsteps tripped lightly. When they reached the bottom Rob held his breath. He did not dare look, but heard the footsteps receding in the opposite direction. He turned and recognised Titus by the jaunty rolling strides he used when out of sight of his master. He was half-way towards the doorway, and fingering the keyring on his belt. Rob waited. His curiosity was returning, but he told himself that he would follow the valet only if he left the door unlocked and only at a safe distance. He wanted no more hidings.

Titus unlocked the door, and pushed it half open to pass through. Rob waited a moment, and then followed. As he approached the door he felt a warm draught on his face, and when he pushed it open he saw that he was in a narrower, darker passage that turned to the right. He walked forward to the turning and looked round to see Titus's figure outlined against the light where the passage ended at a metal grille. He was fumbling with his keys. Rob stood in the darkness, and did not move until the grille was raised, and Titus strode through.

A hoarse whisper close by made Rob spin on his heels. The words had been in a language he didn't understand but the voice conveyed a terrible urgency that commanded his attention. It came again and, looking into the darkness beside him, Rob realised the passage was lined with small doors, each with a metal flap let into the centre. On the door closest to him this flap was open and a pair of eyes was staring out. Rob moved close, heard again the desperate whisper, but still could not understand.

Tears streamed from the eyes, and the imploring whisper continued like the rustle of confession but Rob moved on. Other cell doors had their flaps open, and other eyes stared out in desolation. There were whispers and sobs, words of anger, and yelps of frustration that made grown men sound like children. He recognised a word of French, or German, even a sad plea for mercy in a Yankee drawl, but there were as many tongues as there had been in Babel. Some of the eyes were as blue as his

147

own, others as dark as the tropical night, but there was terror in every pair and not a gleam of hope.

The metal grille was still up, and Rob walked under it with no more foreboding than if he were strolling in a Kentish garden. All fear had left him, and all subservience. What he had seen had aroused in him an indignation that dissolved any sense that he might not be the equal of any other man. With no thought for himself, he strode forward to confront Titus.

But almost at once he came upon a sight that put from his mind even his indignation. He had entered a long passageway with a low, vaulted ceiling. On either side, men sat with their backs to the wall, chained together at the neck and ankles. Some were naked, others wore rags, and some the remnants of fine clothes. Some were thin and ill, others still robust. Slavs with blue eyes shining under brows as broad as their shoulders sat alongside tall Africans whose black skin gleamed under the torchlight. Bearded fair-haired ruffians glared their defiance beside slim youths from the Levant, and here and there Rob noticed tatters of the naval uniforms of France, Sweden or Russia.

Even in his surprise Rob felt he had come upon the scene at some moment of importance. There was a tension that had nothing to do with his appearance. Indeed, his clattering arrival drew few glances. Everyone seemed to be concentrating on something else, perhaps waiting for someone to speak, or for something to begin.

# Twenty-One

---

There was a thud off to one side. Several of the men in chains muttered, and drew threats from the guards.

Another thud, and then another.

These came from a side room, just behind Rob. Slowly, because he had guessed what sight would meet his eyes, he turned to see a man stripped to the waist, chained at the hands and feet, against the end wall. Torches burning on either side shed a bright, flickering light. The floor was covered in sawdust, but the room was otherwise bare except for two wooden buckets. A bald burly fellow, in black breeches and a sleeveless leather jerkin, was wielding a leather whip. He flicked it through the air with casual mastery, and landed it across the man's shoulders, adding a fourth red weal to the white flesh. Such punishment had been a common sight on the deck of the *Dawn Treader*, but those floggings had the merit of being deserved and carried the force of public justice. In the dungeons of the Palazzo Ferri, with strutting Titus in command and where the only witnesses were wretches in chains, the spectacle increased Rob's sense of outrage.

Perhaps sensing this force of dissent behind him, Titus turned. His expression of pious pleasure turned to one of alarm. Even the whip-master hesitated, but with a movement of his arm Titus ordered the punishment to continue. He came towards Rob, his features set in anger, which was undermined by the anxiety showing in his eyes.

'You have no business here.' Titus used his crop to point towards the grille and the passageway beyond. 'Go now, and say nothing of what you have seen here.'

'I am a free man. I demand to –'

Titus stepped closer. Behind him the whip landed again, and a terrible cry rang out. The guards cursed and cracked their whips.

'You will demand nothing.' Titus's voice was steady and commanding, but his lower lip trembled.

The two young men faced one another. Then Titus seemed to relax. 'Very well. Why shouldn't you know? Stay.' He turned back towards the scene of punishment, and called out to the whip-master, '*Quanti colpi?*'

The man barked in Italian as he readied the whip to land another blow.

Titus took Rob by the elbow and led him forward. 'There's another dozen due.'

Rob resisted. 'You forget, Titus, I am a sailor and no stranger to punishment.'

The lash landed once more on a back already marked by a dozen stripes. The poor fellow was coughing and gasping for breath, but the whip-master did not hesitate to swing the lash again. It curled gracefully through the air before cutting into flesh.

Titus smiled, and ran a hand down over the front of Rob's breeches. 'Does the sight not quicken you?'

Rob clenched his fists. He longed to put the bully on the floor. 'It does not.' He fought to control his anger.

'A pity. The cur under the lash . . . He reminds me of you.'

Rob looked at the pathetic figure writhing in the chains. What could Titus mean? The poor man had hair that was black and thick, his shoulders were broader and better made than his own, as were his arse and legs, which were half visible as they trembled beneath tattered breeches. The man was nothing like him at all, except that . . .

There was something about him, even in his dreadful state, that reminded Rob of other circumstances, in quite different places . . . and at other times. It was as if, for a moment, he had been dreaming.

And then the lash fell again.

'Surely that is enough.'

Titus feigned indignation. 'Nonsense. What you see here is a kindness. Where he's bound, the lash will be his close companion.'

'And where is that?'

'You ask too many questions.'

Rob would have turned away, if the nagging sense had not lingered that he had seen the suffering figure before. As the whip-master laid on the final strokes, Rob asked Titus what crime the man had committted.

Titus shrugged, and glanced at Rob. 'This is a dangerous place. It is wise . . . not to understand, and if you do, not to show . . .'

'He heard something?'

Titus nodded, and glanced at Rob. 'He understands English.'

'He is our countryman?'

Titus shook his head. 'He is cargo.'

The flogging completed, the whip-master coiled his length of leather, bowed to Titus, and made his way slowly back along the corridor between the rows of chained men. Another guard came forward and picked up one of the buckets. He positioned himself behind the flogged man, who hung limply on the chains, and tossed water over his back. This induced a paroxysm. The man's legs and arms jerked and shook violently, and his neck fell back as a terrible cry came from his gaping mouth. The second bucket, however, produced no reaction. It was as if the man's capacity to feel pain had been exhausted.

The guard unchained the man, and another stood ready to catch him. As he fell back the guard hoisted him, dazed and semi-conscious, over his shoulder, and carried him back to the main part of the dungeon. As the limp body passed him, Rob could see only the reddened back. The man's head hung down out of sight.

Titus led the way back up to the main part of the palazzo. When they reached the entrance hall, Rob turned to go down to the kitchen where some food would have been left for his supper. Titus placed a hand on his arm. 'You must listen to me.' He spoke in a whisper. 'Forget what you have seen tonight.'

'Not even the devil himself –'

Titus tightened his grip. 'Only a fool disturbs the devil at his work.'

From the look in Titus's eyes Rob knew that he should heed his words. 'Who are those wretched men?'

'Sailors, like yourself. Venice needs strong backs to man her galleys. The pirates on the Barbary coasts are happy to sell those they have not slaughtered or drowned.'

'Slaves?'

'Bought from the traders of Ragusa. You have been lucky, Robert . . . so far. If you hadn't caught his lordship's eye . . .'

Rob had difficulty believing what he was hearing. 'All this in Venice?'

Titus laughed. 'In the city of plagues and dreams, why not? When we arrived here Lord Damiens was as poor a man as you or me. Now he is among the richest.'

'But to trade in men . . .'

'It is in man's nature. There are those willing to sell and others eager to buy.' Titus flicked his whip across Rob's backside and walked towards the main staircase. 'Mention none of this to his lordship – unless you are eager to live your life in chains.'

That night Rob slept well. The milord did not send for him, and the uncovered secrets of the dungeon, far from disturbing his rest, pushed him into that deep slumber that stirs the creatures of the mind from their mysterious landscapes, to give us counsel in our dreams.

When he woke Rob knew what he must do.

# Twenty-Two

The gondolas came at ten. Dinner for twenty had been set for eight, but no one had arrived until nine. The dressing had begun at siesta time, and for once the servants had been busy all day.

It was after eleven before the first of the party set off, and most of the gondolas following on did not reach the palazzo by the Ca' d'Oro until well after midnight.

Lord Damiens had decreed that everyone should go to the ball as German fairies, and there was much construction of elaborate hats and whimsical leather trousers, but after one look in the glass the milord decided his party had better dress as Cossacks.

This caused panic among the milliners, tailors and haberdashers, and the household was in a pretty pickle until Lord Damiens, recalling a disastrous evening at Old Pic's that had left him covered in bruises, dispatched Titus to the bordello. Armed with a purse full of silver, Titus had handed the sly pander a letter begging him to lend the Palazzo Ferri the Cossack costumes worn by the gypsies he had employed that night.

Old Pic had consented graciously, and allowed Titus the run of his stable, while his wardrobe mistress assembled what remained of the Cossack costumes, even adding for good measure such other garments as might remind a reveller of the barbarian hoards.

Titus returned in triumph, much impressed. From then on it was a case of everyone waiting until the milord had chosen for himself, then scrambling for the best pieces that remained. The tailors stood by with haughty disdain until called to assist. Then they went to work and sewed in a fury, with pins stuck between their teeth as they spat insults and stole from one another.

Sure at last of his course of action, Rob was in a cheerful mood. Well rested and untroubled by doubt, he had never looked so handsome, as he conceded to Lord Damiens when they stood in their Cossack garb before the glass in the great bedchamber. Neither wore a wig because of the wide-brimmed hats, and their gaudy pantaloons were as fetchingly loose on their thighs as they were trim around their rumps. Their shirts were open down to their belly buttons, revealing fine broad chests, and their boots reached high on their calves.

The day had been blustery, and the blinds were flapping outside the windows overlooking the Grand Canal. Some discarded garments of fancy dress left on the floor stirred in the gusts, and there was clatter and talk on the stairs, but the two men were alone, for once.

Damiens took Rob in his arms and kissed him. Rob felt the smooth and the rub of a freshly shaven upper lip, and the rich scent the milord always wore when going into society. The arms around him were strong, but did not cling, and the groin pressed against his was stirring, as was his own. Rob closed his eyes, sighed, and rested his head on Damiens' shoulder. He was at peace, as content as a babe in its mother's arms, and while he knew he might never again embrace the milord with an easy heart, he did so at that moment.

The waters on the Grand Canal were troubled by the wind as the five gondolas set off from the Palazzo Ferri. Standing was out of the question, so Rob sat close beside Lord Damiens in the first gondola as it bobbed about on the choppy surface. It took all the oarsmen's skills for the small fleet to reach the Rialto although, once past it, there was shelter from the wind on the broad stretch of water where the Ca' d'Oro stood.

The Polish prince had been generous with his invitations, and even after midnight the canal was crowded with gondolas waiting their turn to land passengers.

Despite the stormy weather the palazzo made a fine sight, its landing-stage lit up by flares while the main entrance stood open and festooned with flowers. Bunting hung from every window, and blew and flapped in the wind, but all such effects were reduced to mere decoration by the two vast flags flying from poles that rose high from the palazzo's roof. One bore the Lion of Venice, stark on a white background against the night sky, while the other was a dazzling affair brought from the distant marches to the north, on which the bold cross of Malta was almost engorged by the massed heraldry of a long, noble line.

This spectacle impressed Lord Damiens, who leant forward from his covered seat like an eager boy as the gondola waited. His chatter more resembled that of an excited debutant than a worldly milord, while Rob, who had quite different expectations of the challenges the night might bring, found himself entirely calm. With his mind made up, he had no need to fret or fear. The outcome would depend upon his valour, his daring, and his certain belief that justice was on his side.

As the gondola neared the landing-stage, and Lord Damiens used a mirror to add a little powder to his flushed cheeks, Rob's thoughts were not on the spectacle that would soon greet him in the palazzo but, rather, his mind's eye was filled with boyhood memories. He saw the swift streams and deep still ditches of Kent, its small fields where sheep grazed, and the orchards with their humming beehives. He saw his father, stern as he puffed on his pipe at the cottage gate, and remembered blustery days under white clouds and sunshine, exploring woods and hills with Roman names. He saw Angus, his cropped dark hair framing a face both honest and open, and flushed with anger at parental injustice. He saw his friend as he waved and walked away that bright morning after the Ashford Fayre.

At the landing-stage Rob and Lord Damiens were helped ashore by red-faced fellows, whose only concession to the occasion was a few ribbons fluttering from their boaters. Others were arriving, and everyone stopped to admire each other and exchange compliments. After the dark journey along the canal, the bright flares made those in fancy dress look like actors striding before the footlights. There was laughter, and much looking in glasses, and cries of anguish at what was seen.

Once past the curtain of flowers hanging over the doorway, Rob found himself entering a crowded courtyard, with a fountain at its centre also decked with flowers. An orchestra was playing, and pageboys dressed as Switzers lined the covered staircase that ran up the outside of the walls. These, too, were strewn with flowers and nightlights, although most of the blooms had been trampled. Rob and Damiens joined those making their way up to the *piano nobile* where the prince would be waiting to greet them.

While good humour prevailed, there was also impatience, and some pushed forward in an unbecoming manner. Most, however, were content to pass the time flirting behind their masks and fans, or admiring one another's costumes.

At the top of the stairs the procession went through a narrow hallway into the main room on the piano nobile. This was a fine chamber, whose generous dimensions were exaggerated by reflections from the mirrors lining the walls. The prince stood at its centre, attended by liveried footmen. He was a tall, willowy man, dressed as a Caesar in a plain toga fastened with a silver belt. He wore plain sandals, and his only concession to extravagance was a gold laurel crown.

Few others showed such restraint. Rob found himself squashed between the Man in the Moon and an Emperor of China, while behind him Neptune used his trident to jab him playfully up the arse. Rob did not react, and rather than wait to be introduced to the Prince, as Lord Damiens certainly would, he decided to escape the crush and explore the upper rooms, where his brief experience of Venice told him the diversions would be more amusing.

Ducking under the Man in the Moon, Rob squeezed himself between a fat blackamoor and a thin-faced troubadour to reach the edge of the crowd. He made his way round the room until he came to the stairs. A footman looked him up and down, perhaps struck by the yellow hair that hung loose to his shoulders. Rob took the stairs two at a time, and on reaching the landing walked straight past the ballroom and up another short flight towards the back of the palazzo. There were fewer ladies here, and a number of young men were lounging on the stairs. At the next landing an elderly steward barred the way to a candle-lit room. Rob bowed and was given permission to enter.

The first thing he noticed was the smell of violets. They were everywhere, bunched in large dishes set along the walls, scattered over the floor and tied to the chandeliers so that the light was filtered through their dark hue. Then there was that pleasing sense of relaxation that comes when young men, whether in exotic or simple dress, naked or partially clothed, are set upon amusing themselves according to their natures and appetites. Although a youth dressed as Apollo played a lute, the room was quiet. The windows were shuttered against the wind, and a fire burned in an open stone grate. Rob took a glass of wine from one of the footmen, and wandered among those who were standing or lounging in small groups, or pleasuring themselves or each other. If the scene was one of peace, it was the calm of anticipation. Rob knew as well as anyone that, with so many young men gathered in a place of licence, sooner or later they would resort to such vices as will delight both the man of refinement, and he who is governed by coarser desires.

It began when a quiet Egyptian took a Circassian's cock in his mouth. Two young fops lying nearby left off fondling one another and shoved their stiff little pricks up the pair's bums. They in turn were mounted by a couple of prowling rogues, who soon found their mouths full as well. Thus the chain grew, and parted, and went on growing.

But still there was silence, apart from the squeak of shoe leather, or pop of limb withdrawing from cavity. There were sighs of pleasure, and delighted bursts of laughter. Footmen went round so that those still with empty mouths might take wine, and others offered dishes of olive oil to ease the way into a back passage.

The scent of violets still reigned, but was challenged by the musk of skin rubbed against skin, and the still richer odour of young men breaking sweat.

Rob did not stand back. With the calm that had been his all

day, he undressed and knelt beside a naked young man whose body was as trim and slender as his own was broad and muscular. He bent and kissed the left nipple, and was pleased to see it tighten, its stem rise. He ran a hand down over the firm belly and took hold of a cock no less trim and slender, and used it to pleasure the fellow until his head hung back and his narrow lips parted. At this, Rob kissed the severe mouth, and used his tongue to explore until, with deft agility, he replaced his tongue with his stiff cock. The young man, too intoxicated by the pleasure to object, lay back and took the full length of Rob's cock in his mouth, as if it were as easy to devour as a fig plucked from the vine.

In order to achieve this pleasing effect, however, Rob had to straddle the fellow, and this left his backside up in the air, and therefore likely to attract attention.

And indeed it did, yet not from some young man's stiff cock but, rather the delicate tongue of a noble young Venetian, recently returned from his studies in Bologna, whose particular delight was to pleasure a strapping lad by means of licking the rim at the rear entrance.

At first Rob found this subtle stimulation more an irritant than a pleasure. Certainly it was nothing compared to having his cock sucked in a most energetic and expert manner. But the nobleman was as tenacious as he was single-minded, and he did not let up. It was as if his tongue were performing the most delicate polka or quadrille, and never simply for the effect of the moment, but rather to build each tiny pinprick of feeling into a rolling mass of sensation. This slowly spread from Rob's hole, both inwards, up his passage so that his bowels began to quiver, and outwards, up his spine and down along the muscles in his legs. Before long his entire body was alight with a sensation unlike any he had previously enjoyed.

But the aristocrat, having achieved his aim, did not linger. It was not in his nature to wish to induce climactic fireworks, or to open the box on whose lid he had lavished such attention. Being an idealist, his pleasure lay in the simple act of using his tongue to allow that other mouth to sing whose daily tasks prevented it from speaking its mind. If he could make one robust young man aware of the eloquence waiting to be set free in his backside, he might also glimpse those natural balances that lay at the heart of his philosophy. And so he slunk away, well satisfied and savouring the salty taste of Rob's rear end.

Deprived of sensations in his backside, Rob grew bored with the efforts of the young man sucking his cock. With a smile of polite thanks he withdrew his member, and with both ends free, set off on all fours to seek fresh pleasure.

He was not long in finding it. As he passed by the fireplace, he noticed a fierce-looking man with a black beard, a barrel chest, and shoulders rounded by physical labour. His chest was a thicket of wiry hair, and his belly was large but solid. A stiff cock stood out over a scrotum the size of two oranges, and his legs were thick hairy trunks of muscle. A quick glance was sufficient for Rob to decide to move on. He did not want to get involved with such a creature.

But the beast stirred. As Rob passed by on all fours a hand slid between his thighs and grabbed his balls. For a moment Rob was paralysed, then he felt himself being drawn backwards. The hand had a firm grip. There was no question of escape.

At first the man was gentle. He ran his horny hands through Rob's hair, and bade him sit before him so that he might be better inspected. Like a child with a new toy, the man ran his hands over every part of Rob's body. Thick stumpy fingers probed his mouth and twisted his nipples, and a palm pressed against his stomach to test the muscles. Red lips protruding from the dense beard kissed his lips and neck, and a hand continued to play with his balls.

A passer-by tried to intervene, and grabbed Rob round the shoulders from behind, but a hiss from the hairy man was enough to send him on his way.

Rob, though, was in no mood to be any man's property. He pushed the brute from him and tried to get to his knees, but the hand holding his balls tightened until he yelped. It tightened still more, until he knew he would have to fight the man for his freedom.

Rob's first attack was to take hold of the man's scrotum, and so give as good as the other had taken, but the man was too quick and Rob found his free hand forced away up behind his back. In this position Rob's chest was exposed, and with the greed of a wild animal the man fell on his nipples, pulling, sucking, biting and licking them until the nerve endings went into a spasm that caused Rob to cry out. But Rob knew the man would have no respect for complaints. Brute force and appetite were all he understood, and with his superior strength the outcome of any battle was not in doubt. But Rob was willing to fight, so he counter-attacked once more, and used his head to butt the man so that he lost his balance and fell back. The hand on his balls jerked and Rob fell on top of his tormentor. There were bravos from those watching the tussle by the fireplace, as several coupling pairs parted to witness the superior contest.

The man laughed, and Rob did not know what to do, but when the man spoke several of those nearby laughed too, then turned away. The body under him relaxed, and Rob sensed the fight was over. He rolled off, and the man said something in Italian and ran a friendly hand across his shoulder.

This sudden change of mood left Rob elated. With a smile for the burly fellow Rob moved on towards a small mound of bodies that heaved and grunted like a single monstrous being. If he were to lose himself safely for a while among the many straining limbs and organs, he would still be ready when the time came to act.

# Twenty-Three

For Lucian the day had been a disappointment. He had had hopes of being buggered by a young Austrian count he had visited on business. His smirking staff had assured him the fellow was ardent in his worship of the male behind, but when the time came to move from official to private negotiations, the stuffy young man had turned prickly.

On his way by gondola to the masked ball, Lucian cursed Austria and all her ambitions, and Venice for harbouring such deceivers. The Grand Canal was in darkness, and as he passed under the Rialto Bridge he could see shadowy figures looking down like devils searching for their prey. It was as if the whole city was out to prove him a fool. Back in London a man was what he seemed to be, as surely as the Thames flowed to the sea. In Venice, however, the way to the sea was as serpentine as a pander's wiles. And yet, when the sun shimmered on still canals and placid lagoons, he could not say he was bored with Venice, or tired of her mysteries. The city was like a wanton woman. It draped itself in glory the more to deceive. It offered everything to the senses, and to the curious, but was no place in which to search for love or redemption. Only those reflections and distortions seen in its gleaming surfaces provided any image of the self.

Lucian arrived too late to be received by the Polish count and wandered through the crowded rooms in the simple costume of a Macedonian shepherd. Over his eyes he wore an ivory mask, while a fine black silk kerchief from the Orient was bound across his mouth and chin. The effect was sinister enough to deter all but the bold. In Venetian society the rules were time-consuming, but at a masked ball a man might be anyone, and all niceties were suspended. Lucian walked past a lady in whose salon he had supped the night before and did not so much as offer her a bow. And when he felt a hand on his groin he recognised its owner as a duke from Milan, who was notorious for standing on ceremony. In such a liberal atmosphere he would soon make up for the rebuff suffered at the hands of the Austrian count.

He walked up a flight of stairs behind two Frenchmen dressed as Roman matrons, and on the landing paused to savour the scent of violets. The room in front of him was in near darkness, apart from a few guttering candles, and a log fire that shed a flickering light. Dozens of men were spread across the floor engaged in acts of carnality. Some were youthful and comely, but many showed evidence of excess.

In two minds as to whether to join in, Lucian walked round the edge of the room, taking care where he put his feet. It was, he decided, as well that the air was perfumed by violets: more acrid scents were also rising. To breathe more freely he untied the silk covering his mouth, but kept the ivory mask in place.

A naked young man was squatting nearby. He was pulling on a long cock to ready himself to enter the arse of an elderly fellow, who had raised his scrawny rump in anticipation. Lucian felt a movement in his loins, and wondered whether he should inter-pose himself. But at that moment the young man, his cock stiff and upright, spat on the helmet and without ado plunged himself up the old bugger's back passage.

Lucian looked away. Why hurry? There would be other opportunities.

In the centre of the room, meanwhile, Rob was beginning to tire. No sooner had he withdrawn his prick from a particularly tight bum, than a hand grabbed hold and tried to guide it up another, but slacker, back alley. Not wishing to draw attention,

Rob pulled away and soon found an empty space where he could lie on his back without being disturbed.

On every side men were penetrating one another, or sucking, licking, probing or pulling on each other. There were gasps and exhalations, yelps of pleasure and pain, whispers, and now and then a stifled laugh or loud refusal. Rob lay in their midst, and wondered when he should act.

The shutters rattled. Outside it might be gusty and cold, but inside among so many bodies exerting themselves and where the fire burnt bright, all was warmth and sweaty intimacy. And in the midst of it all, Rob felt safe. There was no one who would hurt him. Even the fierce man had been play-acting. He felt suddenly tired, and his eyes began to close . . .

A light touch on his cock made him start. He muttered a refusal and put a hand over his eyes, hoping to be left alone.

'Asleep, Robbie? This will never do.'

Rob sat up with a start. Although the face leaning close was masked with ivory, there was no mistaking the bright, cold eyes, the firm chin, the severe lines of the body beneath the peasant's cloak.

'Lucian. You are the very man . . .'

The hand was still on his cock, and it tightened its grip. 'Later, Robbie, there'll be time for all that . . .' The masked face was close, and the thin lips were moist.

'You don't understand, sir, there is something I must tell you, something of the utmost importance.' In his mind's eye, Rob saw the slaves in the dungeon at the Palazzo Ferri, and the young man being flogged. He saw the way the body had shuddered as each lash landed. He saw the black hair drenched in sweat, and the trickles of blood. 'Never in my life . . .'

A hand covered his mouth. 'Shush now, there are ears on every side,' Lucian whispered, but his tone was firm. He did not remove his hand, but edged closer until he was able to kiss Rob's lips.

It was impossible to resist. The lips were cool and moist, and yet yielding and inviting. Fingers played with his nipples, and a stiff cock pressed against him. Rob's whole body remembered the pleasure Lucian had given it, and rejoiced at his return. For a

163

moment Rob let himself go, and began to lie back, and then . . . again . . . in his mind's eye . . . he saw the figure chained to the wall and the lash landing.

'No!' He did not keep his voice down, but let the command ring round the room. It acted like a call to action. On every side, those dallying gently were stirred to displays of passion. Delayed climaxes were hurriedly revived, and lost ones retrieved. Silence was replaced by uproar – curses, blows, blasphemous prayers and cries of sheer pleasure.

Lucian, as much startled by the sharp rebuff as by the general copulation, got to his feet, and was about to reprimand Rob with a slap across the face, when the naked young sailor took him by the hand and led him, with an air of command, to the landing.

While Lucian protested, Rob stooped and picked up a discarded toga. 'You must hear me, sir, it is a matter of life and death.' He held the garment against himself then let it drop.

'Whose life? My own?' If Lucian meant to sound a note of sarcasm, he failed.

'At the Palazzo Ferri, there are slaves held captive.'

'Isn't that the common condition of slaves?' Lucian tore off his mask to reveal an expression of impatience mixed with contempt.

'But these are free men, sir, bound for the galleys.'

'If they are for the galleys they are not free men, that much is certain.' Lucian looked away.

'Some are Englishmen.'

Lucian tossed his head back, so as to look down his nose at Rob. 'How so?'

'I saw a man flogged. The milord's valet said it was done for his being English.'

'I see.' Lucian frowned, then smiled and put a hand on Rob's shoulder. 'My dear boy, the galleys are the very limbs of Venice. Without them she would be nothing. And besides, the riches we enjoy here, every glass goblet or gilded hall, all are purchased with gold earned from human cargo. Do you suppose Venice will ever change her ways?'

'But can it be right for Lord Damiens to sell his countrymen into slavery?'

Lucian shook his head. 'No, it cannot be right.' He patted Rob's shoulder. 'You have done well to tell me this, Robbie. We shall meet later.'

'I shall be gone.'

'Nonsense, Robbie, Lord Damiens will not leave before dawn.'

Rob shook his head, suddenly relieved to be able to confide. 'I've had my fill of Venice. I shall be making my way home to England.'

'Does your master know this?'

'He is not my master, sir. I am a free man.'

'In Venice no man is free.'

'All the more reason to escape. I shall steal a mask and . . .' He paused as a swift shaft of doubt ran through him. Had his father not told him never to trust a gentleman? But on looking into Lucian's eyes he saw only concern. 'After all, the means of disguise lie all around. No one will recognise me.'

'Indeed they will not.' Lucian glanced at Rob's fair hair and blue eyes. 'Very well then, Robbie, I shall speak to his lordship. These are matters best left to those of high rank.' Lucian smiled. 'If we are not to meet again, at least allow me a last kiss.' He took Rob's head in his hands and planted the kiss. But Rob felt no stirring, merely an echo of the doubt that had gripped him when he confessed his plans.

They each went their own way without further ado. Rob rejoined the orgy, and Lucian hurried downstairs.

He was not able to progress far, however, before coming upon an amusing scene. A young man dressed as a Bohemian rustic had been discovered to have between his legs a prick of exceptional size. Rowdies had stripped him below the waist and held him spread-eagled on the stairs so that a group of young ladies, attired as vestal virgins, might take turns to sit on him. This they did two at a time. While one raised her elaborate white gown, and lowered herself on to the astonishing appendage, the other squatted on the rustic's face so that the unfortunate was close to drowning. A group of onlookers stood around, awestruck by the lascivious virgins' antics.

All was not as it seemed, however, and when a spectator went down on one knee to get a better view, he caught a glimpse of both a well-shaved scrotum and a cock of modest size. He cried foul, and in no time the pack that had set upon the rustic turned on the virgins. Off came their flowing robes and wigs to reveal them as young men of slender appearance and effeminate manners. Some burst into tears and were soundly pummelled, while most screamed like poultry as they made a dash for the safety of the upper floors.

A loud cheer went up as the last of the deceivers escaped, and the crowd moved back into the main hall to continue feasting and dancing.

The room was crowded, and reflections from the mirrors lining the walls gave the illusion that the ball had broken free of earthly dimensions. Infinite lines of dancers stretched to impossible horizons, and as some moved forward or sideways others retreated in perfect unison. The candelabra shed a golden light, at once brilliant and diffuse, and dripped hot wax on the bare shoulders and bosoms of the ladies below.

Lucian could see no one who resembled Lord Damiens. In the heat and soft dazzle, with most of the guests masked and in fancy dress, it was not easy to tell a man from a woman, let alone pick out one among so many.

A man with no mask, but wearing a fine silver and black coat, stood close by the orchestra. Lucian recognised but could not place him. Only when the man turned did Lucian see the jewel gleaming in the centre of his fine grey wig, and realise he was face to face with Old Pic.

Lucian greeted the whoremonger with the cool formality he reserved for his dealings with tradesmen, but his aloof façade was quickly undermined when Old Pic, with the instinct of his trade, remarked that it was amusing to see Lord Damiens attired as a savage among so many of lower birth.

'I did not know he was here.' Lucian hoped to affect an indifference that would elicit the information he was after. 'Can he be seen?'

But Old Pic was not one to let go of his advantage without promise of gain. He used a lace handkerchief to fan himself. 'All this heat . . . and how this new music grates on the nerves! Perhaps you will be kind enough to excuse . . .'

Afraid he was about to lose his best chance of finding Damiens, Lucian forgot himself and reached out to place an imploring hand on Old Pic's sleeve. 'I would really be most grateful, sir, if you could show me . . .'

Old Pic looked down at his sleeve as if a reptile were clinging to it. 'Mr Parry, I don't know the customs of your country but . . .'

Lucian withdrew his hand and bowed in defeat. 'I must beg your pardon, sir. The truth is I must speak to Lord Damiens. It is a matter of urgency.'

In an instant Old Pic's manner changed. 'In which case, my dear fellow, we shall find him.' He motioned to a young man nearby, who was dressed and masked all in black. 'It should not be difficult. He is a Cossack for the night.' He spoke in a strange tongue to the young man, who bowed and walked off through the dancers.

'I am much obliged, sir.' Lucian adopted his most humble manner.

Old Pic smiled graciously, but his eyes were hard. 'This urgency, sir, if it is a delicate matter . . .'

'It is, sir, and only for the ears of Lord Damiens.'

It was Old Pic's turn to bow. 'I was merely going to observe, sir, that should the matter require as remedy the use of strong men, I have three such here tonight. They are most obedient fellows.'

Lucian was about to thank Old Pic when he heard a familiar voice. Turning, he saw Damiens disguised as a Cossack. The masked man in black was at his side.

'Charles, how handsome you look.'

Damiens laughed. 'My beauty, Lucian, is but a blown blossom compared to yours.'

As the two men embraced Lucian whispered, 'We must talk – it is most urgent.'

Damiens did not react, and instead acknowledged Old Pic, who bowed low. Damiens turned back to Lucian. 'I have met a most delightful young Swede. He is a hussar in the service of his queen. You must meet him, Lucian. I'll wager he'll beguile you as much as he does me. Come . . .' He put an arm round Lucian's shoulder and was about to lead him away, but he paused when he saw that the man in black was keeping company with two other ruffians in the same uniform. 'Who are these men?'

Old Pic smiled winsomely and put a hand to his wig. 'They are mine.'

'And why do they hover so?'

'A strong arm has many uses.' Old Pic frowned. 'Should you require my services, I shall be downstairs by the landing-stage. It is too hot in here.'

Lucian led the milord to a small side alcove, in which two young men dressed as gladiators were sitting weeping and holding hands.

Damiens affected impatience. 'What is all this? My Swede will think me gone.'

'Your fair-haired sailor tells me of strange cargo at the Palazzo Ferri.'

Damiens showed no surprise, but cursed loudly enough to frighten the gladiators into leaving. 'That household is a cauldron of gossip.'

'But it is the truth?'

Damiens nodded. 'There is a trader in Ragusa who deals with the Barbary pirates. The Venetians pay good money but the trade is secret.' For a moment he was lost in thought. 'Confound the fellow! I should have had him thrown him back into the canal but I pitied him – always a bad idea.'

'Never forget, Charles, who brought you this news.'

Damiens put an arm around his friend's shoulder. 'Of course I shall not. But we must put an end to young Robbie's mischief. He is a pretty fellow but he must not stand in our path.'

'He means to escape tonight, using discarded disguises.'

Damiens showed no surprise. 'We must be careful. He will tell tales in return for money and a passage home.'

'Old Pic's men could dispose of him. It is still night.'

'Bodies in canals draw attention.' Damiens paused, lost in thought. 'But Old Pic and his blackguards may help us, even so.

If they can we must leave at once. I shall reward you well, Lucian.'

The two men left the alcove together and made their way to the stairs leading down to the entrance hall. Old Pic was waiting at the bottom, his three blackguards beside him.

# Twenty-Four

They found Rob copulating with two soldiers of fortune from Hesse. He had meant to find some disguise, remove himself from the house, and then from Venice. But the soldiers had hair as fair as his own, and chests as hard as steel breastplates, and their cocks were stiff and ready for play. He could not bring himself to turn away from their whispered promises of sound solid fucking, so he had lain with them, taken one mighty cock up his arse and another in his mouth, and had soon abandoned himself to the fierce sensations and enveloping warmth.

The blackguards were not subtle in staging their abduction. They strode across the room thrusting naked torches into every face, and used their boots to make a path for themselves. When they found Rob they pulled him from his union with rough hands, so that the two German cocks slid out of him like oysters from their shells. Some complained, but as many found the spectacle amusing or exciting, and went about their couplings with fresh vigour as Rob was dragged away.

On the stairs the blackguards paused to bind his mouth with a length of black silk, and put a coat and pantaloons on him, but did not allow him to fasten the buttons on either. As they passed through the ballroom, those who bothered to look up from their debaucheries saw three fellows all in black marching a handsome young man whose cock hung loose from his flies, and who showed fair hair and a marbled chest that would be a temptation to any person. They smiled, guessing the young cockerel had been caught stealing from another's nest once too often, and would suffer an honest drubbing when his captors got him outside.

But at the landing-stage there was no one except Old Pic, who stood erect in his silver and black coat. The jewel in the centre of his wig flashed in the torchlight.

Rob would have tried to reason with him and appeal to his decency as one adventurer to another, but the gag was too tight, and the blackguards gave him no time. They laid him face down along the bottom of a gondola, then settled themselves so that their feet rested on his shoulders and back.

Those up early on the Rialto saw nothing unusual as the gondola passed under the bridge, carrying three masked figures dressed all in black.

The wind had dropped, and there was little traffic on the canal. The journey did not take long. As they approached the Palazzo Ferri, one of the blackguards ordered the gondolier to deliver them to the entrance at the side, on the narrow canal where Rob had been pulled from the water only weeks before.

But this time he was not led through the gates and into the garden to be greeted by servants; he was marched to the other end of the landing-stage where a low door was let into the palazzo wall. One man removed Rob's gag, while another hammered on the door until it was opened by a grim-faced man holding a whip. There was a brief exchange, and the man stood to one side as the blackguards shoved Rob inside.

The man put his foot out as Rob passed and sent him sprawling on the stone floor. The whip snapped in the air above him and landed on his back. For a moment Rob felt nothing, then his whole body went numb with shock as the crippling pain asserted itself. Another lash was enough to persuade him to get to his feet, despite the agony, and a third made him hurry along the passageway towards the dungeons, where he had seen slaves waiting to be shipped to the galleys.

Other guards, whips at the ready, were patrolling the long

passageways with cells on either side. The last time Rob had walked there the silence had been broken only by the odd cry of anguish or plea for mercy, but now a cacophony was heard of shouts and taunts, and answering curses and threats. Whips cracked in warning. It was a place without a common tongue, a Babel without mercy, where the cruel demands of profit reduced everything to chaos and confusion.

Rob was led to a cell at the far end of the passage, not far from where he had seen the man flogged. As the door opened it scraped the flagstones, as if seldom unlocked, and Rob was pushed inside. The door closed behind him with a terrible heaviness, and Rob found himself in darkness. Too numb with pain and fear to think, with stripes burning on his back, he sank to the floor where he sat motionless.

It was a while before Rob realised he was not alone. At first he thought the rustling might be a rat, but when he opened his eyes he saw that there was sufficient light from the opening in the door to allow him to see the outlines of the cell. It was larger than he had imagined, as deep as three men his height and half as wide. Nor was it empty. Some wooden boxes were piled along one wall, and some sacks were heaped in the far corner. It was from these that the rustling came.

For a while he took no notice, as he did not wish to disturb any rodents, but soon there was a groan and the sacks moved to reveal a human leg. Although only the foot and calf were showing, partially covered by tattered legging, Rob saw that the skin was pale and the calf thick with muscle. Despite having good reason to be fearful, he was overwhelmed by relief: there was something comforting about seeing such a limb at such a time – it was as if something he had dreamt of long ago had come back to haunt him.

The pile of sacks stirred again, and this time did not settle, but became a mass of movement that reached its climax when several sacks were sent flying through the air. One landed on Rob's lap, and he pushed it away with a cry of disgust.

This was met by a similar sound from the far end of the cell. It was as if Rob himself had spoken. Staring through the murky air, now filled with dust, he saw that his companion was not a rat but a young man lying on a heap of sacks, and wearing a ripped shirt and an equally torn pair of light breeches.

For a few moments the two young men stared at each other. Then Rob heard the other curse. He did not reply because he was too startled by what the young man had said, although he could not think why he should be surprised to hear a curse in such circumstances. The young man cursed again, and once more Rob felt both taken aback and somehow relieved.

Then he cursed a third time, and Rob not only heard, he understood, and replied, 'Yes, fuck it.' His own voice sounded strange.

'Fuck, fuck, fuck . . .'

The young man seemed unable to say anything else, but what else was there to say? Were they not both prisoners bound for a life of servitude? So Rob joined in the chorus, and for a while they repeated the word over and over, as they gave vent to their fury, until it began to lose its force and they burst out laughing.

When they fell silent again, neither spoke. But it was not the silence of despair. And when Rob finally did speak his voice was breaking with emotion. 'Are you an Englishman?'

'I am not, and I'll fight the man who says I am.' The voice was as clear and deep as its accent was strong.

'So you are from north of the Border?'

'Born in Leith by the Firth of Forth's clear waters. And you, sir, judging by your accent, must be a Kentish man.'

'I'll fight the man who denies it.'

They were both laughing, and crawling across the floor towards one another. It was as if lightning had struck. They did not know what was happening, because they had no time to think, and they could not feel, because they were too shocked, but those parts of them that lay too deep to ask for proof had already guessed, and when they met in the centre of the cell, both on their knees, and paused to look into each other's eyes, they did know. By then Rob and Angus were content simply to throw their arms around one another, and tighten their grip, as tears streamed from their eyes.

When they parted, and sat back on their haunches, they began to marvel at finding each other. They argued as to whether it was fate that had reunited them or benign intervention. Angus, who had studied the motions of the stars during his watches at sea, was sure that the answer lay in the heavens. Rob was content simply to wonder at the miracle of having his old friend at his side once more.

There was much to be said. The two young men sat on the cell floor, surrounded by filth and every evidence of human squalor and brutality. Outside whips cracked as those condemned to a life of misery cried out in futile defiance. But Rob and Angus were not afraid. The night was not yet over, and whatever the dawn might bring, they would face it together.

Angus told of his life as an able seaman on a ship-of-the-line, of battling against the French, and being taken by the Barbary pirates. He struggled to contain his anger as he described how the pirates had first treated their captives well, but then had tricked them and sold them to the venal traders of Ragusa. Of his suffering he made light, as he did of his many heroic acts, but it was these last that brought the tears flooding to Rob's eyes, while the tales of suffering roused him to righteous fury.

When it was Rob's turn to tell his story, he too made light of many bitter episodes, and was wary of mentioning others, which he reckoned Angus might not understand. But he need not have feared. No sooner had he begun to tell the sad story of the stowaway than Angus cried out that he hoped Rob had made love to the doomed young fellow. At sea he had learnt that a shared hammock was the best comfort a man could find and, in a world as desolate as the ocean itself, only in affection and a lover's caress did a man find ease.

These words, spoken with forthright conviction, acted upon Rob like a balm, and smoothed away the last of his uncertainties. He moved close to Angus and placed a hand on his shoulder. For a moment Angus was still, but Rob had no fear, and was patient until Angus sighed gently and leant forward to kiss Rob on his forehead. It was a gesture at once paternal and fraternal and, for a while, as they looked into each other's eyes and saw the bright lights burning, they held back from any physical expression of the feelings sweeping through them. If neither time nor their beating hearts could stand still, their gazing eyes did, and so did their thoughts and desires. Together they had reached the still centre of their lives, and of themselves, and deep within each of them the moment lasted as long as time itself.

And then, like hungry men who have paused to say grace, they fell upon each other.

# Twenty-Five

They fucked with abandon. The reunion may have left their minds stunned and their hearts full of love and hope, but their bodies were burning. Life at sea had rubbed away all traces of Angus's tender youth. The soft human clay that had formed the comely lad at play in the orchards of Kent had long since set firm in the mould of manhood. It was natural, therefore, that Rob did not hold out for too long in the struggle to see who would make the first running. It was a short contest between friends, albeit as hard fought as any between enemies, but informed by the passions of love and discovery rather than lust for conquest. Angus's strength soon told, and Rob surrendered with a sigh. He rolled on to his stomach and laughed, and promised that any second round would find him a better match.

He was glad when Angus did not delay in pushing his cock inside him. Certainly it was a thick and lengthy rod, and Rob cried out as the hole in his backside was pushed wide open. It was as if Angus was set upon slicing him in two, but once through the gate, the cock set about its task with all the determination Rob would have expected of his friend.

It was not a long fuck. Perhaps Angus was too big, or after so long in chains was too full of come to submit to the disciplines of delay. Maybe the flogging had roused him, or it had simply been too long since he had let his cock feel the inside of another man.

Whatever the reason, Rob soon felt the urgent thrusts of a cock out of control. To help his friend keep command of himself he shouted at the top of his voice, accusing him of being a scurvy son-of-a-bitch, a cunt's man, and fit only for the whorehouse or mounting sheep.

But it was useless. Angus was already on the steep slope to ecstasy, and he, too, was calling Rob a dirty whore born of shit and the devil's spillage. As he let go with the first spurts Angus arched his back and plunged his cock so deep up Rob's backside it seemed that he might break through to the very centre of Rob's being, where both life and pleasure had their source. But the flood broke, and Angus fell writhing on Rob. His obscene words were replaced by a frenzy of jagged thrusts. Rob rejoiced to feel Angus spurting inside him, and his warmth and weight on him. Angus gasped for breath. He pressed his mouth to Rob's ear and whispered that he loved him more than the sun and the moon and the stars.

Then they pulled apart.

Angus lay back against the pile of sacks and closed his eyes. His face wore an expression of sated contentment. Beside him Rob was happy, but far from sated.

From the first time he had set eyes on Angus, when the Scottish lad had appeared one morning in the orchards, full of good cheer but with fists at the ready, and black hair falling over his dark flashing eyes, Rob had been in love. Not that he knew it. They fought more often than they spoke, and tangled with one another in contests of strength and will. But, in the strange way of boys, their friendship had grown among all the false alliances, betrayals and stand-offs. They could no more ignore one another than they could keep from each other's company. What Angus had seen in him, other than a firm friend, he did not know, but Rob had known from the start why he could not take his eyes off Angus.

And still could not. Now, as then, Angus's shoulders and chest were broader than his own, and his neck thicker. His belly was flat, and hardened to withstand any punch. Although a column of black hair now grew from his belly-button down to join the thick thatch at his groin, the arse was still wide enough for the buttocks to snuggle there like two halves of a Cox's Pippin. If nature had ever made a sweeter curve, Rob had not seen it.

There were changes. The hands were harder and callused, and the arms were thick with sinew and muscle. Tattoos decorated the firm flesh below each shoulder, and a mass of dark hair flourished in the armpits. The back was a solid slab of muscled flesh torn by the whip. The legs had grown hairy, with thighs like logs, while the calves were bricks of muscle. If the feet had somehow retained the delicacy of youth, the face had not. The cheeks were thinner under thick stubble, the chin firmer, and the black hair had been cut short. Above all, the eyes had a knowing and hungry look. All in all, the boy had been absorbed by manhood, and the proof of it lay between his legs. A raw seeping cock, thick and flaccid, lay at rest on a bed of wiry black hair.

Although they still had much to say, and there was much to dread, they lay still. After a while Rob noticed that Angus had drifted into sleep. He could not grudge his friend a few dreams, but none the less felt pangs of loneliness. To be deprived even of Angus's consciousness was more than he could bear, and as he edged close against the warm firm body, he swore that, come what may, whether in freedom or slavery, alive or in death, he would never allow himself to be parted from his friend. A separation would be a sacrilege against the powers that had brought them back together. And even if those forces grew forgetful and did not watch over them, there was no torture known to man, nor any force in the spheres, sufficient to uncouple them.

And with the vow still echoing in his mind, he too fell asleep.

The night was drawing to its end. The anguished cries of the darkness gave way to more mundane sounds as bowls of food were shoved under the cell doors. Whips no longer cracked, but harsh voices were raised as the guards busied themselves preparing for the prisoners' departure. The air was thick with the acrid smell of burning coal.

Rob was soon awake. He had not slept deeply, and his mind was hectic with dread. In a few hours they would be on board the galleys from which no man had ever escaped except into death. If they were to survive they would have to act before they left the palazzo, yet his mind could come up with no idea as to what might be done. Men chained and blinded by hoods were no match for those armed with whips and bludgeons.

But on waking Angus seemed not to share Rob's despair. He cursed the stiffness he felt where the lash had done its work, and threw his bowl of food against the wall, but when he pulled Rob close to him, he was gentle. Rob felt the strong arms holding him, and could not prevent himself from kissing his friend on the lips, which stirred Angus to place a hand on Rob's loins, then to feel inside his breeches, take hold of the balls and play with them. When Rob began to mutter about the new day bringing enslavement, Angus stopped him with another kiss, took Rob's hand and pushed it to where his cock was growing.

'We must not.' Rob's voice was hoarse.

'We may never see each other again.'

Rob pulled away and grabbed his friend by the neck. 'We shall never be parted. Do you understand? Never.' His voice rang out with the clarity of his conviction.

All Angus could do was look into Rob's eyes and nod. Suddenly overcome Rob sank back and buried his face in his hands. Tears seeped between his fingers.

'We will be brave . . . when the time comes, but until then . . . so long as we're together . . .'

Rob felt a hand on his balls again, and sank forward so that he pressed his face against Angus's smooth stiff cock. No gleaming sword pulled from its bejewelled scabbard ever looked nobler. Rob's nostrils filled with the warm scent of groin and arse, and he closed his eyes to capture a few last moments of sweetness.

But Angus was not content merely to have Rob lie with him. He had fucked him only hours before, but his sleep had repaired him and he was ready for more. He whispered to Rob that, although the day might bring horrors beyond imagining, for now they had each other, and seeing that they were still young and well, they should therefore pass the time in love-making rather than shedding tears. He wiped Rob's eyes with the back of his hand and, with a cheerful laugh, turned on his side and poked his arse towards Rob.

'There's the last cherry of summer. Pluck it while you can.'

Suddenly stiff, Rob sat up, pulled out his cock, spat on its helmet and, using his hands to force a path between the large hairy buttocks, thrust it at the clenched portal.

'You'll have to do better than that, my lad.' Angus laughed. 'I've been laid siege to a hundred times.'

Rob braced himself against Angus's shoulders, and used his hips to thrust, but still there was no give. The door remained locked. 'I'll need a rod of steel to slip through there.'

'Nonsense, my lad, use the machine God gave you.'

Rob was not used to suffering rebuffs at either entrance, and was not amused by Angus's light-hearted refusal to help. Could he not relax in friendship and so allow a decent entrance?

He used his fingers, but the knot was tied too tightly. He used his cock again, and when there was no progress, grew indignant and thrust himself as hard as he dared, so that his own cock seemed about to buckle. He parted the firm cheeks with his hands and used the dribble from his cock to massage the tight entrance. Then he thrust again, but with no better luck, so he did what he had prayed he would not have to do, and as Angus chuckled in triumph, he placed his face between the cheeks and used his tongue to tantalise the resisting muscle.

Rob could feel nerve endings quivering where his tongue probed, and Angus squirmed – even tried to clench his cheeks but Rob was not having that, and used all the strength in his arms to keep them wide apart. The hole was still tight and closed, but Rob guessed from his own experience that if the tongue did its work well, and for long enough, the siege would be raised.

And when Rob tested the gate with the tip of his thumb, it did give way, and he found he could slip a couple of fingers easily where no man had been before. But such scouting was of no importance unless the cock followed on. Only then would the cherry be taken, and Angus be his.

It was not easy, but in the end, with a mighty thrust, Rob felt the defences give way. The tiny round entrance was breached, and Angus let out a deep groan of surprise. Rob moved in triumph, sending a few hard thrusts so that Angus would be left in no doubt that they would make a pair of equals.

But his sense of triumph was soon overtaken by an urgent need to navigate a proper journey, so that he would arrive at his climax neither so soon that Angus might mock him, nor so late as to be thought a plodder. Above all, he was eager to avoid those doldrums that come after the first excitement of entry, and when the climax is still in the far distance. So he employed all the arts and trickery he had learnt in Venice to ensure that Angus, who was so cocky in the saddle, might be taught to enjoy the more humble satisfaction of being ridden.

To this end he pulled Angus's arse towards him so that it stuck up at an angle that ensured a better passage for his thrust while providing a more stimulating sight. This done he took care to alter both the course and the depth of each thrust. Having never been fucked before Angus would feel the cock moving inside him with unusual intensity, and Rob plunged this way and that to take full possession of his friend, body and soul.

As the novelty of fucking his friend wore off, Rob's fretful mind turned to the strange circumstances of their coupling. They lay on the floor of a filthy cell, surrounded by muck and debris, and took their pleasure while outside the guards were preparing to dispatch them to an earthly hell. But even if they had already been there, Rob would not have felt the fires or tortures. It did not matter that he might never fuck again, because after Angus all men would seen insipid and dull. His only care was that he should have Angus as Angus had him, and that thereafter, no matter what, they would know that they were truly lovers.

But it was not to be. Despite all the skills Rob employed, Angus was not prepared to lie easy and be taken. As Rob's pace quickened, he felt Angus begin to move against his rhythm so that the deep thrusts were thwarted, and his small darts and teasing changes of direction went for nothing. It was sabotage.

For a while Rob pressed on, eager not to fail himself or his lover. But Angus was too restless, and soon he began to rear and jerk so that Rob lost control of his own movements. He cursed Angus and told him to hold still, but it was too late, and with a skilful movement Angus pushed his arse so high Rob found himself lifted into the air. With a twist of his torso Angus dumped Rob on his side, forcing the cock out of his hole.

Rob had no time to sit up, or even work out what had happened, because Angus, his cock rampant once more, had hold of him. Rob was turned so that he was kneeling on all fours, then felt his legs being pushed apart, and a hand running between his cheeks. He knew what Angus had in mind, and fought back with all the strength he could muster, but Angus was the senior of the pair in size, energy and will. Without bothering to moisten the hole he eased his sharp rod up Rob's back passage, and so retook the field he had only recently deserted.

Rob knew it was useless to protest. The better man had won, and consolation had to be found in knowing that he had at least plucked his friend's cherry, and been where no man had gone before. If he had turned out not to be a conqueror, he had proved himself an explorer.

Angus set a spanking pace in the saddle. His thrust was deep and true, and his cock's width ensured ripples of pure sensation were soon coursing through every sinew in Rob's body. He felt himself enveloped in clouds of sensation that lifted him from the squalid cellar floor and sent him flying back to paradise. And Angus was not even exerting himself.

Glancing round, Rob saw him kneeling with hands on hips, and his head thrust back. His eyes were closed and he was using his hips to thrust and pull his cock in and out of Rob's ever more raw backside. Angus was overmastering him effortlessly. It was the role Angus had been born for, just as nature had determined that others should be mastered. It was the divide as old as the garden of Eden, and Rob's only regret was that he had not given Angus more than a moment's doubt as to who was whom.

As Rob surrendered to Angus, the sounds from beyond the cell door grew more alarming. Whips were being used, and cries of anguish were heard. In his state of delirious pleasure it was difficult for Rob to believe that he might find himself under the lash in a few minutes' time. Angus, too, seemed unmoved by the noises, and since his fucking was absolute in its command and efficiency, and demanded an equal concentration, Rob put his fears to the back of his mind. What glory could equal that of being made the instrument upon which so expert a lover spun waves of pleasure refined beyond the limits of imagination or memory? What horror could obliterate the moment? The world and its evils might press close, but as Angus devised a fuck shaped to the grandest design, no other place existed except the paradise they had made of the small damp cell.

Time was lost to sensations. Angus drove on with all the determination of one who knows misery is waiting. He quickened the pace, and grabbed Rob's stiff cock that had been straining against the thin air, and jerked it down and back until it seemed it might snap at its stem. Rob cried again, and this time begged for mercy, but Angus did not relent, any more than did those wielding their whips outside the cell. Rob's cries were lost among those of men being driven to their doom, and suddenly he was aware once more of his predicament. He envisaged the scene outside, the cruelty and hopelessness, the pain and blind fear, and he knew that in a matter of seconds that world would invade and destroy their fragile paradise like cut-throats in a nursery.

Even at his climax Angus did not lose control. Like a ship's captain he navigated a way through the storm using skills born of instinct and concentration. Rob may have felt himself roughly treated, but he reached the summit as Angus did. Then, as Angus coursed in and out of his backside, and used both hands to force Rob's cock and balls to surrender their load, Rob felt himself become a part of Angus. The come was spurting into him, and from him, and he was both the object of his lover's will and its instrument. They were as one, but the one was Angus, and with a raw cry of triumph and regret, Rob knew that those waiting outside with their whips and chains were too late. Angus had already enslaved him.

# Twenty-Six

When the guards burst in on the private paradise, they did not think they had stumbled upon some pretty picture of love's consolations so much as a scene from the inferno. Two young men were rutting with all the defiance of goats. One urged the other on while clasped to his back as if engaged in some stationary race. It was rumoured that buggery was the norm among the sons of Albion, and nothing seen in the upper rooms of the palazzo had challenged this view. It was shocking, nevertheless, to come across men engaged in such a display at the moment of their departure to a life of drudgery.

For all their brutality the guards were God-fearing fellows, who would rather face their maker than the devil, and to find men coupling when they should have been cowering, and oblivious to everything except their union, aroused their deep fears. Worse still, the scoundrel doing the fucking had fresh stripes across his back. Who but the devil himself could be impervious to a flogging?

After they had dragged the lovers apart, they did not treat Angus tenderly, but they remained wary of him and waited until they had him in chains before using their whips to administer their lesson a second time. But even as the lash coiled round him, Angus stood as still and upright as if he were the master and the guards his henchmen. Those wielding the whips soon lost heart and lowered their lengths of ox-hide. There was work to be done, and the sooner the dark-haired fellow was sent to the galleys the better. There he would be met by slave drivers equal to the task of subduing him.

Meanwhile Rob stood as the guards put ragged clothes on him, fixed a heavy shackle round his neck and placed fetters on his ankles. Then they linked him to Angus with chains, and closed the locks with keys. There could be no escaping from such irons.

They were led to the door to join the miserable figures passing by. Rob remembered the night he had woken from dreams to find himself in a nightmare as other wretches were led to their doom. Then he had prayed he might never suffer their fate, but whatever guardians had saved him then had since deserted him. The shackle on his shoulders was so heavy he could not imagine surviving long with it, let alone toiling under the lash until he dropped.

When the time came for them to join the parade, Rob stumbled, and for a moment was too dazed to know which way to turn. A whip across his shoulders showed him, as its smooth punishing surface cut through his shirt to break the skin as easily as a surgeon's knife.

They had not gone far before the line halted. The air was darkened with soot, and the sound of bellows blowing was mixed with cries of anguish from the head of the parade. But all such sounds were as nothing to the piercing scream that rang out a moment later. There was muttering and movement in the line, until the guards spread their whips across a few backs to restore order. But another scream broke the silence, then another. The line began to move slowly forward, and the roar of the bellows grew louder. The blackened air was disturbed so that the flickering torches shed a lurid glow.

Rob was beginning to understand the nature of the horror that awaited him. Even the sight of Angus beside him, still upright and proud despite his fetters and the bleeding weals on his back, offered no comfort. Their moment together may have been a gift of the gods, but nothing could save them from human evil. For the first time he understood that they were doomed, and that no one would save them.

In his despair he did not struggle in his chains, or cry out when he saw the braziers and branding irons. Ahead of him men were being forced to bare their arms so that a crude outline of the Venetian lion might be burnt into their flesh. He did not avert his eyes, but stood calmly beside his lover, sure that the pain would be no worse than that he would suffer every day for the rest of his life.

The noise was terrible. Those who stood waiting protested at the agonies about to be inflicted on them, while those closer to the braziers stood weeping as the red irons were plunged into the beds of bright burning coals. Only those in the clutches of the guards were silent, too terrified to scream as they were led forward between the braziers and forced to their knees. Two men in black leather breeches with bared chests stood on either side waiting to draw the irons. They wore long gauntlets and black masks to shield themselves from the heat. When the irons were red hot, they signalled to the guards, who wrenched the poor fellow's arms back to allow both irons to be planted at the same moment. It did not take long, but the men made sure the irons burnt deep. The screams seared the eardrums of those forced to watch.

The line of wretches moved slowly forward. The bellows hissed, the guards cursed and cracked their whips. Screams were followed by the stench of burning flesh, the rattle of chains, and the ghastly sound of those weeping in pain and despair.

Rob could see the torture, and its effects, and knew that as inevitably as a clock's hands move towards the hour he would soon be kneeling as the irons burnt him. But he felt no temptation to panic or complain. Instead his mood began to lift. With Angus at his side, he had no reason to fear. The pain would come to both of them, and they would suffer. But those seconds of agony would be nothing. Afterwards they would still be together. Nothing else mattered.

The guards took no chances with Angus. He was grabbed on either side while a third seized the chain running between his legs and jerked it backwards. Angus lost his balance and fell forward. His chains were removed and he was dragged towards the men standing ready with the hot irons. As soon as he was on his knees and in position the irons were rammed against his upper arms, burning deep through tattoos of mermaids entwined on anchors. He let out a mighty roar, and in arching his back moved his arms so that the irons were quickly withdrawn. The guard in command shouted in anger and planted his boot on Angus's flayed back so that he fell on his face. Then it seemed the irons might be used on him a second time, but when they pulled him up, the overseer signalled for the next man to be brought forward.

Rob watched Angus endure his trial with serene confidence. It was an ugly sight, but he knew Angus would survive. Brutality was wasted on him. He was as strong in mind as body, and it would take more than whips and branding irons to destroy him. Seeing such fortitude gave Rob the strength to pray that he, too, might endure the pain with as much grace.

He was held by both arms to be unchained, then led briskly forward. The sickening smell of burning flesh hung in the still hot air, and as he was forced to his knees the heat from the braziers scalded his face. There was a pause. One of the men holding him said something, and the other laughed. Rob knew that the irons were being reheated, but he did not dare look. He had hoped to endure the pain as might a dumb animal, but kneeling between the braziers, he was overcome by terror. It rose from inside him, like a bird flapping vast black wings, and turned his stomach to liquid and his heart to a hammering box. His sight went out of focus and the nerve endings in his upper arms tingled.

There was a grunt from one side, and an answer from the other, and the heat intensified. The irons were about to strike. Rob looked up, and as his vision cleared, he saw Angus standing with his back to him. He was about to call his name and have him turn so that he could see his lover as he was burnt, but he was too late and he felt himself pushed hard from either side.

For a moment there was no pain, and Rob began to take in breath, but there was to be no mercy, no shield of numbness or fainting. When the pain came it was like constant cannon fire, or the light of a million suns. It drove through his arms, up into his face, freezing it into a mask of agony. It stopped his heart, and closed his lungs. His legs splayed in panic and his stomach contracted, sending its contents spewing up to be blocked at his throat by air exhaling in a terrible scream. It was pain beyond anything the body alone might generate, and when the scream ended, and he tried to breathe in, he choked on the smoke of his own burning flesh.

Before he knew what had happened he was dragged away, as another was pushed to his knees behind him.

Rob stood shoulders hunched as he tried to nurse his wounds. He did not look at Angus as they were chained together, and he did not care how his lover had suffered. He was entirely alone, and he cursed the day he had been born. Where before there had been pride and hope, and confidence, there was only the simple tyranny of fear. He was afraid to move, to look, or speak. He was afraid of what might happen, and of what had happened. There was himself, and there was fear. Nothing else. He had no loyalty except to fear, no thoughts except to be afraid, and no ambition except to be mastered by fear, and to entrust himself to it.

When Angus touched him, Rob pushed him away. He did not dare glance up, or speak. His only thought was not to attract the attention of the guards and suffer the whip.

Angus said something as he turned away, but Rob did not hear because there was a commotion ahead of them at the far end of the dark passageway. A portcullis was being raised, and beyond it two vast doors were being dragged open. This let in the dawn's silvery light, and against it, like black cut-outs, a group of men was marching in. Unlike the palazzo's guards these men were not ruffians recruited from the streets, but liveried officers of the Republic. They wore wide-brimmed boaters' hats and tunics of red and gold, with lions emblazoned on their chests. Their breeches were brown with thick pleats, and their stockings were white, while their deck shoes were neatly made and polished. Their whips were tucked into their belts, and they strode along with their arms swinging like men with nothing to hide.

As Rob watched he felt the inevitability of his fate. Officers of the Republic were to be his masters, and Venice would return him to the sea as her slave. At the end of the passage he saw a lighter painted in black and gold bobbing on the canal as it waited to take on its human cargo. He remembered seeing the galleys moored at the Giudecca that first morning as he came up on the *Dawn Treader*'s deck. The sight had made him shiver then, as did the prospect of seeing them again. But see them he would, and soon. After all, with his arms branded, his liberty stolen and his courage gone, what was he but a slave? Only hours before he had been a free man ready to set out for home. Now he was resigned to his fate. A few minutes ago he had found comfort and hope in having Angus at his side. Now his friend could be a thousand miles away and it would make no difference.

# Twenty-Seven

Lord Damiens and Lucian had been in no hurry to leave the Polish count's ball. It was the milord's habit to be elsewhere when unpleasantness was afoot, and he did not wish to return to the Palazzo Ferri until he could be sure that everything was in order. He hated confusion, and had made it his rule that if there was dirty work to be done, it should be left to those underlings who best understood such things. What mattered was the purse of gold, not the sordid business of trade.

Lucian, too, had his reasons to linger. There had been concern among His Majesty's officials at the behaviour of certain subjects residing in Venice, and he had been asked to keep an eye on his friend, who was said to be the most dissolute. There was also the question of the young sailor. A friend betrayed is always a danger, and Lucian was anxious to make sure the galleys had him. Once aboard he would be as good as dead. No records were kept, and no names listed. No one escaped, and no one survived.

Titus greeted them on the landing-stage at the Palazzo Ferri with news that all was well. A recruiting party from the galleys had arrived, and its commander was well pleased with the goods on offer. The slaves were freshly branded, and ready to be loaded into the lighters. There had been no mishaps.

Damiens smiled and put a hand on Titus's shoulder. 'The

faithful servant will be rewarded.' He turned to Lucian. 'Shall we see off our troublesome young friend?'

Lucian nodded. 'Indeed we should, for we must wish him well in his new life.' His smile was cold enough for Damiens to feel its chill.

Nor did Titus fail to notice its cruelty. 'Follow me, my lord. We must hurry, or they will be gone.'

All the doors to the lower floors were bolted and locked, and Titus had to find the key for each one. On reaching the lowermost floor they were met by a guard, who warned them that the loading had begun. Titus made no reply but took the man's whip.

They made their way quickly along the passage to where the slaves had been branded. The air was thick with smoke and steam from the doused braziers, and the two men who had used the irons were standing to one side, wrapped in black cloaks, and drinking from large goblets. They pointed towards the long wide passage that led to the portcullis and the great doors that opened on to the canal. A cool breeze blew towards them as they hurried along. The lighter moored at the landing could be seen riding the wash.

Only a few slaves in the passageway still waited to be boarded. A man in full Dalmatian dress was standing to one side with a secretary who was counting the men. Opposite him a black-coated doctor examined each man as he passed, while the commander of the Republic's guards stood on the landing stage with his men on either side. Behind him was another officer of the Republic, no less well guarded, whose severe garb of black trimmed with simple lace was as eloquent of his power and position as was his confident bearing and haughty expression. In his hand he held a leather satchel, embossed in gold with the Lion of Venice.

Lord Damiens bowed to the Dalmatian, who returned the courtesy. It was clear that everything was going to plan. There was an air of formality, of easy command and mutual respect, that pleased the milord. The slaves had been well subdued, and were in good condition. It was unlikely there would be much haggling over the settlement. With such an excellent cargo there should be profit for all.

Seeing no point in conducting his business in such a setting, Damiens dispatched Titus to invite the representatives of the Republic up to the *piano nobile* where they might enjoy refreshments. The Dalmatian, on the other hand, would have to wait where he was for his share of the gold.

Damiens asked Lucian if he had seen the young sailor. For a moment Lucian did not reply, so Damiens turned to him and asked again.

Lucian was staring ahead, his eyes wide and seemingly fixed on some distant horizon, but when Damiens followed his gaze he saw that he was looking at the last of the slaves. At first he did not recognise the stooped figure staring back. He was in rags like the others, and showed the mark of the whip beneath his torn shirt. His body was as filthy as his bedraggled hair. When he tried to take a step forward he stumbled. It was a pitiful sight, and one at which the milord did not wish to gaze long.

And yet those eyes . . . how blue . . . and searching.

Lucian was laughing, not the hearty laughter of enjoyment but the silent rocking mirth of the undeserving.

The milord was not pleased. It was not seemly to laugh in front of officers of the Republic. 'Will you not share the joke? These gentlemen will wonder at us.'

'My lord, do you not see who it is?'

Damiens was losing patience. 'I confess I do not.'

Lucian lifted his arm and pointed at the slave, who was still staring back at him. 'That is your lover, sir. Young Robbie.'

'You are mistaken, sir. I suggest we return.' But Damiens could not continue. He knew that Lucian was right. It was Robbie. Only hours before he had kissed him as tenderly as he had ever kissed a man. How could he have been changed into such a broken wretch? Damiens remembered holding Rob, the strength in his arms and back, his ever-willing cock standing at the ready, the heft of his balls, the smell of sweet burnt milk that wafted from his groin. He had been a good lover, as gentle as could be, as rough as he needed to be, and as beautiful and unknowable as the night sky.

Lucian was no longer laughing. 'How quick the wheel of fortune spins for those who rise too far.'

Damiens did not allow himself a last glance at his lover. Hard as he was in his purpose, he could not trust himself. 'Come, man, we must get away.'

The officers of the Republic stood ready to follow, and the Dalmatian smiled his consent to being left behind. With as much pomp as the circumstances allowed, Lord Damiens led the way back to the palazzo's upper floors.

Rob would not have looked back had he not heard the milord's voice. No man had dared raise his eyes after being burned by the irons, and the guards still stood ready with their whips. The loading had been as slow as the branding, and Rob was the last in the line. All he could do was nurse his throbbing arms, and hope not to attract attention. But when he heard the milord's voice, he turned and saw Lord Damiens standing beside Lucian, and knew that he had been betrayed.

They had used him as their plaything, and afterwards had discarded him for profit. All the caresses, all the fine words and gifts of jewels, all the nights spent in gaming houses and brothels, all the shared laughter, the glances and confidences, all the love and hope, all of it, everything had been lies. Neither had meant a word they had said, and they had even come to mock him in his wretched state.

A fury spread through him that seemed to work like alchemy and transform the pain left by the hot irons back into fire. His cheeks burnt and heavy tears of humiliation dribbled down his face. Every ache was numbed, and a fire of anger burnt in his belly while cold slithers of rage stabbed his heart. His vision was clear.

When the milord went, he took with him his henchmen, and left the last of the loading to be overseen by the Republic's guards. These men, Rob noticed, were well fed and well dressed, and as concerned to make a fine impression as to do their duty. Most had not even pulled their whips from their belts, and several who had were toying with them as if curious to know how to use them. The only member of the household still on the landing-stage was Titus, who stood beneath the raised portcullis with both his whip and ring of keys hanging from his waist.

After a pause, the line moved forward. Angus was three ahead of Rob and would be the next to be taken aboard. Since Rob had rebuffed him after the branding, he had kept his own company and his head bowed, although his broad shoulders were still straight despite the bleeding welts. The doctor stepped forward to look at his back, disturbing the torn shirt as if examining some piece of goods for damage. With a frown and a shrug he nodded to Titus, who directed Angus towards the planks leading up to the lighter.

Rob knew that once Angus was on board all hope was gone and, although he had felt himself bereft and abandoned, it was at that moment that he felt, with utter certainty, that there would be no coming back once Angus was aboard. The Venetians might make lazy guards, but as seamen they were without equal. Escape would be impossible.

He shouted for Angus, and his voice echoed along the passage-way like a trumpet calling the dead. He ran forward and there was confusion as Angus stared back in fearful surprise.

Rob told himself that Angus had not seen the milord and Lucian laughing at them, and would not have known who they were: his defeated heart and mind would still lie dulled by shame and despair. Angus might have been cock of the walk when they fucked, but it would be for Rob to save them.

Titus was the first to notice that something was afoot. He drew his whip and raised it above his head, but Rob was no longer afraid of strips of hide and he leapt at Titus. In the confusion he drew tight the chain between his hands, and rubbed them across the valet's face. Titus drew back, and Rob used the moment to grab Angus and pull him from the line. The Venetian guards were stirring, but they were not used to surprise. By the time they had drawn their whips and made ready to use them, Rob and Angus were half-way towards the branding room, and the stairwells leading up to the palazzo.

But they could not move fast. Their shackles and chains were heavy, and the hot irons had bled their strength. Titus suffered no such impediments, and ran past them, calling out that slaves were escaping.

Rob was soon staggering under the weight of his fetters, and beside him Angus breathed heavily. They stumbled on, fighting their chains, and weeping as thickets of doom closed round him.

In the end they could go no further. The rusty shackles chaffed at their necks, and Rob tripped over the chains between his legs. He fell against the wall and, had Angus not reached out to steady him, would have dropped to his knees.

Angus leant against him. 'We're cornered.' Rob saw that his friend was staring back the way they had come. Beyond their gasps and the rattle of their chains, there was silence. 'They have us.'

Despite his exhaustion and the thick streams of sweat running off him, Rob was still numb with cold fury. He would die before he was taken into slavery. 'We must go on.'

His voice was husky but the words were clear enough to infuriate Angus. He took Rob by the shoulders and shook him. 'Can't you see?' He pointed back along the passage. 'We've come too far. They're waiting for us.'

Rob looked round. Ahead the passage ended in a bolted door and the way back was also blocked. A dozen or more guards of the Republic had formed up on either side of the passageway, their whips at the ready. Beyond them Titus stood guard at the door that led to the palazzo's upper floors. With his legs apart and his hands on his hips, he had the stance of one with no more to fear than a cat when toying with a mouse.

For a moment neither Angus nor Rob moved. Then Angus drew breath. 'Shall we put the bastards to the test?' His voice was hoarse with passion.

A spike of ice ran down Rob's spine. Suddenly he could breathe freely. He was ready to kill. He reached out and took hold of Angus's cock and balls. The prick sprang free, too large and hard to be gathered in the palm of any hand. Rob squeezed the hefty globes until Angus roared his old deep laugh. Rob tightened his grip. 'Are these made of petals and silk, or are they solid oak?'

With a hard smack Angus took hold of Rob's balls, and made

a fist of them. 'Yours may be oak, my English lad, but mine are Scots granite.'

Still gripping one another, they embraced. As their shuddering bodies collided, their lips met in a rich slick of salt and saliva. If this were to be the end, they would go with the taste of each other sweet on their lips.

The guards of the Republic jeered.

With final clenches, Rob and Angus let go of each other's balls. Their eyes met, and for a second smiles played on their lips, before they threw back their heads to let out cries of defiance that were heard even by the doomed souls waiting in the lighter.

They ran into the gauntlet.

The guards had an easy time of it. The task required little skill. They laid the lash on so that some licks coiled round Angus and Rob to bite into their chests and stomachs while others snapped between their legs to bruise and cut like knives.

It was the whips' weight that drove Rob to his knees. He tried to shield himself with his arms, but there was no hiding. The lashes were the licks of the devil's tongue. Twist and turn as he might under the furious assault, he could not escape the punishment. When a whip coiled round him with deadly speed, Rob jerked his head to avoid its leaded tip. He saw a guard raising his thongs, and when it fell across his back Rob was flattened. He did not cry out, and he did not weep. He lay in surrender, and began a retreat to those remote chambers of the mind where the difference between life and death means little.

Angus saved him. While Rob gave himself to dreams, Angus greeted each fresh stripe as his mortal enemy. He cursed, and cried out to God. He fell under the blows and wept. He rose and shook himself, shuddered, and spat white foam in defiance. He was not ashamed to howl like a beaten dog. At the same time he spread himself over Rob, and found the strength to rise again. He lifted his friend and set him on his feet. He saw that the guards were standing back, confident that they had inflicted enough punishment to bring them to heel.

But it was not in Angus's nature to submit to chastisement.

Rather, it made him stubborn and wild, and as he emerged from the gauntlet his only thoughts were of escape.

Titus stood in his way, but even his stern countenance did not deter Angus. He stumbled towards the valet, hissing defiance, and willing to die. Never again would he be careless of his freedom.

Titus looked at the pair with pitying disdain.

'Let us pass.' Angus's voice was sure, and his tone did not beseech.

Titus shook his head. 'I cannot.' But doubt seemed to cross his mind and he frowned.

Angus saw this and took another step. 'We are free men.' He leaned close. Was the valet tempted to help them? Or was it a simple equation of fear: which would be worse, to suffer Angus's rage or that of the milord?

The decision was not long in coming. 'You are slaves.'

'Then so are you.' In his fury Angus spat so that the glob fell on Titus's boot. 'Some spittle for your lick.'

Titus affected disdain. 'Not yet tired of the whip? You crave more?' He raised a hand to order the guards forward.

A smile crossed Angus's face. 'You'll need more than whips!' With a sudden movement at his waist he jerked his head so that his forehead butted Titus on the chin.

The valet fell backwards against the door, and shouted for the guards, who at last began to move forward.

But they were too late. While Angus had been talking, Rob had been watching Titus's fingers as they caressed the keys on the metal ring attached to his belt. There were more than a dozen, but one seemed to deserve all the attention, and as Titus collapsed against the door, Rob made a grab for it, and rammed it in the lock. It turned with well-oiled ease.

Rob pushed Titus out of the way and, with Angus at his heels, ran for the stairs leading to the upper floors.

# Twenty-Eight

Lord Damiens was determined that his new wealth from trading slaves should not diminish his reputation as the most dissolute nobleman in Venice. As soon as he had the gold purse in his possession, he ordered flares to be lit and liveried footmen to parade on the landing stage, so that those returning from the masked ball might take refreshment at the Palazzo Ferri. On the upper floors the windows were thrown open to be festooned with flowers, and an orchestra that happened to be passing on the Grand Canal was enticed from its duty to play at a wedding by the sight of beckoning young men in lascivious disguises. Before long the strains of viols capped by the blare of trumpets filled the morning air. Even the Venetians crossing the canal, whose faces bore the dour expression of those who must work for their living, could not but look up to smile and wave at the brilliant scene.

That only the more debauched elements of Venetian society chose to land did not trouble the milord. Since arriving in Venice while fleeing his creditors he had learnt to fend for himself. In making himself rich, by the cruellest means, he had shed his foppery, and could no longer be dismissed as yet one more exile from debt and an ancient title. He had never been, and did not intend ever to be, dull.

So those who landed, for the most part, were in need of repair after the exertions of the night. Lord Damiens, who had acquired a Venetian's understanding of the need to disguise the more visible effects of human frailty, gave orders that looking-glasses should be stood in the entrance hall, along with tables set with powders, perfumes, rouges, and paint. The footmen had been instructed to encourage the gentlemen to relieve themselves in piss-pots set along a wall, while screens were provided for the ladies to hide behind.

Through this busy mêlée of the masked, the disguised, the exhausted and the undone, Rob and Angus were able to move without drawing attention beyond some disapproving remarks about their choice of garb. Even so they did not wait to be recognised, or arouse the curious to ask how such startling effects of the whip and shackle had been achieved. They made their way to the door leading to the garden, where they were confronted by another class of person no less eager to enter the palazzo.

As news of fresh riches had spread through the kitchens, various skivvies and boys had been dispatched to the markets for provisions. They in turn alerted those with other wares to offer, and soon the narrow paths leading to the Palazzo Ferri were full of tradesmen, hawkers and sundry mongers, all pursued by the usual opportunists, beggars and riff-raff. This crowd jostled at the gatehouse entrance to offer bribes sufficient to gain their entry. Once in the garden they hurried towards the kitchens, unperturbed as they passed two young men in chains and fetters, with torn backs, matted hair and bruised faces. The reputation of the palazzo ensured that no matter what strange sights greeted them, they took no notice.

Rob led Angus to the gatehouse. The keeper was busy taking bribes, and the door had been left open. They walked through to the small room at the back, where they found Silvio lying on his bed reading a work of philosophy. A burly naked man was kneeling beside him, sucking his cock.

Rob was in no mood for niceties, and merely pulled the man off the agent's prick. The poor fellow stood up in alarm. Looking around in confusion to find his clothes, he had to suffer the indignity of having his own stiff cock firmly tugged by Angus. And when the fellow bent forward to pick up his gondolier's breeches, Angus awarded his hairy backside a playful but resounding smack, whose impact was given added weight by the manacles still on Angus's wrist. After that the man fled, without putting on his shirt or boater's hat.

There was no telling whether Silvio was surprised to see Rob in such a state, but he quickly realised what he wanted. He put aside his book and got off the bed with lithe unhurried grace. His splendid stiff cock hung free from his fly as he went through into the gatekeeper's room.

Angus was about to follow him, but Rob signalled him to be patient. The two friends looked around at the bare dusty room. Sunshine lit up two tiny windows and fell on the discarded books and clothes scattered across the floor. They smiled, and then shook their heads in disbelief. Within shouting distance of where they stood, slaves were being shipped to the galleys, and minutes before they had run a gauntlet of whips as they fought to save their freedom and their lives. Now, as they regained their breath in the silence of a scholar's study, they were able to measure their good fortune and decide what to do next.

By the gleam in Angus's eye, Rob had the suspicion that their minds were as one. So long as they kept hold of the initiative, and their luck held, they would endeavour to make themselves free men by the day's end, and to see punished those who had wronged them. After all they had suffered, it did not seem too daunting a task.

Silvio returned with sets of keys, a hammer and a spike. It did not take him long to free the two sailors from their rusty irons. He picked up his book and showed it to Rob, who saw that it was written in French. Silvio stood in silence as Rob turned the pages without knowing what they contained. When he glanced up at Silvio, and saw the fires burning in his eyes, he guessed the scholar was hoping for a comment. But he could think of nothing – no sign or word, that might satisfy such ardour – and was filled with regret that he could not share whatever thoughts and purposes were flooding through the young man's mind. Angus soon put a stop to the impasse by taking hold of the book, closing it, bowing and formally handing it back to its owner. Then he gripped the scholar in a fraternal embrace. This had the effect of unleashing a torrent of impassioned speech that ended as quickly as it had begun. But the act of brotherhood was sufficient to win Silvio to their side.

The agent knelt beside his bed and pulled a case from under it. He sat back on his haunches and stared at Angus as he opened the lid. Inside there were four pistols with double barrels. He took out a pair, and rising, offered them to Angus by slipping them inside his tattered shirt. Rob was offered the other pair, which he also hid about his person. Silvio found them simple robes and wished them luck. They embraced, and left.

Two tables ran down either side of the *piano nobile*. As the guests milled around and the orchestra played, servants brought in gold platters and glossy majolica dishes laden with seafood, fowl, sweetmeats, breads, pies, cooked eggs, fresh and stewed fruits, and hot cakes. Flagons of wine and ale were set among glasses rimmed with gold, and coffee and hot chocolate were served in tiny china cups that required frequent refills.

Such were the civilised arrangements for the breakfast. But Lord Damiens did not have in mind anything so mundane as a simple celebration, with tedious exchanges of platitudes and niceties. He wanted those present to remember the day. It was his ambition to make himself not only the richest, but also the most notorious nobleman in Venice. Rumours would spread across Italy and into France towards England, telling of excesses unknown north of the Alps. Those who were eager for news of his ruin would hear instead of a life lived with music and dancing, of free-flowing wine, exotic foods, and scenes of buggery beyond imagining.

To this end, before he bade his guests sit, he ordered his footmen to strip, half of them below the waist, the rest entirely naked. This was the signal for the ladies to take their leave, which they did with many graceful expressions of regret and disappointment. Some of the men, too, decided that their pleasures had lasted long enough. And even among those who had made the life of the libertine their norm, a few found the instruction to the footmen not to their liking, although they were outnumbered by those curious to witness fresh novelty.

The footmen were beefy, many with hairy legs and chests, and to the discerning eye they made a fine, if savage, spectacle as they draped themselves over the fine linen covering the long tables. Some lay along them, on their sides, so that both their cocks and backsides were on view. Others lay across on their backs or bellies to display the special charms and attraction of their fronts or behinds. Posies of sweet-smelling wild flowers were draped around cocks and balls, while the arses on display were dressed with such delicacies as might appeal to the palate of those wishing to probe between the cheeks with fingers or tongue.

Some of the footmen were made to stretch their arms or legs, and intertwine them with another's, or to stand on the table, and make a sculpture depicting some heroic struggle or rapt embrace. The remainder were dispatched under the table to squat and wait upon the pleasure of any man who might wish to have his cock sucked while he ate or conversed, or even, if he were to eager to expend energy, to fuck an arse or two.

When all was ready Lord Damiens went to the head of the table on the right side. He sat against the dazzle from the open windows overlooking the Grand Canal so that to those lower down the table he appeared like a king in glory.

Lucian sat at the head of the other table, and once he was in place, those who comprised the company Lord Damiens chose to keep hurried to secure places of favour for themselves.

There were plenty of gluttons. Perhaps it was the table laden with food and well-developed nakedness, or the flavour of the wine. Some may have discovered that beyond the walls of their disapproval there lay sunny meadows of sensual delight. And several saw no reason to deny themselves those activities that had seen them through the night. But, whatever the reason, the breakfast party was eager to drink and eat, gossip and jest, and just as the music soothed their jaded senses, so soon they were reaching under the linen cloth for mouths to suck their cocks. Some of the footmen's arses had been painted with fine sauces, which were required to complement the pies and sweetmeats, and others had hard boiled hens' eggs nestling under their balls. Here and there a prick had been covered in a coloured oil, or cruelly seasoned so that its owner had to rub it free of the powder or apply an unguent that made it grow long and stiff. Mounds of fish roe were set on nipples to be licked off. Before long an excitable fellow, unable to contain any longer his fascination with the doe-eyed servant lounging beside him, had jumped up and pulled out his cock and rammed it up the well-made arse, ignoring as he did so the salad leaves decorating the deep crack.

This acted as the signal for an outbreak of sodomy. Servants were bent over the table to be entered by the younger guests, many of them as eye-catching as those they penetrated, while two fops with long black hair and tight breeches decided to have themselves sucked while standing back to back as the centrepiece of Lucian's table. The two slender young men with dark skin who knelt to suck them had fetching buttocks that protruded to form a perfect curve. They went about their work with diligence.

Lord Damiens was well pleased. Who else would have dared stage such a display so soon after a major ball, and who would have brought such imagination to the task? He noticed how an elderly gentleman was feasting off the white meat of a chicken sliced and set among fresh fruit on a servant's hairy chest. Another had managed to bring a youthful servant quickly to the boil, and was holding his wine goblet under the spurting prick so as to add creamy juice to his drink. Two fellows in the uniform of the Doge's guard were using belts to flog the back and arse of a wealthy gentleman from Basel. This fellow had his face pressed to the groin of an impassive footman who was spooning stewed fruit down the cleavage of an ugly man dressed as a courtesan.

Soon the whole room would abandon itself to the exercise of libidos both general and particular. By evening Venice would know only one topic of conversation, and the scandalous name of Lord Damiens would be on every painted lip.

# Twenty-Nine

The milord's bedchamber was empty. All the servants had been called away. The bed had not been slept in, and, as the shutters were closed, the room was in darkness except where light shone through cracks to shed strips of brilliance across the floor. Clothes spilled from the closets, and lay in jumbled heaps. The air was still and heavy with the milord's favourite perfume.

When Rob and Angus found the bathtub left full, they stripped off and jumped in, sending tepid water cascading over both ends. They did not care. Angus had never been concerned to win any man's approval, and Rob was no longer beholden to Lord Damiens. They splashed one another, and used oils both pungent and unguent to cleanse and soothe themselves. They rubbed balms into the weals on each other's backs, and scrubbed their feet until all traces of the dungeon's slime were gone. They plunged one another under the water, used razors on their chins, and shook their heads free of water.

When they got out they fell upon each other on the soaking floor to test their strength and glory in one another's warmth and tenderness. They kissed teasingly, and passionately, and whispered and laughed. Angus got Rob on his back, and pinned his arms above his head, so that he could shake more water from his hair into his friend's face. He threatened dreadful torture if Rob did not kiss both his nipples without delay. When Rob complained that they were out of the reach of his lips, Angus lowered himself a little, and ordered Rob to stick out his tongue so that its tip might tickle the red buttons. But Rob managed to jerk himself free and clamped his front teeth on Angus's chest, so that it was the Scot's turn to beg to be set free.

They dressed quickly and without much thought to impress, but in doing so they raided the closet where Titus kept the milord's finest shirts and coats. Angus, who had never before put on the clothes of a gentleman, burst out laughing at the sight of himself in stockings and silver-grey breeches. And there was a tussle as Rob tried to decide whether his friend should dress to the right or left. But Angus stared at himself in awe when Rob added a linen shirt, a coat of royal blue trimmed with gold, and a grey cravat that was held in place by a silver pin topped by a pearl fished from the Persian Gulf. His face had not changed, his hair was as black and thick as ever and the same white teeth gleamed when he smiled, but the rest of him was transformed.

There was no doubt that he made a fine figure of a man. The braided epaulettes gave his broad shoulders shape and elegance, and his thick frame and deep chest lost no sturdiness in the exquisite coat. Many had admired his fine backside when he wore a sailor's bell-bottoms, but encased in fine tight breeches the muscular cheeks curved to sweet effect. His legs looked all the more powerful in stockings, and even the silver buckles on his shoes seemed to add to his manly distinction.

If Rob had to play the hen to this magnificent peacock, he was determined not to let his friend carry all the lustre. Knowing that his yellow hair and blue eyes always drew admiration, he permitted himself a slightly dishevelled look, as if he were used to wearing a gentleman's garb but had been caught out by the absence of his valet. His cravat was a little crooked, and the pin so simple as to be without a jewel. The coat he chose was of plain silk dyed the colour of his eyes, but half a shade darker. His breeches were a little loose, and his shoes well worn.

Since Angus had black curls that would have been the envy of any rake or desperado, and Rob's fair locks had tempted many a young lady to wish to steal them for her own head, they decided to follow the fashionable preference for things natural and not wear wigs. After some careful mutual tousling before the looking-glass, they decided their hair should fall as it might.

When they were quite satisfied, they armed themselves.

Rob had expected to go downstairs and make an entrance on the *piano nobile*. To confront the milord would be a fine revenge, and one that would surely compel him to offer his escaped prisoners both freedom and compensation. But Angus cuffed him for making such an effeminate suggestion.

Having seen action and been taken by the Barbary pirates, Angus believed pill and plunder to be the only true rites of victory. His heart had grown hard while a prisoner at sea, and chained to the walls of draughty caves above Ragusa. By the time he had arrived in Venice to be flogged and sold as a slave, he had sworn to avenge the crimes committed against him. And since Lord Damiens had been the architect of his suffering, he would die rather than leave the Palazzo Ferri without the booty to satisfy his grievance.

When Rob suggested they might win more by pleading their case, Angus took his friend by the shoulders and told him to think hard how they might find and enter the treasury. 'It's time to take, Rob, not to beg.'

The darkness in Angus's eyes forbade argument, and Rob pointed to the landing. 'The door on the left. His lordship keeps his jewels and papers there. It is locked.'

'Then we must open it.' Angus made for the door. Rob noticed how he walked with a sailor's rolling gait, and how he thrust his chin forward as if ready to take on the world.

But without a key there would be no entry to the treasury.

Two dwarfs were late arrivals at the breakfast. They were tough fellows, and had a will to enjoy themselves. Crowned with laurel, they jumped on Lucian's table and made a pretty picture as they pranced up and down before coupling amid bowls of stewed fruit. When a choirmaster from San Marco made a fool of himself over two blue-eyed Balts, he was rudely upended and pierced with a piece of celery. A wealthy young scholar from Oxford was sick, and a Parisian panicked as he inserted his fingers into a hermaphrodite's fly. A mighty dildo made of polished oak was much in demand after it fell out of a lawyer's bum, and a doctor of medicine found something amiss with the balls of a particularly well-hung Swede. Four gentlemen from Amalfi joined arms to dance, and a Venetian nobleman famous for his impotence suffered a sudden orgasm. The merry mood continued with the arrival of a fashionable torturer and his friend, the Republic's official executioner. Having completed their duties for the day, they had been travelling back to the modest home they shared when they were persuaded to join the festivities by a young man of their acquaintance with unusual tastes. In his capacity as an officer of the state, the executioner at once let it be known that he had never seen such terrible sights. He stood scowling with his axe, while his more sociable friend opened his box of implements and set about explaining their uses. Fearing matters might run out of control, Lord Damiens ordered a side table to be set so that they might eat with their backs to the gathering.

Despite the breakfast's success, Lord Damiens was worried. On his day of triumph he could not afford mishaps. But Titus was nowhere to be seen. The lighters would soon be leaving with their human cargo, and only Titus could bring proof that everything was in order.

Angus had tried throwing himself at the treasury door, and had rammed it with a piece of marble sculpture that broke in two pieces.

Rob scolded his lover: 'What if we are found out? Four pistols will not match a room of a hundred. And what if they are armed?' He was losing patience with Angus's bravado. 'We shall be sent to the galleys after all.'

Angus saw the sense of the argument and slumped to his knees. He sat back and buried his head in his hands. Thick droplets appeared on his eyelashes.

Rob gripped him by the shoulders. 'We could leave by the gatehouse, and be free men. Sooner or later we shall have to put all this behind us.'

Angus looked up at Rob and shook his head. 'After all I've suffered I shall never forget . . . or forgive.' The tears were falling fast. 'I shall die first.'

'We well may . . . and soon . . . chained in rows in the galleys.'

There was silence between them. With nothing to say, and with their own thoughts crowding in, they were as still as the broken statue that lay beside them.

A floorboard creaked. Rob turned and saw Titus at the top of the stairs. He stood with his hands on his hips, and was carrying no whip. He pointed at Rob. 'In fresh disguise – again? You are a conjuror, sir, a one-man crowd, a mob on your own.' He moved closer. 'And yet, somehow, always the same dull clay. We are all as God made us.'

Rob took a couple of steps forward. 'So you are a philosopher, Titus. I had not seen that in you before.' By confronting Titus himself he hoped to restrain Angus. Gunfire would bring servants running.

Titus pointed towards the battered door. 'Digging for treasure?' He raised an eyebrow and snorted in derision.

Rob refused to rise to the bait. 'I need a pin for my cravat.'

'So you do.'

Rob was aware of the unnatural silence behind him. It was not like Angus to sit on his backside when a fight was in the offing. He was about to reply when he realised that Titus was no longer paying him attention. Rob glanced round and saw Angus prowling behind him. His fists hung clenched at his sides, and the whites of his eyes gleamed.

Rob reached out and took Titus's arm. 'Give us the key! We'll –'

But it was useless. Titus brushed Rob's hand away as if fending off a troublesome beggar. He, too, clenched his fists.

It was to be a fight.

For all his grace, Angus was more a brawler than a gentleman of the ring, and in his finery he cut a rather awkward figure. And in Titus he had met his match. The valet went forward to duck and weave. Although Angus landed the first punch, Titus came back with a hook to the chin. Riled by the speed of the retaliation, Angus landed his left fist in the middle of Titus's belly but, rather than buckle, the valet again responded with a hook to the chin, this one heavy enough to put Angus off his balance.

Rob watched with alarm, and also an eye shrewd enough to

judge the contest likely to be long and bloody, its outcome uncertain. And there was something distasteful in seeing a man so dressed up tussling with a valet. There was only one thing to be done if he were to prevent Angus producing his pistols. He would have to enter the fray himself, and see to it that Titus was quickly put on the floor.

His first punch was a swift and accurate upper cut that caught Titus nicely under the cheekbone and sent him staggering backward. He half expected Angus to reprimand him for this ungentlemanly intervention, but instead heard him mutter sincere thanks. Another well-judged blow had the valet sitting on his arse and, there being no one to count him out, Angus chose to place a shoe lightly against his groin, and to lay on a small tap that had Titus wriggling in trepidation.

Rob knelt beside Titus and whispered in his ear that he could not hope to restrain Angus if he was not given the key to the treasury door. Conceding defeat with a patronising sigh, Titus reached inside his tunic and produced a small velvet ring with several keys attached.

'The large one. The others open the caskets.'

The breakfast revellers were showing few signs of fatigue. One or two were asleep and others had fallen into trances induced by sexual shock or exhaustion. But most continued to amuse themselves. Rare were the breeches that had not been torn open at the fly, or cocks that had not seen the light of day. A visitor from the moon might have thought it no more forbidden in Venice to show a cock in public than it was to unglove a hand. Pink and purple pricks stood up, or jutted out in front of every pair of breeches. Not a few drooped, but as many were on the way up as down, and there was no shortage of hands and mouths to coax and stimulate the excitable organs.

With the eating done, and much wine taken, those of a rowdy disposition were making the running. Some young officers of the Venetian Navy had decided to demonstrate one of the more vigorous of their below-deck pastimes. They formed themselves one behind the other, and each stuck their cock up the arse of the man in front. As the orchestra played a slow shanty they moved forward, swaying this way and that and bending their knees. This continued until a cock slid from an arse. As a forfeit the cock's owner had to run to the front of the line, kneel, and take the first man's cock in his mouth. When a second man found himself similarly disconnected, he, too, ran to join the man already kneeling there. His cock was soon up the sucker's arse. In this way the line would slowly reform itself, until it changed direction. The orchestra played faster, and as the young officers became more agitated in their movements, so the danger of over-excitement leading to spillage grew. In the end, a handsome fellow could hold back no longer, and was quickly gathered into the arms of his comrades and, as the come spurted from his cock, was tossed in the air like a tennis ball.

Not all incidents were as good-natured. A willowy fop, whose languor misled a footman into thinking he could ignore an instruction to refill a wine-cup, bent the hapless servant over Lucian's table with his legs well spread to be fucked by a cock of unexpected length and width. The sounds of this angry coupling were heard above the orchestra, and drew the eyes of those who were ready to spice their amusement with more vicious sights.

The fop fucked with wicked skill, his piston driving in and out between the spread cheeks with measured strokes governed by pelvic jerks of the utmost precision. Although the spectacle had more the appeal of discipline than lust, the two bodies made a contrast irresistible to the connoisseur's eye. The fop was not only willowy; he had the limber grace of a thoroughbred, and the easy cruelty of the naturally sensuous. He did not break sweat, and he showed no mercy towards the footman's arse, and instead used it to pleasure himself as much by demonstrating his skill as a cocksmith as by the satisfaction of purely carnal desire. The footman's arse, on the other hand, was the perfect receptacle for a ruthlessly used cock. It did not go slack, or tighten spasmodi-cally, but kept that consistency born either of inexperience or expert drilling. Nor was he a man to be taken without complaint. He reared up and contorted his face in eloquent tribute to the fop's rapier thrusts, and he pushed his arse high, and this way and that, as if hoping somehow to escape the hardened flesh that had captured him.

When the time came for the fop to come, he leaned his thin form backwards, and gripped his own buttocks with both hands. Sending in thrusts ever deeper, and faster, and more ruthlessly, he forced himself over the brink, and as his cries of triumph harmonised with those of anguish from the miserable servant, he pumped himself dry. Afterwards he withdrew his cock with a single pull, and wiped it on the linen tablecloth, using all the care of an assassin cleaning fresh blood from his knife.

Lord Damiens was not pleased. He enjoyed a hard fuck as much as the next man, and used his cock to chastise his servants as often as any, but he considered it unseemly that such rough displays of discipline should be performed in public. If the fop was offended and wished to teach the footman a lesson, he should have asked to be shown to a side room. Although the milord believed that licence, by its nature, would lead to excess, and that the civilised man should have no more fear of it than he should of limitation, he did not want the day undermined by viciousness. In the end the ugly always drove out the beautiful.

Meanwhile, in the treasury, Rob had found jewels to delight the vainest princeling. He held two rubies in his hand, one cut to reveal the deepest shades of red, the other to sparkle under soft light. There were sapphires so blue he demanded Angus compare them to his own eyes, and pearls so warm and soft to touch he could not resist playing with them on his tongue. Some stones puzzled him: they were without colour or sparkle and were rough to the touch. And some were as black as jet, or pale green or yellow, and yet opaque. But he put them all in his coat pocket. Others would tell him their worth.

Angus had no time for coloured stones: he preferred the feel of Spanish pieces of eight on his palm. The heavy English sovereign and gold louis he had seen before, but never in profusion, and the silver and gold ducats were so smooth from use they slipped through his fingers.

Titus stood watching them. He showed no sign of distress, and watched everything the two thieves did with eyes as impassive as a confessor's voice.

# Thirty

Lord Damiens was tiring of his guests. Too many had nothing to offer except a willingness to fuck or be fucked. The spectacle of so many cocks rampant, foaming, or simply dangling had become tedious. He had tried to revive his spirits by having a tough young man from Istria suck him. But even the warmth of a willing mouth, and the sight of one so rugged and well made crouching to pleasure him, while pulling on a fine stick of a cock, failed to excite. It was time to call an end.

He was about to signal to his steward, himself stifling a yawn, when he saw Titus standing in the doorway. This was a welcome sight, and he beckoned his valet with a gesture of urgency. He would want to know where his valet had been.

Titus did not obey his master at once, but turned to speak to two fellows who had appeared behind him. Such insolence was unlike Titus, who knew better than to linger when called. The milord beckoned once more, and did not take his eyes off him as he approached.

'My lord, the cargo is leaving.' Although Titus bowed, he did not bend far.

Lord Damiens would not chastise so senior a servant before the eyes of the footmen. He merely asked if all had gone well.

Rather than answer, Titus glanced back at the two strangers, who were making their way across the room. They were undeniably fine-looking young men, but wore masks over their eyes.

'If it pleases my lord to view the scene from the window, he will see the lighters departing with their cargo.'

There was something strange in Titus's manner, but the milord saw no reason not to follow the suggestion.

Titus led the way and peered down to where the side canal ran in behind the palazzo. Two lighters were emerging, both covered in black tarpaulin. Men in the uniform of the Venetian Navy stood at intervals down either side, and used long oars to propel the vessels out into the Grand Canal. The two craft mingled with the morning traffic. Of their cargo there was no sign.

Lord Damiens gazed down at the scene. He was reassured. After all the effort and danger, all the risks he had taken, and the bad conscience, he was safe. And rich – soon to be richer still, so long as his luck held. The Republic's need for slaves to man their galleys was as inexhaustible as the Barbary pirates' skill in providing them. The trade was clandestine, but the profits great. He had never expected to become a man of trade, but poverty is a harsh master and he had risked all to free himself from its pitiless claws. He breathed in the morning air, and turned to congratulate Titus.

But again, his valet was looking elsewhere. What was the matter with the man?

There was no time to find out. The morning sunshine hurt his eyes and he shielded them with his hand as he turned back into the room. Dazzled, he did not notice the two figures standing close by as he made his way back to his seat. As he sat down he summoned the steward. It was time to send the guests on their way.

From behind their ivory masks Angus and Rob had been watching the milord and his valet as they stood at the window. With no desire to see the sad departure, they were content to wait until the milord had returned to his place. Although they drew all eyes, and their entrance had caused many to stop in their tracks, or in the motions of copulation, they made no effort to show who they were, or why they had come. Those who are sober among the drunken, and determined among the purposeless, have no need to explain themselves. They stood and waited.

Minutes before, on the upper landing, Angus had flipped a gold louis to settle who should have the pleasure of taking the milord, and who his haughty friend. When Rob called tails and Angus saw the upturned image of the old Bourbon king, he called the milord's name. They shook on it.

So while Angus calmly worked out how to subdue and deal with Lord Damiens, Rob directed his attention to Lucian, who was spooning ice-cream into the upturned mouths of two elderly gentlemen dressed as Romulus and Remus. Their wrinkled faces and bulging bellies were ill suited to any imitation of the boy saviours of Rome, and there was applause when Lucian boxed Remus's ear for letting some melted cream dribble on to his chin. Rob smiled beneath his mask. He could not have wished to disrupt a more disgusting scene, especially as Romulus was about to be dragged over the knee of a Bavarian count to be walloped for spluttering while trying to talk with his mouth full.

Although they had not agreed the signal to begin, Rob knew that Angus would, without thinking, take the task upon himself when the moment was right.

Angus had learnt the advantage of a swaggering gait from the officers he served under on his ship-of-the-line, and the Barbary pirates had taught him that the effect of surprise is always heightened by the discharge of a firearm. So he strode forward to where Lord Damiens sat fanning himself as he gave instruction to his steward. Ripping the mask off his face, he produced a pistol from inside his coat and fired it into one of the mighty chandeliers. Shards of glass fell like summer hail.

The effect was all he could have wished for. As the patter of glass and squeals of alarm died away, an utter silence reigned, broken only by the sound of more shattered glass as Angus leapt on to the table. Spinning the pistol on his thumb, he kicked through the debris. Lord Damiens rose to remonstrate, but Angus aimed a shot past his head close enough to make him slump back in his chair.

There was no need for words. Angus made poetry of his

actions, so clear and precise were their intention and execution. He lifted the milord from his chair and set him on a servant's stool. He drew a second pistol and poked it between the lord's teeth. He ripped the coat and shirt of the lordly back, and beckoned to a nearby fop who was carrying a cane.

With an ashen face and shaking hand the dainty fellow walked forward to hand over his thin malacca stick.

Angus had taken punishment on his shoulders and arse, and knew that while the pain is the same, the indignity of having stripes laid across the arse hurts more. So he aimed his pistol at the milord's fly and ordered him to stand and unbutton himself. With the quick obedience of one who expects his suffering to be short-lived, the milord bared himself front and back. Angus took him by his cock and led him back to the table. He motioned him to bend, and immediately laid the malacca across the lordly arse with all the accuracy and confidence of one who knows he has just cause to chastise.

Rob, meanwhile, was tackling Lucian, who had pushed Remus away and was staring in horror at the invaders. As Rob approached he drew his pistol. He did not need to fire the weapon, but simply aimed it at Lucian's mouth as he unbuttoned his fly. In a setting that had seen every vice enacted, the sight of one more cock was hardly cause for surprise, but the fine throbbing tool Rob let spring from his linen looked as much a dangerous device as any firearm.

Lucian did not hesitate when Rob motioned him to his knees. He sat back on his haunches and raised his face, mouth open, with the apprehensive willingness of a man surrendering to the dentist's pliers.

Nor did Rob waste any time. He sank his mighty cock, so proud and upstanding, so seemingly invulnerable in its purple and red bunting, deep into Lucian's mouth. The instrument was no stranger to the orifice and Rob shoved it all the way in, forcing Lucian to gag and wave his arms in protest until, by sheer force, the cock made its own way down his throat.

Rob rode his mount with style and dash, and made no concession to the comfort of the gagging, breathless young gentleman, who had himself shown scant concern when he had fucked Rob's arse no less ruthlessly.

Angus knew that prolonged punishment will make a dreary spectacle for those used to more subtle diversions, and soon loosened his breeches to produce a cock to equal that of his friend. It was not only swollen and purple from excitement, it stuck out from the folds of Angus's clothing at a bold angle eloquent of its owner's health and virility. It would need no pulling or pummelling to make itself ready.

If Lord Damiens had hoped his punishment might be over, he did not make the mistake of standing up but remained bent over the table with his well-tanned arse sticking up like the two halves of some well-ripened fruit.

Angus, after the fashion of sailors, used some dribble from his mouth as a mix for the juice oozing from his helmet. The onlookers were growing rowdy, and it was as much to draw their applause as to ease his passage that he slowly massaged the sticky liquid into his prick. Then, with a hand placed on the small of the milord's back, Angus used a single unguided thrust to send his cock through the lord's tight gateway into the warm void that must be possessed if one man is to own another.

The two young friends fucked. One bore down on a face as lean and handsome as any thoroughbred's; the other lanced an arse whose delicate mounds and tight hole were a tribute to twenty-five generations of strategic coupling. The cocks that took them, however, were the consequence of less carefully constructed unions, and made up in strength and endurance what they lacked in fine, slender elegance.

Being young and free, and suddenly in the best of spirits, Angus and Rob's eyes met as together they climbed the route to the summit. They burst out laughing. To combine justice with pleasure was a rare achievement, and those who were witness gathered round to join in the merriment. They made a strange spectacle. Some were noblemen whose forebears had marched out of Rome with the legions, or had come down from the Alps in the name of the Holy Empire. There were footmen whose parents toiled in the fields and on steep mountainsides, and city folk who knew only the world of the City and its lagoon. Together their cheers would not have disgraced regatta day, and were heard on the far side of the Grand Canal where honest souls waiting to cross turned to one another and smiled. Perhaps, a lawyer suggested, the evil English milord was gone, but others shook their heads, suspecting the truth.

Angus came first. He poured his seed into the milord's arse as copiously as he had filled his pockets with gold. He pulled himself out, and acknowledged the applause. Rob followed him with a mighty groan, as if he were expelling down Lucian's throat the very essence of Venice. As he pumped himself empty he felt himself becoming once more the English lad who only weeks before had stepped ashore from the *Dawn Treader*.

# Epilogue

A gust of wind along the Strand stirred the dust. Two horses reared, and one pranced on to the footpath causing several ladies to seek refuge in a milliner's shop. A carter delivering masonry got into a dispute with a driver eager to proceed towards Knightsbridge, but their ill temper did not mar the gay spring morning. Although there had been rain earlier, the grey clouds had vanished, and seeing the sun shining, Rob and Angus had decided to take their midday coffee at the Adelphi.

They were in town for only a few days – their duties on their estate forbade longer visits – so they took every opportunity to hear the latest gossip. The satisfactions of rural life were true and lasting, but the pleasures to be found among open fields and honest neighbours were not diminished by the regular refreshment of London life.

They lodged in a house off Drury Lane, where the landlady understood the ways of bachelors, and the walk along the Strand to the Adelphi did not take more than ten minutes. Rob enjoyed the crowds, and the variety of strange and tempting sights. In the country, life went plodding by without novelty, but in London it was possible to gratify the desires of the moment, rather than move always in time with nature's slow rhythms. So he was pleased to note a new fashion favoured by the more dashing young bucks. This was to wear breeches made from a fabric so shiny it reflected the sun, and cut so tight it was possible to judge the wearer's likely worth between the sheets.

Angus, who thought all fashion mere tricks of the tailor's trade, and had become more dour in his opinions since being appointed a magistrate, declared that should any rascal show himself in such a saucy outfit at Ashford, he would soon find himself locked in the stocks until market day. Such robust views had not, however, prevented him from sending the kitchen boy with a note to a house near Seven Dials to ensure that a certain young man would be waiting for him at a quarter past five.

The colonnade at the Adelphi was always crowded mid-morning with ladies and their servants out shopping, and gentlemen on their way to do business. Here and there passageways ran back into the building, and some were open through to the far side to allow a glimpse of the traffic on the Thames. The coffee-houses at either end were, by common consent, two of the finest spots in London, and those who gathered there might as easily have come from the Court as from the City, or from Westminster or the Inns of Court. It was not a place to stand and be seen, or to be idle or dream, but the natural convergence for those whose lives were lived to good effect.

Rob preferred to walk the full length of the colonnade and sit close to the coffee-house door where the same smiling young waiter always brought a tray with coffee and fresh cakes. To be served by him was a pleasure typical of many that Rob enjoyed when in London, and he was happy to leave a generous tip to ensure that he would not be denied it the next day. It amused him, too, that Angus would always complain about the tip, despite the much greater expenses he incurred most evenings in the house near Seven Dials.

The young waiter also guaranteed a certain sympathy of temperament among those who chose to sit where he would serve them, and their conversation reflected a shared ease with aspects of man's nature that elsewhere might provoke disapproval.

It was not entirely a surprise, therefore, when Rob saw the Earl of Blansett approaching. As was the custom of the house, courtesy demanded that the greetings be brief and that no man

219

should rise. Nor did the exchanges dwell on private matters, but ranged as widely as was necessary to ensure the free flow of conversation. In the end, but without hurry, a topic was always found that was of interest to both parties, and on this occasion it was the exhibition, in one of the Adelphi's public rooms, of recently imported oils by the Italian master known as Canaletto.

The Earl of Blansett had not been impressed. '. . . views of canals . . . every one of them . . . and all very much a much of a muchness.' His voice had an unforgiving timbre, and his clothes showed an encroaching eccentricity. His coat was wide at the hems and patterned in bright greens and yellows, and his shoes were pink. Even his wig seemed to have been dipped in some reddish dye, while his beauty spots resembled angry pimples.

Angus was keen to see the paintings. 'It's a while since I saw the canals of Venice. If these paintings are accurate, I might have one for myself.'

The Earl raised an eyebrow and shook his knees in agitation. 'The King has yet to see them. They say he will be coming shortly. Until then you will find the pictures reserved – a matter of precedence you see.'

Rob stared ahead and said nothing.

But Angus would not be silenced. 'Gold has a precedence all its own.'

The Earl's knees shook ever faster. 'Indeed, sir, who can deny it? And if the news from France is to be believed the whole world's gone topsy-turvy.' He shook his head and clasped his knees. 'However, to other matters. My son, Lord Humphrey, is about to tour the more tranquil parts of the continent. He is to visit Venice, and hopes to lodge at the Palazzo Ferri with a certain Lord Damiens. I believe you know him.'

Angus looked glum and shook his head, but Rob nodded and smiled. 'Indeed I do, quite intimately. I lodged there myself a while ago.'

Angus muttered something that the Earl did not hear.

'I knew Damiens as a boy.' The Earl smiled as if remembering a naughty child play a prank. 'He was headstrong then. I'm told the poor man fell among thieving guttersnipes, and must now take in paying guests. It's not the first time he has found himself among the weaker brethren. Gambling, you see. He always had a passion for the tables . . . and for the pleasures of the night.'

'How did you know of our acquaintance with him?' Rob's voice betrayed no tension.

The Earl let out a brief laugh in the soprano register. 'My dear fellow, don't you know? He uses your name as an introduction.'

Angus rose. He pushed the table away, spilling coffee and causing the Earl to emit another high peal of sound. With the slightest of bows Angus walked off.

'Your friend is a grumpy fellow. Pining for Scotland, I expect.'

Rob stood and fumbled for the coins to pay the waiter, who was leaning over the table to wipe away the spillage. Rob noticed that the Earl's left pink shoe was rubbing against the young fellow's calf. 'I think I had better go before Angus buys a painting.'

But the Earl of Blansett did not hear. He was busy ordering more refreshment from the waiter.


Rob found Angus standing before a canvas on which was spread a scene of the Grand Canal on a sunny day. The brilliant spectacle had a light of its own that shone in on Rob's memories to bring back the sounds and smells of Venice. Peering close he could make out the Palazzo Ferri, and the landing-stage, and the tower on the roof where he had dallied. And on the Grand Canal he could sense the movement and ever-changing light suggested by the artist's hand.

'You must not buy it.' Rob spoke softly, as he always did when serious.

'Now I've seen it I do not want it.' Angus's voice was almost gentle, and Rob could hear the sadness in it. 'Too much dazzle, and too much to hide.'

Rob placed a hand on his friend's shoulder. 'Let's go home.'

Angus stared at him in surprise. 'This minute?'

Rob nodded.

'But at five I have to go to Seven Dials.'

'Come home.'

★

As they were leaving they were intercepted once more by the Earl of Blansett, this time in the company of a handsome young fellow wearing a scholar's sober garb.

'This is my son, sirs, Lord Humphrey.'

They exchanged bows, and Lord Humphrey silenced his father to ask, 'Should I stay with Lord Damiens when I am in Venice?' There was an appealing simplicity about the young man.

Angus began to say something, but Rob interrupted. 'My answer to your question must depend on what you hope to learn during your stay there.'

'Whatever was taught to you.' For a second, a smile flickered across the solemn face.

'Then I see no reason not to recommend the Palazzo Ferri. There is no better place in Venice for a young man who has curiosity and a willingness to learn through experience.'

The Earl of Blansett bowed deeply and was full of thanks, but his son lingered. When his father was out of hearing, he burst out laughing. 'My dear sirs, I will always be in your debt. From what I've heard, life at the Palazzo Ferri is never dull, and you must agree, on this earth, tedium is always our enemy.' With a cheerful smile, and more thanks, the young lord strode off.

Angus was standing, hands on hips, staring at Rob as if in disbelief, and as stern as any boy's father. 'Robert, why in God's name, did you – ?'

But Rob silenced him with a glance. 'You stay another day – go to Seven Dials if you must – but I must go home.'

Angus frowned, but knew argument was useless. He sighed. 'Very well, home it is. And if we must go, we may as well go now.'


The weather was changeable. Clouds sped in from the Channel across Romney Marsh, driven by a wind that troubled the woods along the ridge above Appledore.

Rob had been out all morning in the orchards, and had returned to the manor house for lunch with his brothers and father. It had been a hearty meal, eaten with gusto and good humour. With Angus on duty as magistrate in the courthouse at Ashford, Rob had been able to play the plain son of Kent, to joke with his brothers and freely show his father the respect that was due.

And after he had watched them ride away up the drive, he had walked down through the orchards to the river where the oak stood. He sat on its twisted roots and paid no attention to the blustery showers, or even the frisky lambs. He lit his pipe and stared into the wind. He remembered the nights on the *Dawn Treader* when he had danced on deck under swaying lamps to the tune of the stowaway's penny-whistle. The old ship had creaked and bucked her way through the darkness, and the wind was always warm, the rum plentiful. He had been young then, and the stars overhead only faded with the dawn.

## IDOL NEW BOOKS

*Also published:*

### THE KING'S MEN
Christian Fall

Ned Medcombe, spoilt son of an Oxfordshire landowner, has always remembered his first love: the beautiful, golden-haired Lewis. But seventeenth-century England forbids such a love and Ned is content to indulge his domineering passions with the willing members of the local community, including the submissive parish cleric. Until the Civil War changes his world, and he is forced to pursue his desires as a soldier in Cromwell's army – while his long-lost lover fights as one of the King's men.

ISBN 0 352 33207 7

### THE VELVET WEB
Christopher Summerisle

The year is 1889. Daniel McGaw arrives at Calverdale, a centre of academic excellence buried deep in the English countryside. But this is like no other college. As Daniel explores, he discovers secret passages in the grounds and forbidden texts in the library. The young male students, isolated from the outside world, share a darkly bizarre brotherhood based on the most extreme forms of erotic expression. It isn't long before Daniel is initiated into the rites that bind together the youths of Calverdale in a web of desire.

ISBN 0 352 33208 5

### CHAINS OF DECEIT
Paul C. Alexander

Journalist Nathan Dexter's life is turned around when he meets a young student called Scott – someone who offers him the relationship for which he's been searching. Then Nathan's best friend goes missing, and Nathan uncovers evidence that he has become the victim of a slavery ring which is rumoured to be operating out of London's leather scene. To rescue their friend and expose the perverted slave trade, Nathan and Scott must go undercover, risking detection and betrayal at every turn.

ISBN 0 352 33206 9

### DARK RIDER
Jack Gordon

While the rulers of a remote Scottish island play bizarre games of sexual dominance with the Argentinian Angelo, his friend Robert – consumed with jealous longing for his coffee-skinned companion – assuages his desires with the willing locals.

ISBN 0 352 33243 3

# CONQUISTADOR
## Jeff Hunter

It is the dying days of the Aztec empire. Axaten and Quetzel are members of the Stable, servants of the Sun Prince chosen for their bravery and beauty. But it is not just an honour and a duty to join this society, it is also the ultimate sexual achievement. Until the arrival of Juan, a young Spanish conquistador, sets the men of the Stable on an adventure of bondage, lust and deception.

ISBN 0 352 33244 1

# TO SERVE TWO MASTERS
## Gordon Neale

In the isolated land of Ilyria men are bought and sold as slaves. Rock, brought up to expect to be treated as mere 'livestock', yearns to be sold to the beautiful youth Dorian. But Dorian's brother is as cruel as he is handsome, and if Rock is bought by one brother he will be owned by both.

ISBN 0 352 33245 X

# CUSTOMS OF THE COUNTRY
## Rupert Thomas

James Cardell has left school and is looking forward to going to Oxford. That summer of 1924, however, he will spend with his cousins in a tiny village in rural Kent. There he finds he can pursue his love of painting – and begin to explore his obsession with the male physique.

ISBN 0 352 33246 8

# DOCTOR REYNARD'S EXPERIMENT
## Robert Black

A dark world of secret brothels, dungeons and sexual cabarets exists behind the respectable facade of Victorian London. The degenerate Lord Spearman introduces Dr Richard Reynard, dashing bachelor, to this hidden world. And Walter Starling, the doctor's new footman, finds himself torn between affection for his master and the attractions of London's underworld.

ISBN 0 352 33252 2

# CODE OF SUBMISSION
## Paul C. Alexander

Having uncovered and defeated a slave ring operating in London's leather scene, journalist Nathan Dexter had hoped to enjoy a peaceful life with his boyfriend Scott. But when it becomes clear that the perverted slave trade has started again, Nathan has no choice but to travel across Europe and America in his bid to stop it.

ISBN 0 352 33272 7

# SLAVES OF TARNE
## Gordon Neale

Pascal willingly follows the mysterious and alluring Casper to Tarne, a community of men enslaved to men. Tarne is everything that Pascal has ever fantasised about, but he begins to sense a sinister aspect to Casper's magnetism. Pascal has to choose between the pleasures of submission and acting to save the people he loves.

ISBN 0 352 33273 5

## ROUGH WITH THE SMOOTH
Dominic Arrow

Amid the crime, violence and unemployment of North London, the young men who attend Jonathan Carey's drop-in centre have few choices. One of the young men, Stewart, finds himself torn between the increasingly intimate horseplay of his fellows and the perverse allure of the criminal underworld. Can Jonathan save Stewart from the bullies on the streets and behind bars?

ISBN 0 352 33292 1

## CONVICT CHAINS
Philip Markham

Peter Warren, printer's apprentice in the London of the 1830s, discovers his sexuality and taste for submission at the hands of Richard Barkworth. Thus begins a downward spiral of degradation, of which transportation to the Australian colonies is only the beginning.

ISBN 0 352 33300 6

## SHAME
Raydon Pelham

On holiday in West Hollywood, Briton Martyn Townsend meets and falls in love with the daredevil Scott. When Scott is murdered, Martyn's hunt for the truth and for the mysterious Peter, Scott's ex-lover, leads him to the clubs of London and Ibiza.

ISBN 0 352 33302 2

## HMS SUBMISSION
Jack Gordon

Under the command of Josiah Rock, a man of cruel passions, HMS *Impregnable* sails to the colonies. Christopher, Viscount Fitzgibbons is a reluctant officer; Mick Savage part of the wretched cargo. They are on a voyage to a shared destiny.

ISBN 0 352 33301 4

## THE FINAL RESTRAINT
Paul C. Alexander

The trilogy that began with *Chains of Deceit* and continued in *Code of Submission* concludes in this powerfully erotic novel. The evil Adrian Delancey has finally outwitted journalist Nathan Dexter in his deathly game of cat-and-mouse – destroying Nathan's relationship with student Scott in the bargain. From the dungeons and saunas of London to the deepest jungles of South America, Nathan Dexter is forced to play the ultimate chess game – with people as sexual pawns.

ISBN 0 352 33303 0

## HARD TIME
Robert Black

HMP Cairncrow prison is a corrupt and cruel institution, but also a sexual minefield. Three new inmates must find their niche in this brutish environment – as sexual victims or lovers, predators or protectors. This is the story of how they find love, sex and redemption behind prison walls.

ISBN 0 352 33304 9

# ROMAN GAMES
Tasker Dean

When Sam visits the island of Skate, he is taught how to submit to other men; acting out an elaborate fantasy in which young men become wrestling slaves – just as in ancient Rome.

ISBN 0 352 33322 7

## WE NEED YOUR HELP . . .

### to plan the future of Idol books –

Yours are the only opinions that matter. Idol is a new and exciting venture: the first British series of books devoted to homoerotic fiction for men.

We're going to do our best to provide the sexiest, best-written books you can buy. And we'd like you to help in these early stages. Tell us what you want to read. There's a freepost address for your filled-in questionnaires, so you won't even need to buy a stamp.

---

# THE IDOL QUESTIONNAIRE

## SECTION ONE: ABOUT YOU

1.1 Sex (*we presume you are male, but just in case*)
Are you?
Male ☐
Female ☐

1.2 Age
under 21 ☐ 21–30 ☐
31–40 ☐ 41–50 ☐
51–60 ☐ over 60 ☐

1.3 At what age did you leave full-time education?
still in education ☐ 16 or younger ☐
17–19 ☐ 20 or older ☐

1.4 Occupation _____

1.5 Annual household income _____

1.6  We are perfectly happy for you to remain anonymous; but if you would like us to send you a free booklist of Idol books, please insert your name and address

_____

_____

_____

_____

## SECTION TWO: ABOUT BUYING IDOL BOOKS

2.1  Where did you get this copy of *Venetian Trade*?
    Bought at chain book shop   ☐
    Bought at independent book shop   ☐
    Bought at supermarket   ☐
    Bought at book exchange or used book shop   ☐
    I borrowed it/found it   ☐
    My partner bought it   ☐

2.2  How did you find out about Idol books?
    I saw them in a shop   ☐
    I saw them advertised in a magazine   ☐
    I read about them in _____
    Other _____

2.3  Please tick the following statements you agree with:
    I would be less embarrassed about buying Idol
    books if the cover pictures were less explicit   ☐
    I think that in general the pictures on Idol
    books are about right   ☐
    I think Idol cover pictures should be as
    explicit as possible   ☐

2.4  Would you read an Idol book in a public place – on a train for instance?
    Yes   ☐     No   ☐

## SECTION THREE: ABOUT THIS IDOL BOOK

3.1  Do you think the sex content in this book is:
    Too much   ☐     About right   ☐
    Not enough   ☐

3.2   Do you think the writing style in this book is:
Too unreal/escapist    ☐     About right    ☐
Too down to earth    ☐

3.3   Do you think the story in this book is:
Too complicated    ☐     About right    ☐
Too boring/simple    ☐

3.4   Do you think the cover of this book is:
Too explicit    ☐     About right    ☐
Not explicit enough    ☐

Here's a space for any other comments:

---

## SECTION FOUR: ABOUT OTHER IDOL BOOKS

4.1   How many Idol books have you read?

4.2   If more than one, which one did you prefer?

4.3   Why?

---

## SECTION FIVE: ABOUT YOUR IDEAL EROTIC NOVEL

We want to publish the books you want to read – so this is your chance to tell us exactly what your ideal erotic novel would be like.

5.1   Using a scale of 1 to 5 (1 = no interest at all, 5 = your ideal), please rate the following possible settings for an erotic novel:

Roman / Ancient World    ☐
Medieval / barbarian / sword 'n' sorcery    ☐
Renaissance / Elizabethan / Restoration    ☐
Victorian / Edwardian    ☐
1920s & 1930s    ☐
Present day    ☐
Future / Science Fiction    ☐

5.2 Using the same scale of 1 to 5, please rate the following themes you may find in an erotic novel:

Bondage / fetishism ☐
Romantic love ☐
SM / corporal punishment ☐
Bisexuality ☐
Group sex ☐
Watersports ☐
Rent / sex for money ☐

5.3 Using the same scale of 1 to 5, please rate the following styles in which an erotic novel could be written:

Gritty realism, down to earth ☐
Set in real life but ignoring its more unpleasant aspects ☐
Escapist fantasy, but just about believable ☐
Complete escapism, totally unrealistic ☐

5.4 In a book that features power differentials or sexual initiation, would you prefer the writing to be from the viewpoint of the dominant / experienced or submissive / inexperienced characters:

Dominant / Experienced ☐
Submissive / Inexperienced ☐
Both ☐

5.5 We'd like to include characters close to your ideal lover. What characteristics would your ideal lover have? Tick as many as you want:

| | | | |
|---|---|---|---|
| Dominant | ☐ | Caring | ☐ |
| Slim | ☐ | Rugged | ☐ |
| Extroverted | ☐ | Romantic | ☐ |
| Bisexual | ☐ | Old | ☐ |
| Working Class | ☐ | Intellectual | ☐ |
| Introverted | ☐ | Professional | ☐ |
| Submissive | ☐ | Pervy | ☐ |
| Cruel | ☐ | Ordinary | ☐ |
| Young | ☐ | Muscular | ☐ |
| Naïve | ☐ | | |

Anything else? _____

5.6 Is there one particular setting or subject matter that your ideal erotic novel would contain:

_____

5.7 As you'll have seen, we include safe-sex guidelines in every book. However, while our policy is always to show safe sex in stories with contemporary settings, we don't insist on safe-sex practices in stories with historical settings because it would be anachronistic. What, if anything, would you change about this policy?

_____

_____


## SECTION SIX: LAST WORDS

6.1 What do you like best about Idol books?

_____

6.2 What do you most dislike about Idol books?

_____

6.3 In what way, if any, would you like to change Idol covers?

_____

6.4 Here's a space for any other comments:

_____

_____

_____

_____


*Thanks for completing this questionnaire. Now either tear it out, or photocopy it, then put it in an envelope and send it to:*

**Idol**
**FREEPOST**
**London**
**W10 5BR**

*You don't need a stamp if you're in the UK, but you'll need one if you're posting from overseas.*